Darkfall

Cindy Bond

Published by Cindy Bond, 2024.

This is a work of fiction. Similarities to real people, places, or events are entirely coincidental.

DARKFALL

First edition. November 12, 2024.

Copyright © 2024 Cindy Bond.

ISBN: 979-8230115564

Written by Cindy Bond.

Chapter 1: A Storm in the Making

As the tempest rolled over the coastal town of Windward Bay, I stood at the edge of my family's old pier, watching the waves crash violently against the wooden posts. The storm mirrored my turbulent emotions. Just last week, I was certain of my decision to leave this place for a new job in the city, but a chance encounter with Nathan Hale, the man I had always considered my nemesis, made me question everything. His arrogance, his smirk—it grated on my nerves like nails on a chalkboard. Yet, beneath that brash exterior, there was something unsettlingly magnetic that pulled at my curiosity. I felt it in the way his dark eyes seemed to penetrate my defenses, leaving me breathless and confused.

The wind howled, tugging at my hair, and the salty spray of the ocean mist danced around me like a mischievous spirit. Each gust seemed to whisper my doubts, a cacophony of "What ifs" swirling in the stormy air. I had always been the sensible one, the responsible daughter, the reliable employee. But the way Nathan had challenged me that night—his words teasingly daring me to reconsider my escape—stirred something within me that had long been buried under layers of duty and expectation.

I kicked at the loose pebbles scattered along the pier, feeling the rough textures underfoot as they skittered into the waves. Just a week ago, I had envisioned my life in the city, filled with high rises and endless possibilities, where I would be free from the whispers of small-town gossip. Yet here I was, staring into the roiling sea, feeling every bit as trapped as the crabs scuttling beneath the pier, prisoners of their own rocky homes.

"Why do you always have to be so dramatic?" I muttered to myself, glancing back at the town, where the quaint houses with their weather-beaten shutters stood as stoic witnesses to my inner turmoil. Each window was a pair of eyes, watching my every move, judging my indecision. But as I turned back to the ocean, my heart raced at the thought of Nathan's smirk. It was maddening, infuriating, and yet—thrilling.

A flash of lightning split the sky, illuminating the churning water below. The clouds roared overhead, an ominous choir of nature's fury. The storm was advancing, but it was more than the weather that churned within me. It was the nagging thought of Nathan, of how he always seemed to find me at the most inconvenient moments, his presence like a storm cloud that refused to drift away. We had grown up together, two stubborn kids sparring on the playground, trading barbs like currency. But somewhere between those childhood squabbles and the present, our rivalry had morphed into something far more complicated.

I remembered that last encounter vividly—the way he leaned against his truck, arms crossed, that infuriatingly confident smirk on his face. "You're not really going to leave, are you?" he had asked, the question laced with disbelief. The way he'd challenged my plans made my blood boil and my heart race simultaneously, an exquisite mix of frustration and intrigue.

"Of course I am. Not everyone wants to rot away in this sleepy town," I had snapped back, trying to mask my wavering resolve with indignation. But even as I spoke, I could see the flicker of something in his eyes, a spark of recognition, as if he understood the weight of my words and the truth behind them. There was a bond there, thick and undeniable, one that tugged at my heartstrings even as I fought against it.

Now, as the wind picked up, tearing at my clothes and sending shivers down my spine, I knew I had to decide. I could turn back, retreat to the safety of my family home, where expectations loomed large and dreams were often eclipsed by practicality. Or I could stand my ground, face the storm—both outside and within—and make a choice that might change everything.

Just then, a voice broke through the howling wind. "You know, standing out here like a shipwrecked sailor isn't going to help anyone." It was Nathan, his silhouette emerging from the shadows of the pier, the very embodiment of chaos and charm.

"Shouldn't you be somewhere safe?" I shot back, not bothering to hide my annoyance, but my heart quickened at the sight of him. His tousled hair whipped around his face, and raindrops beaded on his skin, giving him an uncharacteristically vulnerable appearance. "Or are you just here to gloat?"

"Maybe I'm here to save you from drowning in your own melodrama." He stepped closer, his voice low and teasing, the hint of a smile playing at the corners of his lips. "You're about to throw away everything for a job that might not even be what you want. Doesn't that strike you as a bit... hasty?"

"Hasty?" I echoed, my voice rising with the wind. "What do you know about hasty? You've spent your life stuck in this town, too scared to try anything new."

He tilted his head, that infuriatingly charming smirk unwavering. "And you think running away is the answer? What if I told you there's more to this place than meets the eye?"

For a moment, I faltered, the tension between us thick enough to slice. The rain began to fall in earnest, each drop a small reminder of the feelings I had kept bottled up for so long. He was right—there was a world here, rich with memories and connections that had shaped who I was. But did that mean I should stay?

"Maybe," I replied, my voice barely above a whisper, "but sometimes staying is just as scary as leaving."

The storm raged on, the waves crashing beneath us like a heartbeat, each pulse matching the rhythm of our conversation. I could see it in his eyes—the hesitation, the understanding. There was something unspoken hanging in the air, a connection that defied the very reasons we had fought against each other for so long.

And just like that, the storm transformed from a backdrop of chaos into a metaphor for our own entwined fates, each wave crashing against the shore like the heartbeat of our unresolved tensions.

The rain fell harder, each drop a reminder of the uncertainty swirling within me. Nathan stepped closer, the distance between us shrinking like the divide between two rival factions forced to coexist. I could feel the heat radiating from his body, an unexpected warmth amid the cold drizzle. Our gazes locked, and I half expected him to laugh, to throw another jibe my way, but instead, there was an intensity in his eyes that made my stomach twist.

"Are you always this dramatic, or is it just when I'm around?" he quipped, breaking the silence, his voice teasing yet somehow sincere.

I rolled my eyes, but I couldn't suppress a smile. "Oh please, this isn't drama. This is just me processing a life-altering decision while standing on the edge of a pier during a storm. Totally normal."

He chuckled, and the sound sent an unexpected thrill through me. "Normal for you, maybe. Most people would be inside, sipping hot cocoa or something."

"Hot cocoa? Really?" I scoffed, shaking my head. "How cliché. I'd take a glass of wine over cocoa any day."

"Wine it is, then." He stepped closer, and I noticed how the rain had darkened his shirt, clinging to his form in a way that was entirely distracting. "What if I told you I could give you a reason to stay?"

"Are you trying to manipulate me with your devilish charm?" I shot back, unable to resist a playful grin. "Because if you are, it's working."

His smile widened, and in that moment, I was reminded of all the reasons I had fought against this inexplicable connection. It felt too easy, too comfortable, and that scared me more than the storm brewing above us. I shook my head, trying to dispel the warmth blooming in my chest. "But seriously, Nathan, what could possibly make me want to stay in this town?"

He opened his mouth to respond, but the wind whipped around us, drowning out his words. Suddenly, a particularly strong gust sent a spray of seawater crashing into my face, and I shrieked, instinctively stepping back. "Well, that was rude!" I exclaimed, wiping my eyes.

"Nature's way of reminding you to pay attention," he teased, the glimmer in his eye dancing with mischief. "But really, you should think about it. This town has more to offer than you realize."

I narrowed my eyes, intrigued despite myself. "Oh? And what exactly do you think I'm missing?"

He stepped back slightly, the rain tracing rivulets down his face. "For one, there's this place called The Crow's Nest. It's a dive bar, but it has the best live music on Friday nights. I'm not sure if they serve wine, but they definitely have cheap beer."

I laughed, shaking my head at the absurdity of it all. "You think a bar is going to convince me to stay in Windward Bay? I'm looking for a career, Nathan, not a nightlife adventure."

"Careers can happen anywhere, but life? That's what we're talking about. You're about to trade your life here for a job, and I'm not sure that's the right move."

I studied him, the rain pooling in the crevices of the pier beneath our feet. He looked sincere, almost vulnerable, a surprising contrast to the confident facade he usually presented. "You don't know me," I countered, my voice steadier than I felt. "You don't know what I want or need."

"Maybe I don't know everything," he replied, his tone softening, "but I know you've been restless for a while. You've got that spark—just look at you. You'd set this town on fire if you stayed."

The compliment caught me off guard, and I felt my cheeks flush, either from the rain or the sincerity of his words. "You're saying I'm too hot to handle?" I shot back, unable to resist turning the moment playful again.

"Something like that," he replied, smirking. "And let's be honest, you could use a little chaos in your life. You've been so focused on plans and responsibilities, you've forgotten how to just... live."

"Chaos? Is that what you call your brand of charming mischief?" I arched an eyebrow, matching his playful tone. "Because I'm not sure that's what I need."

"Maybe it's exactly what you need. Life isn't meant to be a straight line, you know. Sometimes you've got to embrace the twists and turns, even if they lead you back home."

His words hung in the air, and the storm around us seemed to quiet for a moment, creating a bubble where it felt like only we existed. I wanted to argue, to hold onto my determination to leave, but something in his expression made me pause. There was a sincerity there, a depth that made my heart race with the possibility of something more.

"Okay, fine," I said, folding my arms defiantly. "You've intrigued me. What's your big plan to show me that this place isn't the backwater I've always thought it was?"

"Tomorrow night, you're coming to The Crow's Nest with me. You can't say no," he said, his tone suddenly serious, as if it were a dare.

"Who says I'm not busy? I could be packing my bags and writing resignation letters," I countered, knowing full well the prospect of a night out with Nathan was far more tempting than any mundane task.

"Right, because that's how you want to spend your last night in Windward Bay," he replied, shaking his head as if he were seeing right through my excuses. "Come on, indulge me. If you hate it, you can leave. If you like it, well... we'll see where that takes us."

"Is this your grand seduction plan? Luring me in with promises of bad music and cheap beer?" I asked, feigning indifference even as my heart thumped faster.

"Absolutely," he said with an exaggerated seriousness, "because nothing says romance like sticky floors and overpriced nachos."

We both laughed, the sound cutting through the stormy air, making the moment feel lighter. For a heartbeat, I allowed myself to entertain the possibility of staying. Maybe Nathan was right. Maybe there was more to this town than I had ever allowed myself to see.

"Okay, fine. You win," I said, trying to keep my tone light, but inside, my heart was racing with excitement and trepidation. "I'll go to this bar of yours. But if it turns out to be a disaster, I'm holding you responsible."

He extended his hand, that charming smirk back in place, and for a moment, I hesitated, contemplating the weight of that simple gesture. Then, with a nervous laugh, I took it, my pulse quickening as our fingers intertwined. The storm raged on around us, but in that moment, standing on the edge of my old world, I felt something shift deep within me—a tremor of hope, the first crack in my resolve, as if I were finally allowing myself to embrace the chaos.

The following day was a study in contradiction. The sun emerged from the depths of the clouds, casting a golden hue over Windward Bay that felt almost mocking in its cheerfulness after the previous night's storm. I stood in front of my bathroom mirror, wrestling with a tangle of emotions as I brushed through my damp hair. The reflection that stared back at me was a mixture of defiance and uncertainty, and I couldn't help but smile as I remembered the spontaneous agreement I'd made with Nathan. How had I gone from a meticulously planned exit strategy to a last-minute invitation to a dive bar?

I pulled on my favorite faded jeans and a sweater that felt like a hug against my skin. The soft fabric enveloped me in comfort, which felt almost necessary given the whirlwind my life had taken on since Nathan had shown up on the pier. Was it foolishness to let a single encounter disrupt my carefully laid plans? Perhaps, but something deep within urged me to explore this unpredictable path. After all, it wasn't every day that Nathan Hale, my childhood rival, suddenly transformed into my unexpected ally—or, dare I say, friend.

The sunlight flickered through the trees lining our family's old house, illuminating the dust motes dancing in the air. The aroma of fresh coffee wafted through the kitchen, mixing with the familiar scent of salt from the ocean just a few blocks away. I found my mother standing by the window, a soft smile gracing her face as she gazed out at the horizon.

"Are you excited about your new job?" she asked without turning, her voice light and hopeful.

I hesitated, the excitement that had once surged within me now feeling muddied with uncertainty. "I am, but I'm still figuring things out."

Her brow furrowed slightly, and she turned to me, her eyes a mix of concern and curiosity. "You know you can always talk to me, right? About anything."

"Of course, Mom. It's just..." I bit my lip, wrestling with how much to reveal. "I met someone, and he's kind of made me rethink things."

"Someone? A boy? Tell me more!" she chirped, leaning in, her interest piqued.

"It's not like that," I rushed to clarify, the flush creeping up my cheeks. "It's Nathan Hale. We've had a rivalry since we were kids, and now he wants me to go to this bar with him."

"Nathan Hale? The one you used to argue with on the playground?" Her eyes twinkled with mischief. "You always said he was insufferable."

"He is! But it's complicated now," I admitted, the words tumbling out faster than I could catch them. "He challenged my decision to leave, and for some reason, I agreed to this ridiculous outing. I just need to see what it's all about."

"Sounds like more than a rivalry to me," she teased, winking as she poured another cup of coffee.

I rolled my eyes but couldn't shake the giddiness that bubbled within me. "It's not like that! At least, I don't think so."

"Just promise me you'll be careful," she said, her tone shifting to seriousness. "I know how you can get swept away when you're excited."

"Mom, it's just a night out." I held up my hands in mock surrender. "Nothing to worry about."

The clock ticked steadily as the hours drifted by, and the excitement that had been bubbling under the surface began to crystallize into something more tangible. The afternoon melted into evening, and as the sun dipped below the horizon, painting the sky in hues of orange and pink, my heart raced in anticipation.

When I arrived at The Crow's Nest, the dive bar lived up to its name. It was an unassuming structure, weathered by years of salt and storms, its neon sign flickering in the dim light. The raucous laughter and music spilled out onto the street, creating a warm, inviting atmosphere that drew me in. Nathan was already inside, leaning casually against the bar with a drink in hand, and the moment I stepped through the door, our gazes locked.

"Look who decided to show up," he said, his voice playful, a slight challenge in his tone as he approached me. The dim light caught the contours of his face, the play of shadows highlighting the intensity in his dark eyes.

"Try not to look too smug," I retorted, crossing my arms. "It was a tough decision to leave my plans behind for this."

"Too late for that," he replied, gesturing to the barstool beside him. "Have a seat. You'll thank me later."

I rolled my eyes but obliged, feeling the energy in the room swirl around us, a blend of excitement and anticipation. I ordered a glass of wine, a choice that Nathan watched with an amused smirk.

"I knew you had it in you," he quipped. "Who would have thought you'd trade your perfectly brewed coffee for a cheap glass of wine in a dive?"

"Everyone needs to step out of their comfort zone sometimes," I shot back, savoring the cool liquid as it slid down my throat, warming me from the inside out. "Besides, this place has a certain charm, don't you think?"

"It's got character, I'll give you that," he said, leaning back, a hint of mischief dancing in his eyes. "Just wait until the band starts. They're a local favorite, but don't expect anything polished."

"I'm ready for whatever this place throws at me," I replied, feeling bold and adventurous. "Bring it on."

And just as the anticipation peaked, the band began to play—a raucous blend of rock and blues that sent ripples of energy through the crowd. Laughter and cheers erupted, and I couldn't help but sway slightly to the music, feeling lighter than I had in weeks. Nathan's gaze was steady, a spark of appreciation lingering in his eyes as we navigated the chaos together.

"This isn't so bad, right?" he shouted over the music, his voice thick with enthusiasm.

"Not bad at all!" I shouted back, caught up in the moment, an unexpected wave of joy washing over me.

As the night unfolded, we shared stories, laughter, and an easy camaraderie that felt effortless. The more we talked, the more the past faded into the background, leaving only the thrill of the present. But beneath that surface, I sensed the unspoken tension building—a current that crackled between us, alive and electric.

Just as I was starting to let my guard down, my phone buzzed on the table, jolting me from my reverie. I picked it up and saw a text from my father, the words abrupt and unsettling: We need to talk. It's important.

"Everything okay?" Nathan asked, noting the shift in my expression.

"Uh, yeah. Just... family stuff," I stammered, my mind racing. "I should probably..."

"Finish your drink first," he interjected, a knowing look in his eyes. "You've been planning to leave this town, remember? Don't let a text derail your night."

As if on cue, the music swelled, a surge of sound that seemed to resonate with my emotions. I weighed my father's message against the warmth of the moment, the promise of laughter still echoing in the air. But just as I raised my glass to clink it against Nathan's, a loud crash from the back of the bar shattered the atmosphere, and the crowd's laughter turned to gasps.

"What was that?" I asked, my heart pounding.

"I don't know," Nathan replied, his demeanor shifting to concern as he stood. "Let's check it out."

We pushed through the throng of people, adrenaline kicking in as we moved toward the commotion. As we neared the back, the sight that greeted us froze me in place—two figures, cloaked in shadows, arguing fiercely, one of them gripping a baseball bat, the other clenching a small, glinting object.

"Get back!" one of them shouted, their voice laced with aggression.

And just like that, the night turned from exhilarating to terrifying, my heart racing as the implications crashed over me like the very waves I had stood beside just days before. As Nathan instinctively moved closer, I felt an unsettling sense of dread settle in the pit of my stomach. Something was about to change—whether I wanted it to or not.

Chapter 2: The Unwelcome Reunion

The annual Windward Bay Carnival unfolded before me like a kaleidoscope of chaos and color, a dizzying swirl of laughter and shrieks that clashed against the backdrop of twinkling lights strung between the weathered trees. Each stall, draped in brightly colored fabric, beckoned with promises of fried delights and carnival games, where the air was thick with the scent of cinnamon and sugar. My best friend Sarah had dragged me along, her enthusiasm bubbling over like the fizzy sodas in the cups we held, and though I tried to mask my reluctance, the festive atmosphere was hard to resist.

We weaved through the crowd, the sounds of the carnival—a blend of cheerful music and excited chatter—creating a rhythm I found oddly infectious. Children darted past us, their faces painted like wild animals, clutching prizes they'd won at games I'd rather avoid. The ring toss, the dart throw, and the ever-elusive balloon pop haunted my thoughts as I recalled my past failures. Still, as I took in the scene, I couldn't shake the feeling that I was stepping back into a chapter of my life I thought I'd left behind.

"Look at that," Sarah said, her voice rising above the cacophony. She pointed toward a stall where a man was juggling flaming torches, his movements as smooth as the waves that lapped at the nearby shore. "Can you believe how talented these people are?"

I nodded, forcing a smile, but my mind was elsewhere, tangled in memories I had hoped to forget. The festival was a yearly reminder of what I had lost, of friendships frayed and dreams deferred. Just as I was about to escape into my thoughts, a familiar voice cut through the noise, rich and warm, wrapping around me like a favorite sweater.

"Julia! Fancy seeing you here."

The world tilted on its axis, and my heart plummeted as I turned to face him. Nathan stood at the ring toss booth, the very embodiment of charisma and casual confidence. His tousled hair caught the light, framing his face in a way that made my breath hitch, as if my lungs had forgotten how to function. He wore a relaxed smile, one that could ignite sparks in the most jaded heart. He always had a way of lighting up a room, and that irked me to no end.

"What's the matter, Julia? Afraid you might have fun?" His grin was teasing, his blue eyes glinting with mischief, the type that sent warmth flooding through me and infuriated me simultaneously.

I rolled my eyes, crossing my arms in a futile attempt to shield myself from the weight of his gaze. "Fun isn't on the agenda, Nathan. I'm here under duress."

"Duress? I thought you loved the carnival! The fried dough? The cotton candy?" He feigned shock, a hand placed dramatically over his heart as if I'd just proclaimed a life-altering revelation.

"Let's not exaggerate. I tolerate it for Sarah's sake. If it were up to me, I'd be home with a book and a cup of tea."

"Ah, yes, the 'homebody' persona," he replied, his tone playful. "Tell me, does that book come with a side of bitterness? Because I think I detect a hint of it right now."

"Bitterness? Please, it's called self-preservation. I'd rather not endure the sensory overload." I gestured toward the cotton candy vendor as if it were a demon lurking in the shadows, ready to pounce. "Or the crowds, for that matter."

"Aw, come on! You can't seriously tell me you're going to let the fear of sugar-induced chaos ruin your night? Just think of all the funnel cake." His smile was infectious, and against my better judgment, I felt my lips twitching into a reluctant smile.

"Funnel cake?" I repeated, feigning deep contemplation. "It is tempting, but I'd rather not spend the rest of the evening with powdered sugar all over my face. Last time I looked like a ghost, and not the cute kind."

"Maybe you could scare off a few clowns while you're at it," he shot back, laughter dancing in his voice. "But honestly, you're missing out. You can't spend your whole life avoiding fun."

"Fun doesn't mean funnel cake and ridiculous games," I shot back, the spark of our familiar banter igniting my competitive spirit. "Fun could mean winning at something for a change."

"Is that a challenge I hear?" His eyes gleamed, an ever-present twinkle of mischief flickering in their depths.

"It could be. I'm not afraid to lose in public," I said, taking a step closer, my heart racing at the thought of facing him in a competition. "You know, just to show you how it's done."

"Bring it on," he grinned, clearly relishing the prospect. He gestured toward the ring toss booth, where a small crowd had gathered, each onlooker waiting with bated breath as their friends attempted to land a ring on one of the bottles. "Let's see if you can handle it."

With a determined nod, I stepped up to the booth, the sounds of the carnival fading into a low hum as I focused on the task ahead. The rings glimmered under the string lights, and for a brief moment, all that mattered was the challenge before me. Nathan's voice faded, and the laughter of the crowd melted into the background as I narrowed my gaze.

"First ring to hit a bottle wins," I declared, my voice steady as I picked up the first ring, feeling the weight of it in my hand. "Loser buys dinner."

"Dinner? I like the stakes." His voice was a low, enticing drawl, and despite the banter, I felt an unexpected thrill at the challenge. "Prepare to lose, Julia."

"Not a chance." I released the ring with a flick of my wrist, the arc of it a graceful dance through the air, destined for victory.

And then, as if the universe had conspired against me, the ring sailed past the bottles, a mere whisper of hope amidst the laughter that erupted from the crowd.

"Nice throw," Nathan teased, a mockingly impressed expression on his face.

"Just warming up," I replied, my competitive fire igniting even brighter. "Let's see what you've got, Mister 'I'm So Charming'."

I watched as Nathan sauntered over to the ring toss, a playful grin plastered on his face, clearly reveling in the competition. The crowd around us buzzed with excitement, children squealing in delight as their parents cheered them on. I felt my heart thump in time with the rhythm of the carnival, a strange mix of dread and thrill coursing through my veins. Somehow, the stakes had risen beyond just a simple game.

"Here comes the master of disaster," I muttered, watching as Nathan confidently picked up a ring. The way he held it, relaxed yet purposeful, sent a jolt of unease through me. The sun dipped lower, casting a golden glow that seemed to spotlight him. It was infuriating how he managed to look effortlessly charming while I was a bundle of nerves wrapped in a jacket too warm for the season.

With an exaggerated flourish, he tossed the ring, and it sailed through the air, perfect in its trajectory, only to bounce harmlessly off the edge of the nearest bottle. The crowd erupted into laughter, and for a moment, I couldn't help but join in, despite the rising tension between us.

"Careful there, Casanova. You might need to stick to juggling," I teased, my voice lighter than I felt.

"Ah, the ring toss! A true test of skill," he retorted, brushing off the mishap with a charming wave of his hand. "Let's not forget, I'm not the one who just fluffed it."

"Oh, please! One bad throw doesn't define me," I shot back, scooping up the next ring. "I've got this."

Nathan watched as I tossed my second ring, this time aiming with precision. It struck a bottle, wobbling precariously before toppling over with a satisfying crash. The crowd cheered, and I turned to Nathan with a triumphant smirk.

"Looks like I'm the one who should be buying dinner," I declared, feeling the sweet rush of victory surge through me.

"Beginner's luck," he said, but I caught the gleam in his eye—he was impressed. "Let's see if you can do it again."

"Let's see if you can actually land one," I countered, reveling in the banter as I handed him a ring.

With exaggerated concentration, Nathan squared his shoulders and aimed. The ring slipped from his fingers and landed—right in the dirt. The laughter from the crowd grew louder, a chorus of delight at his expense.

"Nice aim," I laughed, doubling over as I clutched my stomach. "You sure you want to go for dinner after that?"

"Okay, okay! One more round," he said, feigning indignation but unable to hide his own amusement. "Third time's the charm."

Just as he bent down to pick up another ring, a sudden commotion erupted nearby. A group of teenagers burst into the ring toss area, shoving each other and shrieking with laughter. In the chaos, one of them knocked into Nathan, sending the ring he was holding flying—right toward my face.

"Watch out!" Nathan yelled, his eyes wide with horror.

I instinctively ducked, but it was too late. The ring grazed my cheek, and I stumbled backward, nearly losing my footing. The laughter that followed from the teens felt like a sharp blade against my skin, and I felt the heat of embarrassment bloom across my face.

"Great aim, champ," I mumbled, forcing a smile even as my cheeks burned.

"I'm so sorry!" Nathan rushed over, concern etched on his features. "Are you okay?"

I straightened, brushing off the remnants of my dignity. "Just peachy, thanks." I threw him a playful glare, trying to mask the embarrassment with bravado. "Though maybe you should switch to a less dangerous sport."

The teenagers, still caught up in their antics, offered half-hearted apologies before scampering off, leaving the ring toss booth in a mild uproar. The carnival felt like a whirlwind, pulling me in every direction as I tried to regain my composure.

"Are you really okay?" Nathan asked again, his voice softening. "I didn't mean for that to happen."

"It's fine," I assured him, dismissing the moment with a wave. "Just another day in my wonderfully chaotic life."

"You know, it's kind of cute how you pretend to be unfazed by this," he replied, his gaze lingering on my face. "But I think you secretly love the chaos."

"Maybe I do," I said, daring to meet his eyes, a mischievous grin tugging at my lips. "But I also know when to duck."

He chuckled, shaking his head as he leaned against the booth. "So what's next? A spin on the Ferris wheel? Or do you prefer your amusement rides less... dizzying?"

"I'll pass on the Ferris wheel," I said, glancing toward the towering structure that loomed over the carnival. "I'm not in the mood to lose my lunch. How about the haunted house? Nothing like a few jump scares to clear the air."

Nathan raised an eyebrow, a mix of amusement and challenge dancing in his expression. "A haunted house? You really are a glutton for punishment."

"Only when it comes to you," I shot back, trying to keep the tone light. But beneath the surface, a different kind of tension pulsed between us, a flickering spark that felt both exciting and dangerous.

"Lead the way, brave one," he said, stepping back to let me take the lead.

As we approached the entrance of the haunted house, I felt a rush of adrenaline. The façade was ominous, with creaking doors and flickering lights that seemed to mock the brave souls daring to enter. I took a deep breath, determined not to show any fear as I glanced back at Nathan.

"You ready to scream like a little kid?" I challenged, feeling more confident than I had moments before.

"Only if you are," he replied, his tone teasing, but I caught the flicker of something deeper in his eyes, something that ignited the air around us with an unspoken promise.

Together, we stepped through the threshold, the darkness swallowing us whole. The scent of damp wood and the distant sound of moaning echoed around us, the atmosphere charged with an intensity that felt almost electric. My heart raced as we moved deeper into the shadows, but this time, it wasn't just the haunted house that made me feel alive—it was the thrill of being close to Nathan, the familiarity of our banter wrapping around us like a protective cloak.

"Just remember," I said, the darkness closing in around us, "if you scream, I'll never let you live it down."

"I'm counting on it," he whispered, laughter lacing his words. And in that moment, I knew the night had only just begun to unfold its surprises.

The interior of the haunted house was a labyrinth of shadows, filled with flickering lights that seemed to dance in sync with my racing heartbeat. The air was heavy, thick with the smell of damp wood and artificial fog. I moved cautiously, my fingers brushing against the cool, textured walls as I felt my way through the darkness, adrenaline coursing through me. The thrill of uncertainty hung in the air, igniting a nervous energy that made my skin tingle.

"Are you scared yet?" Nathan's voice broke through the dimness, laced with playful mockery.

"Scared? Please," I replied, my tone a little too confident as I peered into the gloom ahead. "I'm just… cautious."

"Cautious? In a haunted house?" He chuckled, the sound reverberating oddly in the confined space. "That's like being careful with a roller coaster—it's counterproductive."

I couldn't help but smile despite the creeping sense of unease. "Maybe I just enjoy the thrill of the chase," I said, my voice low as I led the way deeper into the darkness.

Suddenly, a loud crash echoed from behind us, and I froze, my heart leaping into my throat. The sound was followed by the unmistakable clattering of what I hoped was just props. But the uneasy feeling crept in, wrapping around my nerves like a cold fog.

"Did you hear that?" I whispered, suddenly aware of how the shadows seemed to close in on us.

"Relax, it's just a haunted house," Nathan said, though there was a slight tremor in his voice that made my stomach twist. "Probably just the actors messing around."

"Right," I said, forcing a laugh even as my heart raced. "I mean, who wouldn't want to jump out and scare us while we're trying to enjoy the ambiance?"

We rounded a corner, and I immediately regretted my bravado. An eerie figure leaped from the shadows, a ghoul with exaggerated features and hollow eyes that glowed faintly in the dim light. I shrieked, more surprised than scared, and instinctively grabbed Nathan's arm, clutching it like a lifeline.

"Now that's the spirit!" he exclaimed, laughter bubbling up as he pulled me closer to him, the heat of his body radiating through the layers of fabric between us.

"Very funny," I retorted, my voice shaky as I released his arm, feeling a jolt of embarrassment. "Just what I needed—an unexpected hug from a creepy phantom."

"Next time, I'll warn you," he teased, though there was an unmistakable warmth in his gaze that made the air feel electric.

As we navigated through the twists and turns, I couldn't shake the feeling that something was off. The shadows seemed to loom larger, more alive, as if they were watching us, biding their time. The laughter from outside faded, replaced by a heavy silence that settled uncomfortably around us.

"Hey, do you think we should go back?" I asked, glancing over my shoulder as a shiver ran down my spine.

"Are you kidding?" Nathan grinned, his eyes sparkling with mischief. "This is the most fun I've had in ages. You're not backing out now."

Just as I was about to retort, a door creaked open to our left, revealing a hidden passageway cloaked in darkness. Nathan took a step toward it, and a flash of instinct pulled me back. "Wait, we should stick to the main path."

But he was already peering into the darkness, curiosity etched across his features. "What's the worst that could happen?"

Famous last words, I thought, but I felt an inexplicable pull toward the unknown. "I don't know. Ghosts? Spirits? Or worse—getting trapped in a horror movie?"

"You know I'd protect you, right?" His words were half-teasing, but the earnestness in his eyes made my heart race for a different reason.

I took a deep breath, nerves tingling as I approached the passage. "Fine. But you're leading the way. I'm not taking any responsibility for whatever terrors await us."

"Fair enough," he chuckled, stepping into the gloom with an exaggerated bravado. I followed closely, trying to mask my unease as we ventured deeper into the passage.

The air grew cooler, and the walls felt damp against my fingertips. Whispers seemed to echo through the corridor, sending chills skittering down my spine. I was hyper-aware of every sound, every flicker of light, every brush of air. The ambiance shifted, becoming thick with an unspoken tension.

"Okay, maybe this was a bad idea," I murmured, my bravado starting to wane as an uneasy feeling settled in my gut.

"Nonsense," Nathan replied, a playful lilt in his voice as he turned to face me, his expression serious yet amused. "This is where the magic happens. Just think of all the stories we could tell."

"Or the nightmares we could live through," I shot back, trying to keep the mood light even as my heart raced.

We pressed on, and the whispers grew louder, more distinct. It was a chorus of soft voices, weaving in and out like a distant melody. I strained to catch their words, but they eluded me, swirling in the air like smoke.

"Do you hear that?" I asked, my voice barely a whisper.

"Yeah, but it's probably just sound effects," he said, though I could see the unease flickering in his eyes.

"Right. Just sound effects," I echoed, my heart pounding as we moved deeper. Then, a sudden flicker of light illuminated the passage ahead, revealing a door at the end, slightly ajar.

"Should we check it out?" Nathan suggested, his voice a mix of excitement and apprehension.

"What if it's a trap?" I shot back, though my curiosity battled against my common sense. "What if we open that door and—"

Before I could finish my sentence, the door swung open with a loud creak, and a rush of icy air swept through the corridor, snuffing out the flickering lights behind us. We were plunged into darkness, the whispers rising to a crescendo that felt like a cacophony of warning.

"Julia!" Nathan's voice was now laced with urgency, and instinctively, I reached for him, grasping his hand tightly.

"What's happening?" I breathed, panic clawing at my throat as I felt the shadows swirl around us, the whispers growing louder, almost pleading.

"Stay close!" he urged, but even as he spoke, the door slammed shut behind us, sealing us in the darkness.

My heart raced as I felt the walls close in, the whispers morphing into a chaotic symphony of disembodied voices. Fear gripped me, threatening to overwhelm my senses. "We need to get out of here!"

In that moment, the air grew thick with an unnatural chill, and I felt a presence looming just beyond the veil of darkness. Something was watching us, waiting.

And then, just as abruptly as it had begun, the whispers fell silent. The absence of sound echoed in the void, leaving only our heavy breaths and the pounding of my heart.

"What just happened?" I whispered, my voice trembling as I squeezed Nathan's hand tighter.

But before he could respond, a low rumble reverberated through the floor beneath us, shaking the ground. The shadows shifted, swirling into a vortex of darkness, and I realized we were no longer alone.

As the atmosphere crackled with tension, I felt a cold breath against my neck, sending a shiver of dread down my spine.

"Julia..." Nathan's voice was barely a whisper, full of fear and uncertainty, and just as I turned to face him, the shadows lunged forward, engulfing us in their depths, leaving nothing but a chilling silence in their wake.

Chapter 3: Shadows of the Past

The morning sun spilled through my window, casting golden light across the floorboards of my small apartment. It felt like a scene ripped straight from a movie, where everything appears perfect until the inevitable twist comes crashing down. As I pulled myself from the tangled sheets, a flicker of unease snagged at my gut. Something about today felt off, like the calm before a storm.

The moment I stepped into the kitchen, my eyes caught the glint of something beneath the door. I knelt down, heart pounding, and pulled a folded piece of paper from under the threshold. My hands trembled as I opened it, the handwriting scrawled in a hasty, erratic manner that felt all too personal. "Leave Windward Bay immediately," it read, each word heavy with a threat I couldn't quite grasp.

My pulse quickened, and a rush of cold air seemed to sweep through the room. It felt surreal, as if I had stumbled into a mystery novel instead of my own life. Had I unwittingly stumbled upon something? My thoughts spiraled, playing out scenarios more fitting for a suspense film than my quiet existence. Was this a prank? A warning? I couldn't tell which idea terrified me more.

After a few minutes of pacing like a caged animal, I grabbed my phone and texted Sarah. She was my rock, my grounding force, always able to coax me back from the edge of my anxiety. Within moments, my phone buzzed.

"Breathe, Ember. I'm on my way," her response came quickly, practical as always. I nodded to myself, as if she could see me through the screen. I didn't want to be alone right now.

While waiting, I stared out at the world beyond my window, watching as the early morning bustle of Windward Bay unfolded. Children rode bikes, their laughter echoing off the walls of the buildings. Couples walked hand in hand, their smiles wide and genuine. How could all of this carry on when I felt like I was standing on the precipice of something dark?

Sarah arrived moments later, bursting through the door with her usual flair. "You look like you've seen a ghost," she said, tossing her bag onto the kitchen counter and approaching me. She was a whirlwind of energy, a stark contrast to the unease wrapped around my shoulders like a heavy blanket.

"It's worse than that," I murmured, handing her the note. The moment her eyes skimmed over the paper, her expression shifted, the playful sparkle replaced by something serious. "What does this mean? Who would do something like this?"

"I don't know," I admitted, my voice barely above a whisper. "But it feels... personal. I can't shake the feeling that someone is watching me."

She leaned against the counter, her arms crossed, contemplating my words. "Maybe it's just a prank. I mean, this is Windward Bay, not the set of a horror movie. People are usually more concerned with beach parties than scaring each other."

I wished I could believe her. "It just doesn't feel right. I've had a strange vibe ever since I got here."

"Okay, let's think about it logically," she said, straightening up and putting on her most serious face. "Is there anyone you've upset? Anyone you've clashed with?"

That was when Nathan's face flashed in my mind, and I felt a strange mix of annoyance and longing. He was the last person I'd expected to feel anything for, yet our arguments had turned into something deeper, a connection forged in the fire of our banter. His teasing had transformed into an unexpected warmth, leaving me feeling both exhilarated and utterly confused. But had I unknowingly crossed a line with him?

"I don't think it's him," I replied, shaking my head, though I felt a twinge of doubt creeping in. "But what if he's somehow involved? Or worse, what if he's the one sending these messages?"

Sarah rolled her eyes, as if I had suggested I was in a spy thriller. "Nathan? Please. He might have a knack for ruffling your feathers, but I can't imagine him as some sort of shadowy villain."

Before I could argue, my phone buzzed again. It was a message from Nathan, his name lighting up my screen. "Hey, what's up? You seem off. Everything okay?"

I hesitated, the note weighing heavily in my mind. Should I let him in on my fears? Or would that just complicate our already tangled relationship? With a deep breath, I decided honesty was the best policy. I quickly typed back, "Just got a strange note. Someone wants me to leave Windward Bay."

Moments later, my phone buzzed again, Nathan's response coming through with a speed that almost made me smile. "What? That's ridiculous! You're not going anywhere. Meet me at the café in twenty. We'll figure this out."

His protective tone sent a flicker of warmth through my chest, but it was swiftly overshadowed by the tension in my gut. "I'll see you there," I texted back, attempting to ignore the way my heart fluttered at the thought of seeing him.

Once Sarah left, I quickly dressed, trying to shake off the unease that clung to me like a shadow. The café was a lively hub, full of the rich aroma of coffee and the soft hum of chatter. But today, it felt like a stage set for a play where I was the only one aware of the dark script unfolding behind the scenes.

As I approached Nathan's table, I could see his brow furrowed in concern. The moment our eyes met, a spark of understanding passed between us, igniting a complicated mixture of emotions. I took a seat across from him, trying to push aside the noise of uncertainty and the note's chilling warning. Whatever shadows loomed over

Windward Bay, I was determined to face them head-on, even if it meant confronting the most unexpected feelings in the process.

The café buzzed with energy, a stark contrast to the storm of thoughts swirling in my mind. The scent of fresh pastries mingled with the rich aroma of coffee, tempting me to let my guard down for just a moment. But the note lingered, a dark cloud hovering over what should have been a carefree Saturday. I sat across from Nathan, who had already ordered two steaming mugs of the house special, his brows knitted in concern.

"You look like you just stepped off a horror movie set," he said, his voice teasing yet laced with sincerity. "Tell me you didn't find a dead body or something."

I couldn't help but smile, despite the gravity of the situation. "Not yet, but I've got a lovely note telling me to skedaddle. So, there's still time."

His expression shifted from playful to serious, the humor draining from his features. "What do you mean, 'skedaddle'? You're not going anywhere. This town is too charming to leave behind."

"It's charming until someone starts sending me threatening notes," I shot back, unable to suppress the bite in my tone. "You're the last person I expected to care, anyway."

He leaned forward, his elbows resting on the table, an earnestness in his eyes that made my heart flutter despite myself. "Ember, just because I enjoy tormenting you doesn't mean I want you to vanish. You're like the only spark of excitement in this sleepy town."

The compliment caught me off guard, and I felt my cheeks warm. "Well, thanks for the vote of confidence. Maybe I should set up shop as the town's drama queen."

His lips curled into a grin, and for a moment, the tension between us faded. But the fleeting moment of levity didn't last long as the enormity of my predicament reasserted itself. "Have you ever received anything like this before?" he asked, his tone shifting to something more investigative.

"Not even close," I admitted, running a hand through my hair in frustration. "I just moved here. Who would even want me gone?"

"I'm not sure, but we should find out. You can't let some random note dictate your life," he insisted, his determination infectious. "How about we do some digging? Together."

"Together? You mean like a buddy cop duo?" I quipped, raising an eyebrow.

"Exactly! You can be the brains, and I'll be the brawn," he declared with an exaggerated flex of his biceps. I couldn't help but laugh, imagining us running through the streets, solving crimes like we were living in a sitcom.

But even as I chuckled, an unsettling feeling nestled in my stomach. "I don't know if that's the best idea. What if it turns out to be something dangerous?"

"Then we'll handle it," he said simply, his gaze unwavering. "Look, if someone is watching you, we need to know why. If nothing else, it'll keep me entertained."

"Great, because I'm sure your idea of fun involves hunting down creepy note writers," I replied, sarcasm dripping from my voice.

He smirked. "Absolutely. And if we're lucky, we might uncover a secret society operating out of the local library. Think of the plot twist!"

"Or we could just get coffee and leave the drama for another day," I suggested, a half-hearted smile tugging at my lips.

"Where's the adventure in that? We're living in a thriller, and you want to make it a rom-com?" he challenged, leaning back in his chair, crossing his arms.

For a moment, I was struck by how his humor balanced out my worries. There was a spark of something between us that was undeniably magnetic, and despite my anxiety, I found comfort in his presence. "Fine. Let's play detective," I relented. "But if we end up in a horror movie situation, I'm blaming you."

Nathan laughed, and I felt the tension lift a fraction as we finished our coffees, plotting our next move.

Our first stop was the local library, a quaint brick building nestled between a bakery and a vintage clothing store. It exuded an old-world charm, with ivy creeping up its walls and large windows framed by white shutters. As we stepped inside, the musty scent of paper and ink wrapped around me like a warm blanket.

"Do you think they have a 'how to find stalkers' section?" Nathan joked, scanning the shelves as I rolled my eyes.

"Maybe check the self-help section for clueless people," I shot back, playfully nudging him with my shoulder.

As we wandered through the aisles, I felt a strange thrill at the prospect of uncovering something—anything—that might help explain the note. We eventually found the librarian, a middle-aged woman with glasses perched on her nose, immersed in a stack of books.

"Excuse me," I said, clearing my throat. "We were wondering if you might have any information about the history of Windward Bay? Anything... unusual?"

Her eyes widened, curiosity piqued. "Unusual? This town is full of secrets, dear. I could tell you stories that would make your hair stand on end. But what are you looking for specifically?"

I hesitated, unsure of how to phrase my request without sounding completely paranoid. "Just anything about... people who might want to keep others from sticking around."

She leaned back in her chair, her interest clearly engaged. "Ah, you mean the local legends. We do have a few tales about folks who didn't quite fit in. But don't let the stories scare you. Windward Bay is also known for its hospitality."

"That's comforting," Nathan chimed in, feigning an air of relief. "You're saying we might get chased off by ghostly figures or something?"

The librarian chuckled, her laughter a soft melody in the stillness of the library. "More like gossipers, if anything. There's a tight-knit community here, and people can be protective. If you're new and don't play by the unspoken rules, you might attract some unwanted attention."

I felt a chill creep down my spine. "Do you think that could be what this is about?" I asked, gesturing to the note in my pocket.

She studied me for a moment, her expression turning serious. "It's possible. But don't let it weigh you down. If you're determined to stay, you'll find your place here. Just remember, every town has its shadows."

As she spoke, I couldn't shake the feeling that her words were laden with meaning, a veiled warning wrapped in kindness. We thanked her and left, my mind racing with possibilities.

The afternoon sun bathed the streets in a warm glow as Nathan and I stepped back outside, the weight of the note still heavy in my thoughts. "So, what's our next move, detective?" I asked, trying to lighten the mood.

"Let's hit up the local diner. I need sustenance if we're going to tackle this mystery together," he declared, determination sparking in his eyes.

"Only if you promise not to make any ridiculous requests like ordering the 'secret special,'" I teased.

"Deal! But only if you admit you're secretly enjoying this little escapade," he shot back, grinning widely.

As we strolled down the street, the banter flowed easily, momentarily masking the unease gnawing at my insides. With each step, the shadows of Windward Bay seemed to deepen, and I realized that unraveling the truth would require more than just courage. It would mean confronting the past—my own and perhaps the town's—layer by layer, until we reached the heart of whatever threat lingered just beneath the surface.

The diner was a nostalgic slice of Americana, with its red vinyl booths, chrome accents, and walls adorned with vintage photographs of Windward Bay's past. The bell above the door jingled cheerfully as Nathan and I stepped inside, the inviting smell of freshly brewed coffee mingling with the scent of sizzling bacon. It was the kind of place where everyone seemed to know each other, where familiar faces exchanged smiles like currency. I felt a strange mix of comfort and tension, as if I were stepping into a scene from a film that had already been scripted long before I arrived.

As we slid into a booth, I took a moment to absorb the ambiance, my senses buzzing with the lively chatter and the clatter of plates being served. A waitress with bright blue hair and a cheerful disposition approached us, her notepad at the ready. "What can I get you two lovebirds?" she asked, winking at Nathan.

I almost choked on the sip of coffee I'd just taken. "Lovebirds? We're just friends," I stammered, heat flooding my cheeks. Nathan smirked, leaning back with a casual air that only added fuel to the fire.

"Just friends? Sure, whatever you say," he replied, his eyes glinting with mischief.

"Okay, Mr. Casanova," I shot back, rolling my eyes. "I'll take a stack of pancakes and—" I paused, glancing at Nathan. "What's your poison?"

"Double bacon cheeseburger, no onions, and make it messy," he replied, grinning as if he were ordering a secret mission.

The waitress jotted down our orders, her smile unwavering. "Coming right up!" She whisked away, and I turned back to Nathan, my heart still racing from the waitress's playful banter.

"You could tone down the charm a notch," I teased, trying to mask the flutter in my stomach. "You're making it hard for me to focus on the actual mystery here."

"Charm is just a tool in my detective toolkit," he shot back, leaning forward conspiratorially. "Besides, if we can distract the locals with our 'lovebird' act, we might just avoid attracting any real trouble."

As we settled into a rhythm of playful banter, my thoughts drifted back to the note. I couldn't shake the feeling that something sinister loomed just beyond the warm glow of the diner's lights. "So, about that note," I said, forcing my voice to steady. "What's our first move?"

"Let's start with the locals," Nathan suggested, his demeanor shifting from playful to serious. "If there's gossip to be had, the diner is where it'll be. We just need to listen and blend in."

I nodded, reluctantly accepting the plan. It was a small town; secrets had a way of escaping even the tightest lips. As we waited for our food, I observed the patrons, their conversations punctuated by laughter and the occasional heated debate over local politics. I felt a growing sense of unease as I noticed a table in the corner—a group of older men casting furtive glances our way.

"Are they staring at us?" I whispered, nodding subtly in their direction.

Nathan followed my gaze. "Looks like they are. Probably curious about the newcomers."

"Or plotting our downfall," I muttered, a shiver running down my spine.

He chuckled softly. "Or maybe they just want to know if we're as ridiculous as we look. You know, the classic newcomer analysis."

Just then, our waitress returned with our orders, the plates piled high and steaming. "Dig in, lovebirds!" she said, a mischievous smile still playing on her lips.

"Thanks!" Nathan said, flashing her a grin before turning to me, his voice lowering conspiratorially. "Let's eavesdrop. It's time to see if these 'locals' have any juicy intel."

I took a bite of my pancakes, half-heartedly enjoying the taste while keeping an ear tuned to the older men's conversation. Their voices were low, but every so often, a snippet of a phrase would drift toward us. "...the newcomers...better watch their backs..."

"Did you hear that?" I whispered urgently, leaning closer to Nathan.

"Yeah, I did," he replied, his expression shifting to one of concern. "Do you think they're talking about us?"

Before I could respond, the door swung open, a gust of cold wind rushing in. A figure stepped inside, momentarily blocking the sunlight, casting a long shadow across the floor. It was a man in a long coat, his hat pulled low over his brow. He scanned the room, his gaze lingering on us for a heartbeat too long before he moved to the counter.

"Do you know him?" I asked, my pulse quickening.

"Never seen him before," Nathan said, his voice tight. "But he looks like trouble."

I turned my focus back to the older men. They were now whispering amongst themselves, casting sidelong glances toward the newcomer. It was as if the atmosphere in the diner had shifted, a sudden tension thickening the air.

Just then, the man at the counter spoke up, his voice a gravelly rumble. "Anyone know where the girl went? The one who just moved into the old Baker place?"

A chill ran down my spine, and I felt as though the ground had shifted beneath me. My stomach twisted, and I glanced at Nathan, who looked equally unsettled.

"What do you think he means by 'the girl'?" I asked, my voice barely above a whisper.

"Could be anyone, but I doubt it," he replied, his eyes narrowing as he leaned in closer. "It could be you."

"Great. Just great," I said, my heart racing. "What should we do? Should we leave?"

"Not yet," Nathan said, determination etched on his face. "Let's stay put. We need to hear more."

As I took a sip of my coffee, my mind raced with possibilities. The notes, the stares, the ominous man in the diner—it all pointed to a bigger picture I couldn't yet see. I glanced around the room, trying to keep my composure, but every instinct told me that whatever was unfolding in Windward Bay was far from over.

Nathan's gaze was fixed on the man at the counter, his expression a mask of concentration. Suddenly, the man turned, his gaze locking onto us with unsettling intensity.

"Hey!" he called, his voice cutting through the chatter like a knife. "You two! I need to talk to you."

Panic surged through me. My instincts screamed at me to run, but there was nowhere to go. My heart raced as the weight of his words settled over me like a heavy fog.

"What do we do?" I asked, my voice shaking.

Nathan's jaw tightened, and he nodded slowly, his resolve unwavering. "We face him. Together."

Before I could process what that meant, the man strode toward us, every step deliberate, his presence commanding and ominous. I could almost feel the eyes of the entire diner on us, the air thick with anticipation. The conversation faded into a murmur, but the tension rose, leaving only the sound of my heart pounding in my ears.

"Didn't you get my message?" the man asked, his voice low and filled with an unsettling authority.

I blinked, caught between confusion and fear. "What message?" I managed to ask, though dread coiled in my stomach like a serpent ready to strike.

"The one that tells you to leave," he replied, his gaze unflinching, the weight of his words hanging heavily in the air.

Suddenly, the room felt like it was closing in around us, the laughter and chatter fading into a distant echo. The world had shifted on its axis, and I realized in that moment that I was no longer just an observer; I was now a part of the unfolding drama. And whatever came next would change everything.

Chapter 4: Torn Between Choices

The storm battered the windows of my small apartment, the rain a relentless percussion that drowned out all thoughts but one: escape. Each gust of wind howled like a banshee, a haunting reminder of the chaos that had spiraled my life into this tumultuous moment. I paced the floor, my thoughts a whirlwind of fear and longing, caught between the tantalizing prospect of freedom and the magnetic pull of Nathan's presence. He had begun to carve a space in my mind and heart that I never anticipated, like vines creeping over a forgotten trellis, beautiful yet invasive.

His visits had started innocuously enough, a simple request for help with a project I had unwittingly sparked during one of my late-night brainstorming sessions. I had no idea then that this would lead to late afternoons filled with laughter and competition. Nathan, with his tousled hair that always seemed to defy gravity, had a knack for turning mundane tasks into a delightful game. The way he teased me—his smile crooked and his eyes sparkling with mischief—ignited a warmth within me that fought against the chill of the storm outside. Our exchanges morphed from sharp barbs to playful nudges, the kind of banter that wrapped around us like a favorite blanket on a cold night.

Tonight, however, was different. The storm felt almost personal, a physical manifestation of the turmoil within me. We had huddled under the old gazebo in the park, its weathered wood a testament to countless storms weathered in silence. The rain drummed above us, creating a private symphony that muted the world. I watched the water cascade in sheets, the sky a swirling mass of gray, and I couldn't help but feel that I was caught in a tempest that mirrored my internal struggle. Nathan leaned closer, his presence an anchor amid the tempest, and I felt my heart race, thrumming against my ribcage as if it too had taken on a life of its own.

"So, what's your grand plan for this weekend? More solitary brainstorming?" he asked, the teasing lilt in his voice almost playful, yet I detected a hint of sincerity beneath it. I glanced at him, catching the earnest look in his eyes—a depth I hadn't noticed before. He always had this way of making me feel seen, as if he could peel back the layers of my guarded facade to reveal the vibrant, chaotic core beneath.

"Maybe I'll just pack my bags and escape to a cabin in the woods. No storms, no distractions. Just me, the trees, and my thoughts," I replied, the idea both liberating and terrifying. I didn't expect the heaviness of reality to creep back in, but the thought of the threatening note lying on my kitchen counter loomed over me like a dark cloud, ready to unleash its fury.

"Is that what you really want?" he asked, his tone shifting, no longer playful but genuinely curious. "To run away? Or is it just easier than facing whatever is waiting for you here?"

I hesitated, caught off guard by the directness of his question. "I just want to feel safe," I admitted, my voice barely above a whisper. The words hung between us like the storm, heavy with unspoken fears. The truth of my situation felt too raw, too fragile to expose to the light. My heart hammered in my chest, battling against the wave of vulnerability crashing over me.

Nathan studied me with an intensity that made my stomach flutter, and I couldn't tell if it was fear or excitement. "Safe from what, exactly?" His gaze pierced through the tension, probing for something deeper, and I found myself torn between sharing my fears and retreating into silence.

"Just... life," I murmured, the simplicity of the statement belied the complexity of my emotions. "Sometimes it feels like everything is spiraling out of control."

"I get that," he replied, his voice low, almost conspiratorial. "But running doesn't solve anything. You have to confront it, whatever 'it' is." His earnestness was disarming, and I felt an unfamiliar urge to let him in, to share my burdens rather than carry them alone.

As the rain poured down around us, I caught a flicker of something in his eyes—a promise of understanding, of acceptance. For a brief moment, the storm faded into the background, and it was just the two of us, suspended in a cocoon of shared vulnerability. I wanted to reach out, to bridge the gap between us, to let him see the real me—the scared, tangled mess I had become. But then reality crashed back like a wave, cold and unyielding. The note lingered in my mind, a stark reminder of the dangers lurking beyond the warmth of this moment.

"Sometimes," I finally said, trying to keep my voice steady, "facing it means stepping back. I just need to figure things out on my own."

He nodded slowly, but there was a flicker of disappointment in his gaze, a fleeting sadness that twisted my heart. "Just don't forget that you're not alone in this," he murmured. "You have people who care, whether you want to admit it or not."

The intimacy of his words wrapped around me, warm against the chill of the storm, and I realized that Nathan had become one of those people—unexpectedly, yet undeniably. The air crackled between us, an electric charge that made my skin tingle and my breath hitch in my throat.

But just as quickly, the weight of uncertainty fell back over me. Could I allow myself to be drawn into this connection while the shadows of my past loomed large, threatening to pull me under? Would I be able to weather the storm, both outside and within? As I looked at Nathan, his earnest expression framed by the pattering rain, I felt a mixture of hope and fear. I wanted to lean in, to explore the possibilities that danced just beyond my reach, but the nagging sense of danger held me back, like a lifeline tethering me to the safety of my solitude.

The rain had settled into a steady rhythm, a gentle whisper now rather than the frantic clamor it had been earlier. Beneath the gazebo, a tentative peace enveloped us, as if the world beyond had muted its chaos to allow a moment of clarity. I couldn't shake the weight of Nathan's words from my mind, and the sincerity in his gaze lingered, wrapping around my heart like a warm scarf. The way he looked at me—like I was a puzzle he was determined to solve—both thrilled and terrified me.

"Do you think we'll float away if it keeps raining like this?" I quipped, trying to lighten the mood as I pulled my knees up to my chest. "I've always wanted to go on an unexpected adventure."

"Float away?" Nathan chuckled, his laughter warm and rich, cutting through the damp chill that had settled over us. "More like we'd be swept down the river and end up in a very unglamorous swamp. Imagine the mosquitoes. Not exactly the grand adventure you're looking for."

"I can think of worse things," I said, a playful smirk on my lips. "Like being stuck in a room with a bunch of salespeople trying to pitch me their latest pyramid scheme."

He raised an eyebrow, amusement dancing in his eyes. "Oh, come on! You know you'd secretly enjoy the chaos. The banter alone would keep you entertained."

"True, but only if I had a good escape plan," I replied, the playful exchange lifting my spirits, if only momentarily. The storm outside felt less oppressive in that moment, our shared laughter creating a bubble of warmth amidst the chill.

As the rain continued to fall, I let my mind wander to darker thoughts, the threat of that note shadowing our lighthearted moment. It was a tangible reminder of the danger I could not shake off. "But really," I said, my tone shifting to something more serious, "what if life just keeps throwing storms at us? I mean, what do we do then?"

Nathan's smile faltered slightly, a flicker of understanding crossing his face. "Then we find a way to weather them. Together. You can't control the storms, but you can choose how you respond to them." His gaze locked onto mine, earnestness radiating from him like heat from a fireplace.

I felt an inexplicable warmth bloom in my chest. It was a simple sentiment, yet it echoed with such weight, and it reminded me that even in my solitary world, I didn't have to face the tempest alone. "You make it sound so easy," I said, tilting my head, scrutinizing his expression. "Like you've never had to deal with anything messy."

He laughed, a genuine sound that sent ripples of joy through me. "Oh, trust me. My life is a masterclass in messiness. I'm just really good at pretending I have it all together. The trick is to keep a steady supply of coffee and sarcasm."

"Coffee? Now that's a survival tactic I can get behind. But sarcasm only works if you have someone to share it with." I couldn't help but grin at him, the lightness returning to my voice.

"Then consider me your sarcasm supplier," he said, his smile widening. "And coffee is on me, if you ever decide to join the land of the living again."

His jest sparked something within me—hope, perhaps. I found myself wanting to lean into the connection we had formed, to let it unfurl like the petals of a flower stretching toward the sun. But the reminder of the darkness waiting just outside our moment together made me hesitate.

As we sat in silence for a heartbeat, a shiver ran through me, not from the cold but from a realization I couldn't quite articulate. "It's hard, you know?" I finally murmured, the vulnerability creeping back in. "Letting someone in when you're so used to locking everyone out."

"I get it," Nathan replied softly, his voice steady as the storm raged on. "But sometimes, the risk is worth it. People can surprise you. They can hold you up when you're ready to crumble."

"I don't know if I'm ready to be surprised," I admitted, looking down at my hands. The tremor of uncertainty rippled through me. "Especially not after everything that's happened."

"Whatever it is, you don't have to face it alone. I mean, I'll even wear a cape if that helps." His grin was infectious, the playful spirit of it grounding me amidst my spiraling thoughts.

"Really?" I laughed, warmth flooding my cheeks. "You'd look fantastic in a cape. Something vibrant, with sparkles?"

"Definitely sparkles. It's all the rage." He leaned in slightly, as if the absurdity of the image was a shared secret just between us. "But in all seriousness, let me help you. We can tackle whatever is throwing shade at you. Together."

I bit my lip, uncertainty clawing at my insides. "What if I drag you into my mess? What if I'm not worth the trouble?"

"Look, I may be a lot of things, but a coward isn't one of them. I thrive on trouble. It's what keeps life interesting." He nudged my shoulder playfully, his teasing demeanor wrapping around me like a cozy blanket.

The storm outside began to fade into the background, and for the first time, I considered the possibility that I might actually let someone in. "You're infuriatingly charming, you know that?"

"It's a talent," he replied with a mock bow, an exaggerated flourish that made me chuckle despite the seriousness of our conversation.

Just then, the downpour outside shifted into a lull, the rain easing into a light drizzle, and the tension in the air around us shifted as well. My heart raced as the moment expanded, stretching taut like a bowstring. I looked up, meeting Nathan's gaze, and felt the weight of unspoken words hovering between us. There was something there—an undeniable chemistry that sent my pulse racing and my mind whirling.

Before I could second-guess myself, I leaned in closer, almost instinctively. "You really mean it? About being there for me?"

"Always," he replied, his voice a gentle promise. The sincerity in his eyes felt like a balm to my weary soul, washing away the doubts that had clung to me like shadows.

But just as I allowed myself to feel a glimmer of hope, a crack of lightning illuminated the sky, followed by a deafening roar of thunder. It felt like an omen, a reminder that life wasn't going to make it easy for me to embrace this newfound connection.

"Guess the storm isn't done with us yet," I said, forcing a lightness into my voice, though inside I felt a turbulent mix of fear and longing. "Should we make a run for it?"

Nathan smirked, the corners of his mouth quirking up in that endearing way I was quickly coming to adore. "And miss this riveting conversation? Never!"

As the rain began to fall in earnest again, I realized that beneath the layers of fear and uncertainty lay something rich and vibrant—a connection that, while terrifying, was undeniably beautiful. The choice stretched out before me, raw and pulsating, demanding to be faced. With Nathan by my side, perhaps I could confront whatever lay ahead. After all, maybe the storm wasn't merely an obstacle but a pathway to something new, something worth fighting for.

As the rain pelted down around us, the world outside morphed into a blur, a canvas of gray and green. Within our cozy sanctuary, Nathan and I were cocooned in our own universe, the air thick with unspoken words and tentative possibilities. The light flickered, casting playful shadows that danced along the edges of our little haven, and I could feel the warmth radiating from him, a beacon against the storm's chill.

"Are you a witch?" he asked suddenly, breaking the silence with a mischievous grin. "Because it feels like you've cast a spell on me, and I'm not entirely sure how to escape."

I raised an eyebrow, half-amused and half-intrigued. "A witch? Really? I don't think I'd look good in a pointy hat."

"True, but you could totally pull off the broomstick." He leaned in closer, his eyes glinting with mischief. "Besides, it's the power to make a storm feel like a gentle breeze that really counts. You've definitely got that."

Laughter bubbled up between us, lightening the heaviness in my chest, but as quickly as it came, I felt the weight of reality settle back in. His words hung in the air, shimmering with warmth and possibilities, but they also reminded me of the peril lurking just outside our makeshift refuge. "If only I had magical powers to make this storm go away," I said, letting my smile falter slightly. "Or to make all my problems disappear."

Nathan's expression shifted, a flicker of seriousness breaking through his playful demeanor. "You don't need magic for that. Sometimes, facing the storm head-on is the only way to break free from it." His sincerity was almost disarming, yet the looming threat of that note gnawed at my thoughts, a persistent echo of danger reminding me that life was rarely as simple as choosing to face it.

"What if the storm is too strong?" I challenged, my voice trembling with uncertainty. "What if I'm not strong enough?"

He studied me for a moment, and I could see the gears turning in his mind, as if he were wrestling with the right words to say. "You are stronger than you think. Strength isn't just about muscles or bravado; it's about resilience. It's about allowing yourself to feel everything—fear, joy, uncertainty—and still choosing to move forward."

I let his words wash over me, the wisdom of them sinking in. Perhaps there was something to what he said. Yet the shadow of that note clung to my thoughts, whispering threats of danger and regret. "You make it sound so easy. But it's complicated. There's so much at stake," I said, shaking my head slightly, my brow furrowing with the weight of my dilemma.

"Nothing worthwhile is ever uncomplicated," he replied, a gentle urgency threading through his voice. "But you're not facing it alone. You have me, remember?" His eyes held mine, and for a moment, I felt a flicker of hope ignite deep within.

"What if I'm the storm? What if I'm the reason everything around me is chaotic?" I asked, my voice barely above a whisper, the admission heavy on my tongue.

He reached out, taking my hand in his, warmth radiating from the simple contact. "You're not chaos, you're life. And life is messy, beautiful, and unpredictable. Embrace it. Embrace the chaos."

I blinked back the sudden wave of emotion that threatened to spill over, my heart racing as I leaned into his touch. There was something incredibly soothing about being here with him, amidst the chaos of my world, yet every reassuring word was underscored by the weight of the note. "I want to, Nathan. I really do. But I have to get past this... this thing that's haunting me."

His expression shifted again, the shadows of concern flickering in his eyes. "Whatever it is, we'll face it together. You have to trust me."

Before I could respond, a sudden gust of wind slammed against the gazebo, rattling the structure and sending a chill through me. I shivered, drawing my hand away from his as an involuntary shudder ran through me. "Trust," I echoed, grappling with the concept. It felt like stepping into the unknown, a leap into the abyss, and the reality of the note haunted me like a specter.

Suddenly, my phone buzzed in my pocket, an unwelcome intrusion into our moment. I fished it out, my heart plummeting when I saw the notification—another message from an unknown number. My fingers trembled as I swiped to open it, dread pooling in the pit of my stomach.

"Are you having fun? You can't run forever. I'll find you."

Panic clawed its way up my throat, choking the air from my lungs. I glanced up at Nathan, whose expression shifted instantly from curiosity to alarm. "What's wrong?" he asked, the warmth of our earlier conversation evaporating as urgency filled the space between us.

I showed him the screen, my hands shaking, the gravity of my situation crashing over me like the relentless rain outside. "It's... it's that note. They're watching me. I can't do this."

"Who is it?" Nathan's eyes narrowed, his voice low and fierce. "Do you know?"

"No, I thought it was just a sick joke, but now..." My voice broke, the fear spilling over. "It feels real. I can't stay here."

"You're not going anywhere," he said firmly, stepping closer, a protective stance taking form around him. "We need to figure this out together. You can't let fear dictate your choices."

I shook my head, my pulse quickening. "But what if it's dangerous? What if I put you at risk too?"

"Then let me share the danger with you," he replied, determination etched across his face. "We'll report it, figure out who's behind it. But you can't just run away from it all. You'll regret it."

I stared at him, my heart pounding, the reality of his words clashing with my instinct to flee. The storm outside raged on, but it paled in comparison to the tempest within me. Could I truly face this darkness head-on?

Just then, a loud crack of thunder shook the ground beneath us, and for a brief moment, I felt as though the heavens themselves were echoing my doubts. The power flickered, the gazebo illuminated in strobing bursts, casting our faces in and out of shadow. I felt the weight of uncertainty creeping back in, like a tide threatening to pull me under.

Before I could respond, the wind whipped through the gazebo, tearing away the security of our refuge. My breath hitched as I caught sight of a dark figure standing at the edge of the park, silhouetted against the lightning flashes. My heart raced, and fear clawed at my insides.

"Nathan…" I gasped, my voice barely a whisper as the figure stepped closer, their face obscured by the downpour. "We need to go. Now."

Nathan's eyes darted to the figure, his expression morphing into one of fierce protectiveness. "Stay behind me," he commanded, his posture rigid and determined.

As the figure moved closer, I could feel my heart pounding, each beat a frantic reminder that the danger I had tried to escape was now standing right before us, shrouded in rain and shadows, and I was faced with a choice: confront my fears or flee once again into the chaos.

Chapter 5: The Mask of Danger

The lighthouse stood sentinel against the swirling winds of the Atlantic, its paint peeling like the layers of forgotten memories. Nathan and I approached, the salty breeze tousling our hair and carrying the scent of brine and adventure. I had always imagined this place cloaked in mystery, but standing before its weathered door, I felt the weight of something deeper, more potent.

"Are you sure about this?" I asked, trying to mask the quiver in my voice with a bravado I didn't quite feel.

He flashed a grin, his eyes twinkling with mischief. "What's life without a little danger? Besides, legends don't come to life without someone to stir the pot."

With a push, the door creaked open, revealing a darkened interior that smelled of dampness and nostalgia. The floorboards groaned underfoot, a chorus of age echoing our every step. I clutched Nathan's arm as we moved deeper into the lighthouse, our laughter ricocheting off the walls, mingling with the distant crash of waves.

The spiral staircase twisted upward like a serpent, each step steeped in history and secrets. I glanced back at Nathan, whose expression was a mix of determination and delight. "Do you think it's true?" I mused, my voice barely above a whisper. "The stories about the ghost? They say she wanders the cliffs, searching for her lost love."

He chuckled, the sound warm and familiar. "You mean the one who fell to his doom after a storm? Sounds like a classic tale to me. Just another reason to keep away from the edge, right?"

As we ascended, the light from a small window flickered with the setting sun, casting golden rays that danced across the dust motes swirling in the air. We reached the top, breathless from the climb and the intoxicating thrill of being together in such an eerie place.

"Look at this view," Nathan breathed, stepping towards the window. My heart swelled as he gazed out at the endless horizon, the sky ablaze with oranges and pinks. In that moment, he was everything—captivating, adventurous, and oh so dangerously alluring. I took a step closer, drawn to the warmth of his presence, my pulse racing with a mix of excitement and something more profound.

But just as I felt the distance between us shrink, an unsettling noise broke through the magic—a low rustling that sent a shiver down my spine. We both turned, instinctively leaning closer to each other.

"Did you hear that?" I asked, my voice barely a whisper, laced with a tension that seemed to hang in the air like the last note of a haunting melody.

Nathan nodded, his expression shifting from playful to serious. "Yeah. It's probably just a raccoon or something. Old buildings attract all sorts of wildlife."

Yet, my instincts screamed otherwise. I could feel something lurking beyond the sanctuary of our shared warmth, a sense of foreboding wrapping around me like a cold fog. "I think we should go," I suggested, though my heart raced at the thought of leaving the thrill of our moment behind.

"Just a little longer," he urged, his tone coaxing. "Let's see what it is."

Reluctantly, I followed him to the narrow doorway leading to the stairs. The dark shadows cast by the sunset made it feel as if the lighthouse itself were watching us, its silence deepening. Just as Nathan reached the edge of the door, I caught a glimpse of movement below.

My heart stopped. A figure was crouched in the shadows, its outline blurred and menacing against the backdrop of the dimming light. Panic surged through me like a bolt of lightning, sharp and relentless.

"Nathan!" I gasped, my voice breaking the spell of silence.

He turned, following my frantic gaze, and the playful glint in his eyes vanished. "What the hell?"

The figure remained motionless, shrouded in darkness, but I could feel the weight of its gaze upon us. Fear coiled in my stomach, and without thinking, I grasped Nathan's hand tightly. "We need to go. Now."

His grip tightened around mine, a silent promise of safety as we retreated back down the staircase. Each step felt heavier than the last, the eerie quiet amplifying our hurried breaths. The air buzzed with an unspoken tension, as if the very walls of the lighthouse could sense our rising panic.

As we reached the bottom, the sense of being watched only intensified. Nathan pulled me closer, his heart beating in sync with my own, a chaotic rhythm of fear and adrenaline. "We should call the police," he suggested, his voice low and steady despite the urgency in his eyes.

I nodded, but the thought of facing whoever—or whatever—was outside made me hesitate. "What if it's nothing? What if it's just someone curious about the lighthouse?"

His brow furrowed as he considered this, but I could tell he wasn't convinced. "Curiosity doesn't usually lurk in shadows. Let's just get to my car."

With every step toward the door, I felt the chill of danger wrapping around us, a tangible thing that made my skin prickle. The lighthouse's walls seemed to lean in, listening, as if to say that secrets were not to be taken lightly.

The door creaked open, and we spilled out into the fading light, the familiar landscape now transformed into something otherworldly. Shadows danced along the edge of the rocky cliff, and the sound of the waves crashing against the stones was a symphony of chaos.

But as we hurried toward Nathan's car, the figure emerged from the shadows, stepping into the light. My breath caught in my throat as I recognized the wild hair and tattered clothing of a local I had seen around town—a drifter with a troubled past.

"Wait!" Nathan shouted, his voice cutting through the thickening tension.

I glanced back, the fear coiling tighter in my chest. "What do we do?"

Nathan stepped forward, his stance protective. "Hey, are you alright?"

The drifter's eyes were wide, but it wasn't fear I saw there; it was desperation. "You shouldn't be here," he rasped, his voice raw and shaky. "You don't know what's coming."

Confusion wrapped around me like a fog, drowning out the panic that had spiked moments before. The lighthouse, with all its legends and shadows, held more than just a haunting tale. It held a warning—a premonition of something dark lurking just beyond the horizon, and we were caught in the eye of the storm.

The air around us crackled with an energy that felt like a thunderstorm about to break. The drifter's presence shifted everything; his eyes bore a haunted look, like a man who had seen the worst of what the world had to offer. I could feel my heart pounding, each beat urging me to retreat into the safety of the lighthouse's embrace, yet the urge to understand this stranger kept me rooted in place.

"Listen, buddy," Nathan said, taking a cautious step forward, his tone a mixture of concern and assertiveness. "What do you mean, we shouldn't be here?"

The drifter's gaze darted between us, as if he were assessing the sincerity of our intentions. "You don't know what the lighthouse is," he rasped, the words coming out in a low, gravelly whisper that sent a shiver down my spine. "It's not just a building; it's a beacon of curses."

My brow furrowed at his cryptic warning, my logical mind grappling with the fear creeping into my thoughts. "Curses? Seriously?" I couldn't help but inject a hint of skepticism into my voice. "Are we in some sort of horror movie?"

Nathan chuckled lightly, trying to ease the tension, but it came out more like a nervous laugh. "Yeah, well, if this is a movie, then I demand a better script." He turned back to the drifter. "What are you talking about?"

"Every light has its shadows," the drifter continued, his voice barely rising above a whisper, as though the very words might draw the malevolence he spoke of closer. "People have gone missing around here—lost to the sea, lost to the lighthouse." He paused, drawing in a shaky breath. "You shouldn't have come here. It stirs things that are better left asleep."

A chill wrapped around me, tightening like a noose. "What things?" I pressed, curiosity tinged with fear driving my inquiry. "What do you mean, lost?"

The drifter stepped closer, his eyes wide and frantic. "You've already woken them. The moment you set foot inside, you disrupted the silence. The lighthouse doesn't take kindly to intruders."

"Great," I muttered, glancing at Nathan. "So, we're cursed. Fantastic vacation we've got going here." I tried to keep the sarcasm light, but my heart raced with unease.

"Look, we'll be careful," Nathan said, trying to pacify the stranger while keeping me anchored. "We didn't mean any harm. We just—"

"It doesn't matter what you meant!" the drifter shouted, suddenly erupting with a fervor that sent us both stumbling back a step. "It's what you've done! You've disturbed the spirits that watch over this place. They'll come for you when the sun sets. You'll see."

The weight of his words hung heavy in the air, and I exchanged a worried glance with Nathan. "Maybe we should go," I suggested, my voice a whisper, the thrill of our adventure now overshadowed by an impending sense of doom.

"Wait!" Nathan said, clearly struggling with the shift in our reality. "We can't just leave. What if he's telling the truth?"

"Or what if he's just a paranoid local?" I countered, the skepticism battling the instinctive fear creeping into my gut. "Let's not forget he's been living in the shadows for a reason."

Nathan hesitated, glancing at the drifter, whose eyes bore the weight of truths I couldn't begin to fathom. "What's your name?" he finally asked, attempting to ground the situation.

"Eli," the drifter replied, his voice quieter now, yet still laced with urgency. "You don't have to believe me, but if you stay, you'll regret it."

As he spoke, the sun dipped lower on the horizon, a fiery orb casting long shadows across the ground. The light waned, and with it, my bravado began to flicker.

"Fine," Nathan said, his voice resolute yet cautious. "We'll go. But we want to know what you mean by all of this. What's really out there?"

Eli's expression softened, a flicker of gratitude illuminating his wild features. "You're in danger, but it's not too late to leave. The tide changes, and with it comes the darkness."

I couldn't shake the feeling that our playful day had morphed into something far more sinister. The lighthouse loomed behind us, its once inviting silhouette now grotesque against the deepening twilight. As we made our way to Nathan's car, I felt a strange pull toward the lighthouse, as if it were beckoning me back, whispering promises of secrets and hidden truths.

Once inside the car, the doors clicked shut, a small cocoon of safety in the gathering dusk. Nathan turned to me, his expression fraught with concern. "What do you think? Do we take Eli's warning seriously?"

I sighed, running a hand through my hair in frustration. "I don't know. Part of me thinks he's just... well, not all there. But then there's that other part, the one that remembers the stories about this place."

"Maybe we should just get out of here and come back during the day," he suggested, starting the engine, the hum of the car's engine bringing a sense of normalcy amidst the tension.

As we pulled away, I couldn't help but glance back at the lighthouse, its silhouette dark and foreboding against the fading sky. It felt as if the very structure had a heartbeat, pulsing with secrets that I was somehow drawn to uncover. The stories of missing people, the whispered legends—what if they weren't just tales to scare children?

The drive back into town was punctuated by an uncomfortable silence, my mind racing with thoughts I couldn't articulate. Nathan's fingers drummed restlessly against the steering wheel, his concentration visibly shattered. "What if Eli was right?" he finally broke the silence, his voice low. "What if something really does happen at night?"

"Then we'll deal with it," I replied, trying to inject a note of reassurance into my tone. "It's not like we're going to spend the night there."

"But what if we should?" Nathan's eyes flicked to me, and I could see the familiar glint of mischief returning. "What if we camp out nearby? Just to prove Eli wrong?"

I shot him a pointed look. "You mean camp out in the middle of a ghost story?"

"Why not? It could be fun. Think of the stories we could tell later!"

"You really think ghost stories are fun?" I quipped, unable to suppress a smile despite the tension still thrumming in the air.

His laugh broke through the unease, lightening the mood. "I do. And if we get scared, we can run back to town and tell everyone about the spooky lighthouse. It'll be legendary!"

I couldn't help but laugh, the ridiculousness of it all brightening the heaviness that lingered in my chest. "Fine, but if we end up haunting that place, I'm blaming you."

He grinned, that familiar spark igniting once more. "I'll take my chances if it means I get to spend the night under the stars with you."

The warmth of his words wrapped around me, and I felt the clouds of dread parting ever so slightly, revealing a sliver of hope. We would face whatever lay ahead together, navigating through the twists and turns, the shadows and secrets. The lure of the lighthouse might be dangerous, but so was our bond—a blend of courage and curiosity, a willingness to confront whatever specters awaited us in the dark.

The drive back to town blurred by in a haze of thoughts, adrenaline still thrumming in my veins. I could see Nathan's jaw set, the worry lines on his forehead deepening. His usual playful demeanor had slipped, and I could sense the weight of the drifter's warning clinging to him like a second skin.

"What if we really did go back?" he suggested, a reckless glint in his eye that both thrilled and terrified me. "Just to check it out? Make sure nothing weird is actually going on?"

"Right, because nothing says fun like a midnight excursion to a haunted lighthouse." I rolled my eyes, but deep down, the idea excited me. "And if we get sucked into a ghost story, do we get a sequel?"

Nathan chuckled, the sound almost reassuring, but I could see he was serious beneath the jest. "What's life without a little danger? Besides, you said you didn't believe Eli. Prove him wrong."

"Prove him wrong while possibly becoming the main characters in a horror film? Sounds like a winning plan."

He shot me a sideways glance, a smirk tugging at his lips. "You've got to admit, it'll be a story for the ages. Imagine telling our friends we braved the lighthouse at midnight!"

The thought sent a rush of excitement through me, igniting the flicker of courage hidden beneath the surface of my fear. "Okay, fine. Let's do it," I said, surprising myself with the boldness in my voice. "But if we run into any ghosts, I'm blaming you."

We set off again, the familiar roads morphing into shadowy paths lined with towering trees, their branches entwined like fingers reaching toward the sky. The vibrant colors of the day faded into a palette of blues and blacks, the night swallowing everything whole. I could feel the anticipation building in my chest, each beat thrumming with a cocktail of dread and excitement.

As we approached the lighthouse, the ominous silhouette loomed larger than before, the air thickening with the weight of the unknown. Nathan parked a short distance away, the headlights cutting through the darkness and illuminating the path to our destination. The car's engine fell silent, leaving only the sound of the wind rustling through the grass, creating a symphony of whispers that seemed to beckon us closer.

"Ready?" he asked, his voice a mixture of bravado and uncertainty.

"Not really," I admitted, stepping out of the car. The chill of the night wrapped around me, the warmth of the day already feeling like a distant memory. "But when has that ever stopped us?"

"Exactly," Nathan replied, flashing a confident smile that made my heart flutter despite the apprehension gnawing at my insides.

We made our way to the lighthouse, the crunch of gravel beneath our feet mingling with the distant crash of waves against the cliffs. The structure towered above us, its weathered walls whispering stories of old, tales of loss, love, and perhaps something darker. The door creaked open as if inviting us inside, and the air shifted with the scent of salt and damp wood.

"Let's do this," I said, stepping over the threshold, the light from Nathan's phone illuminating our path like a guiding star.

Inside, the darkness enveloped us, the atmosphere thick with suspense. Every creak of the floorboards sounded like a ghostly echo, and I couldn't shake the feeling that we were being watched. "Eli was right about one thing," I murmured, glancing around. "This place is seriously creepy."

Nathan moved closer, his shoulder brushing against mine. "But we're not here for ghosts, remember? We're here to prove Eli wrong."

"Right," I replied, though my heart raced at the thought of what might be lurking in the shadows. "Let's just get this over with."

We ascended the spiral staircase, each step resonating with the weight of our fears and the thrill of the unknown. The air grew colder as we climbed, the chill seeping into my bones, but I pressed on, driven by the intoxicating rush of adventure and the thrill of being so close to Nathan.

Reaching the top, we stepped into the lantern room, where the shattered glass windows revealed the sprawling ocean, a dark expanse stretching to infinity. The moon hung low, its silvery light reflecting off the waves like a million dancing diamonds. "This is beautiful," I breathed, taking a moment to soak it all in, the haunting beauty of the night washing over me.

"See? Not so scary," Nathan said, grinning. "Just us, the moon, and maybe a few ghosts."

A sudden gust of wind howled through the room, rattling the remaining panes of glass and sending a shiver down my spine. "Maybe we should head back down?" I suggested, feeling the air shift, as if something was about to unfold.

Just as I spoke, the sound of a heavy thud echoed through the lighthouse, vibrating the floor beneath us. My heart jumped into my throat, and I clutched Nathan's arm, panic surging within me.

"What was that?" I whispered, my voice trembling.

"Probably just the building settling," he replied, though his tone lacked conviction. "Right?"

We stood frozen, the silence stretching out around us, heavy and expectant. I could hear my heartbeat pounding in my ears, each thud resonating with the growing unease. "Let's go check it out," I suggested, trying to sound brave despite the fear creeping into my voice.

"Are you insane?" Nathan shot back, his eyes wide. "We just heard a noise, and you want to investigate?"

"Someone has to," I argued, adrenaline coursing through me. "What if it's just a raccoon or something? If we don't go, we'll never know."

"Great logic," he replied dryly, but I could see the curiosity sparking in his eyes. "Fine, let's go. But if I see a ghost, I'm throwing you at it."

"Thanks for your unwavering support." I rolled my eyes, the humor serving as a brief distraction from the tension coiling between us.

We descended the staircase, each step feeling heavier than the last, and moved cautiously toward the source of the noise. The air grew thick with anticipation, a tangible force that urged us to move faster. As we neared the entrance, the faint sound of murmurs reached our ears, low and indistinct, like a forgotten conversation.

"Do you hear that?" I whispered, my heart pounding in my chest.

Nathan nodded, his expression shifting from playful to serious. "It's coming from outside."

We edged closer to the door, the wood creaking beneath us. The murmurs intensified, and my pulse quickened. Was it the wind, or were there indeed voices beyond the threshold?

Before I could even consider turning back, Nathan swung the door open, revealing the darkened exterior. The moonlight cast an eerie glow, illuminating a figure standing on the rocky outcrop just below the lighthouse.

I squinted, trying to make sense of the scene. The figure turned slowly, and my breath hitched as recognition flooded over me. "Eli!" I gasped, stepping out into the cool night. "What are you doing here?"

But Eli's eyes were wide with terror, his voice barely above a whisper as he reached out, panic radiating from him. "You have to get out! They're coming!"

Before I could respond, the ground trembled beneath us, a deep rumble resonating from the depths of the sea. The waves crashed violently against the rocks, and a shadow rose from the water, looming larger and darker than the night itself.

"Run!" Nathan shouted, grabbing my arm as the shape surged toward the lighthouse, and I could feel the air crackle with an energy that sent a jolt of fear through me.

We turned to flee, but the ground shook again, and I could hear the whispers intensifying, wrapping around us like tendrils of smoke. "What is happening?" I screamed, my heart racing as the darkness engulfed us.

With one last glance back, I saw the figure rising, an amalgamation of nightmares and legends, and I knew we had awakened something far more dangerous than we could have ever imagined. The night was alive, and we were caught in its relentless grip, with nowhere to hide.

Chapter 6: Allies in Chaos

The air crackled with the salty tang of the ocean as I stood in the small, cluttered office of Windward Bay's historical society, my fingers tracing the spines of dusty tomes and yellowed newspapers. Nathan leaned against the doorframe, his arms crossed, a playful smirk tugging at the corner of his lips, as if he were waiting for me to acknowledge the absurdity of our situation. "You know," he began, his voice a low drawl that sent a familiar shiver down my spine, "for a town that thrives on secrets, we sure are digging up a lot of dirt."

I shot him a glance, my brow furrowing in annoyance, though a reluctant smile tugged at my mouth. "A lot of dirt? You're underestimating the potential for catastrophe, Nathan. This isn't just a summer beach read. These are people's lives. Not to mention the potential for public outrage if we don't uncover who's behind those notes."

He pushed himself off the frame and ambled over, the scent of cedar and sun-kissed skin wafting off him, both disarming and distracting. "You've got a flair for drama, you know that? Maybe you should consider a career in fiction," he teased, leaning over my shoulder to scan the faded newspaper clippings sprawled across the table.

"Thanks, but I think I'll stick to the thrilling life of amateur sleuthing," I replied, rolling my eyes, though I felt a surge of warmth creep up my neck. It was impossible to ignore the way his proximity sent my heart racing, how the shadows of the past seemed to pale in the light of his undeniable charisma.

The door creaked open, drawing our attention away from the pile of clippings. Margaret, the town's aging historian, shuffled in, her silver hair a wild halo around her head. She clutched a stack of documents to her chest like they were the Holy Grail. "I heard you two were digging into old scandals," she said, her voice thick with curiosity, "and I have something you might want to see."

As she laid the papers on the table, the familiar musty scent of old paper filled the air, mingling with the ocean breeze that drifted through the open window. I peered at the documents, my heart racing as I spotted a series of letters addressed to various residents of Windward Bay, each one dated back to the early 1900s. They were filled with accusations of betrayal, greed, and even darker implications—threats of retribution that sent chills down my spine.

"Where did you find these?" I asked, my voice barely a whisper, as if speaking too loudly would shatter the fragile connection we were forming with the town's murky past.

"Clearing out the attic of the old courthouse," Margaret replied, a twinkle in her eye. "You'd be surprised what people toss aside in the name of progress. It's as if they believe forgetting will erase their sins."

Nathan flipped through the pages, his expression shifting from casual amusement to genuine intrigue. "These are like the town's skeletons, rattling in the closet," he mused, glancing at me with a newfound intensity. "Could it be that our mystery is tied to the past?"

"Everything in this town is tied to the past," I said, the gravity of his words settling over me like a heavy fog. "But why now? Why these notes?"

As we poured over the letters, it became clear that each one carried a weight of history, a tapestry woven with threads of betrayal that resonated within the walls of Windward Bay. We exchanged glances, the unspoken understanding of the danger we faced binding us closer together. The thrill of discovery danced in the air, each revelation a new layer added to the chaotic masterpiece that was our partnership.

"I never imagined we'd be doing this," Nathan said softly, his eyes reflecting a sincerity I hadn't seen before. "I thought you were just some spoiled city girl who wouldn't know hard work if it hit her in the face."

"Yeah, well, I could say the same about you, Mister 'I-know-it-all-about-the-sea.' But here we are, sifting through dusty secrets like a couple of amateurs," I shot back, the teasing lilt in my voice cutting through the tension.

He chuckled, the sound rich and warm, and for a fleeting moment, I felt a spark ignite between us, the air thick with unsaid words and hidden desires. "Maybe we make a good team after all," he said, his gaze lingering on mine longer than necessary.

"Don't get used to it," I replied, trying to keep my tone light, but I could feel the blush creeping up my cheeks. "I'm still trying to figure out how you went from my biggest annoyance to my reluctant partner in crime."

"Maybe it's the way you keep underestimating me," he quipped, a mischievous glint in his eyes. "Or maybe it's the way you look when you're passionate about something."

I felt my heart thump loudly against my ribs, the implications of his words settling in. "I'm just here to solve a mystery, Nathan. Nothing more," I asserted, though I wasn't sure if I was convincing him or myself.

"Sure, keep telling yourself that," he replied, his tone teasing but his eyes serious, piercing right through the facade I desperately tried to maintain.

The air grew thick with an unspoken tension as we returned to our research, the weight of the town's secrets surrounding us like an invisible fog. As the afternoon sun began to dip towards the horizon, casting a golden hue over the sea, I couldn't shake the feeling that our journey was only beginning. Each revelation felt like a step deeper into the storm, pulling us further from the safety of the shores we once knew, and I could only hope that when the waves crashed, we would be ready to face whatever chaos awaited us.

The sun rose over Windward Bay like a promise, casting warm hues over the cobblestone streets that wound between weathered houses, each one whispering tales of the past. As I made my way to the coffee shop, the familiar scent of roasting beans mingled with the salty breeze from the ocean, awakening a sense of urgency within me. Nathan was already there, seated at our usual corner table, an array of papers sprawled out before him like a battlefield. He looked up, his expression unreadable, and for a moment, I was taken aback by the intensity of his gaze.

"Good morning, Sunshine," he greeted, the corner of his mouth curling up in a playful smile. "Ready to crack the case of the century?"

I rolled my eyes, feigning annoyance, though the flutter in my chest betrayed me. "You know, some of us prefer coffee before we dive into chaos. It's an important step in the crime-solving process."

He laughed, the sound deep and infectious, and I couldn't help but smile back. "Then let's get you caffeinated before we unleash your inner detective. I'm sure the townsfolk would appreciate it."

As I ordered my coffee, the barista shot me a knowing glance, clearly aware of the sparks flying between Nathan and me. I tried to ignore the heat rising to my cheeks, reminding myself that we were allies now, dedicated to unearthing the truth behind the threatening notes that had sent shockwaves through our peaceful town.

Back at the table, I took a sip of the steaming cup, the rich flavor grounding me as I scanned the papers strewn across the table. "So, where do we start?" I asked, leaning forward, my curiosity piqued.

"Right here," Nathan said, pointing to a faded article that detailed a long-forgotten feud between two prominent families in Windward Bay. "The Hawthornes and the Caldwells. Seems like they had a rather nasty falling out back in the day, complete with accusations and threats that echo eerily to what we've been seeing recently."

I leaned closer, the headlines blurring in my vision as I focused on the words. "They fought over land, wealth... and something else. A woman?" I questioned, sensing the complicated web of emotions that had tangled those families together.

"Isn't that always the way?" Nathan replied, his eyes sparkling with mischief. "Nothing drives people to madness quite like love and property disputes."

"Or a lack of coffee," I quipped, grinning as I thought of my earlier comment. "How do we tie this back to our current mystery?"

As we poured over the details, I felt a rush of adrenaline course through me, our conversation punctuated by the sound of paper rustling and our voices rising in excitement. Nathan pointed out the repeated names in both the past and present, each one a potential lead that could unravel the tangled mess we found ourselves in.

Suddenly, a shadow loomed over our table, and I looked up to find a figure standing there, arms crossed tightly across her chest. It was Marissa, the town's self-appointed watchdog and gossipmonger, known for her razor-sharp tongue and a nose for scandal. "What are you two up to?" she demanded, her eyes darting between us like a hawk spotting its prey.

"Just investigating a little bit of town history," I said, trying to keep my tone light, though I could feel Nathan tense beside me.

"Yeah? Is that what they're calling it these days?" she shot back, her tone dripping with skepticism. "Because I saw you two at the lighthouse, and it didn't look like a history lesson to me."

Nathan raised an eyebrow, a smirk playing on his lips. "We're just looking for some old ghosts, Marissa. Care to join us?"

Her expression shifted slightly, caught off guard by his easy charm. "You think this is a game?" she asked, though the edge in her voice had dulled.

"No, but we could use a new perspective. Care to lend yours?" I suggested, attempting to pull her into our investigation rather than dismiss her outright.

Marissa's gaze narrowed, but curiosity sparkled in her eyes. "I might know a thing or two about the Hawthornes. They were practically my neighbors growing up. If you want to hear the juicy bits, I might be able to help."

As we huddled closer, the air thick with anticipation, Nathan caught my eye and winked. I couldn't help but chuckle, feeling a surge of camaraderie, even if it was laced with the unpredictability of involving Marissa. This chaos felt oddly exhilarating, and for the first time in days, the weight of the threatening notes lifted slightly.

With Marissa spilling details about old feuds and clandestine meetings, our investigation began to take shape. The atmosphere in the coffee shop shifted from one of mere speculation to something more tangible, electric. Nathan leaned in, his shoulder brushing against mine as we shared notes and ideas, our conversation flowing seamlessly from one theory to the next.

"Okay, so what if the notes are a continuation of the past? Someone stirring up old grudges?" Nathan proposed, a spark of inspiration lighting up his features.

"Or someone trying to warn others?" I countered, the gears in my mind turning. "What if they're afraid of history repeating itself?"

"Either way, we need to find out who's behind those notes before things escalate. We could be dealing with a modern-day vendetta." Marissa chimed in, her eyes glinting with excitement.

"Which means we need to dig deeper into the Hawthornes and Caldwells," Nathan said, a determined look crossing his face. "They may be long gone, but their legacy isn't. It's alive and kicking, and we have to track it down."

The three of us quickly formulated a plan, excitement buzzing between us like electricity. As we exchanged banter and ideas, a bond began to form—one built not just on necessity but also on shared intrigue and the thrill of the chase. Each revelation felt like peeling back the layers of a hidden world, one that had been overshadowed by gossip and resentment.

As we finished our coffees, a new resolve settled in the air. This was more than just an investigation; it was a journey into the heart of Windward Bay itself. A journey that, despite the chaos, was bringing us closer—strangers becoming allies against the currents of time, secrets weaving us into the fabric of the town's story. And as I glanced at Nathan, something flickered in his eyes that suggested he felt it too, a shared understanding that this was just the beginning.

The morning sun glinted off the ocean waves, casting shimmering patterns across the shoreline as I and Nathan walked side by side toward the old Hawthorne estate. Each step echoed the heartbeat of Windward Bay, a town rich in history and mystery, and my pulse quickened with the thrill of discovery. Armed with our notes and Marissa's insights, we were determined to unearth whatever secrets lay buried beneath the dust of time.

"What's the plan, oh great leader?" Nathan joked, nudging me playfully with his shoulder. His easy confidence was disarming, a reminder of how far we had come from our initial animosity.

I smirked, trying to hide the flutter of excitement at his proximity. "Let's start with the library. If we're going to crack this case, we need to know everything about the Hawthornes. You can't fight ghosts without knowing their names."

"Are we really doing the ghost metaphor?" he replied, feigning seriousness. "I thought that was just for campfire stories."

I raised an eyebrow, a grin playing at the corners of my mouth. "Just wait until the fog rolls in. Then we can add a few jump scares for good measure."

We reached the library, a charmingly dilapidated building that seemed to lean into the wind as if it were in conversation with the ocean. Inside, the scent of aged paper and ink wrapped around us like an embrace. Dust motes danced in the shafts of sunlight, giving the place an ethereal quality.

"Let's split up," Nathan suggested, glancing around the room. "You take the biographies; I'll handle the archives. I'll meet you back here in an hour."

"Deal," I agreed, secretly pleased at the prospect of unearthing something valuable. "But don't get lost in there. I wouldn't want to have to rescue you from the clutches of the Dewey Decimal System."

He laughed, the sound reverberating through the quiet library, and I found myself smiling as I set off toward the biography section. I skimmed through titles, hoping for something that would shed light on the Hawthornes' legacy. Most of the accounts were bland, chronicling their achievements with all the excitement of a tax audit. It wasn't until I stumbled upon a worn book tucked away at the back of the shelf that my heart raced.

"Whispers of Windward: The Untold Stories of the Hawthorne Family" it read in faded gold lettering. I carefully pulled it from the shelf, the spine creaking in protest. Flipping through the pages, I discovered a collection of letters and journal entries, the ink still dark and vivid. The voices of the past flooded into my consciousness, each word pulsing with emotion.

I lost myself in the tales of betrayal and heartache, stories of love lost and family feuds that had shaped the very fabric of our town. Each entry painted a picture of the Hawthornes not just as wealthy landowners, but as flawed, passionate individuals ensnared in a web of desire and deception.

Time slipped away, and I nearly jumped when Nathan's voice broke the spell. "You're going to need a shovel if you keep digging through that book," he quipped, leaning against the shelf, arms crossed with an amused expression. "What did you find?"

"I think this family was embroiled in much more than we realized," I replied, excitement bubbling in my chest. "They weren't just fighting over land; there were affairs, secret meetings, even accusations of betrayal."

"Sounds like a soap opera," he said, his gaze flickering over the pages. "So what do you think? Someone trying to revive the drama for a reason?"

"Maybe," I pondered aloud. "But it feels deeper than just revenge. There's a pattern here—each family member felt they were wronged, and now those sentiments might have resurfaced. We need to find a way to connect the dots."

Nathan nodded, his brow furrowed in thought. "And if we can find the last living descendant of the Hawthornes, they might hold the key to unlocking this mystery."

"Right," I said, my mind racing. "If only we knew who that was. Let's check the records for any surviving family members."

We made our way to the town clerk's office, a quaint building that had seen better days but still stood resolute against the elements. Inside, the air was thick with the scent of musty files and paper. A woman behind the counter looked up from her computer, her eyes brightening with recognition.

"Back again, are we?" she asked, a smile stretching across her face. "What can I help you with this time?"

"We need to find the current descendant of the Hawthorne family," I said, my heart racing at the prospect of a breakthrough.

Her fingers flew across the keyboard as she pulled up records, the glow of the screen illuminating her face. "It looks like there's one listed here, but it's been years since anyone has filed anything. Her name is Lila Hawthorne."

"Lila Hawthorne," I repeated, rolling the name over in my mind. "Do you have any contact information?"

The woman paused, her smile fading. "I'm afraid that's not public information. But I do know she used to own a little cottage on the outskirts of town. You might be able to find her there."

With a new sense of purpose, Nathan and I left the office, our plans shifting toward the cottage. The sky had begun to cloud over, and a chill crept into the air. I felt a strange combination of excitement and trepidation as we made our way through the winding streets, the clouds swirling ominously overhead.

"Do you think Lila will even want to talk to us?" Nathan asked, his voice steady despite the encroaching storm.

"Only one way to find out," I replied, though doubt gnawed at my insides. "We need her perspective, and if she's the last of her line, she might know more than anyone about what's been happening."

The cottage came into view, a quaint, ivy-covered structure nestled among towering trees. A sense of foreboding settled over me as we approached, the wind howling through the branches, as if whispering warnings of the past.

"Here goes nothing," Nathan said, reaching for the door, and I couldn't shake the feeling that we were stepping into a web spun long ago, one that would ensnare us before we even realized it.

He knocked, the sound echoing eerily in the stillness. Moments stretched out like elastic, and just as I was about to suggest we leave, the door creaked open. A woman stood before us, her hair a cascade of silver, eyes sharp and assessing, as though she were measuring the weight of our intentions.

"Can I help you?" she asked, her voice steady but laced with something unidentifiable—a mixture of curiosity and caution.

As we exchanged glances, I felt a shiver run down my spine. In that moment, I understood: whatever answers we sought, we might not be prepared for the truth. The weight of the past hung heavy in the air, and the storm brewing within our hearts mirrored the tempest gathering outside.

Before I could speak, a distant rumble of thunder echoed ominously, and Lila's expression shifted, darkening as she looked beyond us into the encroaching shadows. "You shouldn't have come here," she said, her voice suddenly taut, filled with an urgency that set my heart racing.

Just then, the sky opened up, rain pouring down in sheets, drenching us instantly. The world outside blurred into a watercolor of grays and blues, but the tension inside the cottage was palpable.

Lila stepped back, the door swinging wider, an invitation laced with warning. "Come in, before it's too late."

As we crossed the threshold, I knew the storm had only just begun.

Chapter 7: A Dance of Deception

The night of the Windward Bay Gala was wrapped in a lavish cloak of glittering elegance and unspoken promises. I stepped into the grand ballroom, the scent of polished wood mingling with the sweet aroma of champagne and floral arrangements. Striking chandeliers cast a golden glow over the room, their crystals shimmering like stars fallen from the sky, illuminating the laughter and chatter that danced through the air.

My heart raced with an exhilarating mix of excitement and apprehension as I scanned the crowd, searching for Nathan. The mere thought of being with him sent butterflies fluttering in my stomach. It wasn't just the anticipation of a night spent together; it was the weight of the secrets lingering between us, their sharp edges cutting into the delicate fabric of our connection. Despite the growing closeness that had blossomed in the weeks leading up to this event, I couldn't shake the unease that lingered in the back of my mind, like an unwanted guest at a party.

And then, there he was. Nathan emerged from the throng, his dark hair slightly tousled, a confident smile gracing his lips that sent warmth flooding through me. He wore a perfectly tailored suit that hugged his frame, enhancing the defined muscles I had only dared to imagine before. As he approached, the world around us blurred, and in that moment, it felt as if we were the only two souls in existence.

"Ready to show off some serious moves?" he teased, his voice smooth like velvet, playful yet carrying an underlying intensity that sent shivers down my spine.

I smirked, rolling my eyes in mock annoyance. "Are you suggesting I'm out of practice? I'll have you know that my salsa game is legendary."

"Legendary, huh? I might need to see some proof of that," he challenged, stepping closer, the warmth radiating from his body a welcome distraction from the swirling thoughts in my head.

Before I could respond, he swept me onto the dance floor. We twirled and spun beneath the cascading lights, lost in the rhythm of the moment. The music enveloped us like a warm embrace, each note pulling us deeper into a world where the looming shadows of doubt could not reach. Laughter bubbled between us, mingling with the music and the chatter of the crowd, and I felt alive, free from the weight of my anxieties.

But as I swayed in his arms, the euphoria was abruptly interrupted. My heart dropped, and the warmth of the evening evaporated as I caught sight of a figure lurking at the edge of the ballroom, cloaked in shadows. A chill crept along my spine, the familiar silhouette igniting an unwelcome sense of dread. It was them—the last person I wanted to see, and yet here they were, watching with cold, calculating eyes that glinted like shards of ice.

"Nathan," I murmured, my voice barely a whisper, the carefree joy draining from my expression as I tilted my head toward the figure.

He followed my gaze, his smile fading as a crease formed between his brows. "What's wrong?"

"I think... I think we're being watched," I replied, my heart pounding not from the dance but from the rush of adrenaline. The presence in the corner was suffocating, pressing in on me like a vice.

"Who is it?" he asked, his tone shifting to something more serious.

I couldn't tear my eyes away from the figure. It was hard to make out details in the dim light, but the tight-lipped smile was all too familiar—a twisted echo from my past that I had hoped to forget.

"I—I don't know. But I think I recognize them."

With a sudden determination, Nathan took my hand, his grip reassuring yet firm. "Let's get out of here. We can talk somewhere private."

Before I could protest, he led me through the sea of guests, the vibrant music fading behind us as we slipped out of the ballroom and into a quieter corridor. The air here was different—cooler, infused with an undercurrent of anticipation that thrummed beneath my skin. I leaned against the cool marble wall, my breath hitching as I tried to compose myself, desperate to shake off the remnants of panic that clung to me like a second skin.

"What do you mean you recognize them?" Nathan asked, concern etching lines across his forehead.

I shook my head, unwilling to confront the memories that threatened to resurface. "It's complicated. They're someone from my past—a person I thought I'd left behind."

"Then we'll face this together," he said, his voice low and steady. "Whatever it is, you're not alone."

His words wrapped around me like a protective shield, igniting a flicker of hope within me. I took a deep breath, feeling the warmth of his presence bolstering my resolve. "I appreciate that, but this is different. This person doesn't play by the rules."

"I'm not afraid of a little chaos," he replied, a spark of defiance lighting his eyes. "But I need you to be honest with me. What's the story?"

I hesitated, the weight of my past bearing down heavily on my chest. I could see the determination etched on Nathan's face, his fierce loyalty palpable. With a deep inhale, I decided to reveal just enough to ease the tension. "There are things I haven't shared—people I thought I was done with. I thought they were behind me."

"Whatever they are, we'll deal with it together," he assured me, his voice strong.

But as his words echoed in the silence, I couldn't shake the feeling that the real storm was yet to come, brewing on the horizon, waiting to unleash its fury on our fragile bubble of trust and connection.

I pressed my back against the cool marble wall, the thrum of the gala fading into a distant hum as I wrestled with my thoughts. Nathan's expression mirrored my own confusion and concern, yet there was a resolute strength in his gaze that anchored me in the storm of uncertainty. Just as I opened my mouth to share the weight of my past, a sudden crash echoed from the ballroom. The sound shattered the moment, drawing our attention to the chaotic whirl of colors and laughter just beyond the doorway.

"Did you hear that?" I asked, a knot of dread tightening in my stomach.

"I did, and it sounds like it came from the dance floor," Nathan replied, his tone shifting into that of a protector, the flicker of worry igniting a fierce spark within him.

Without a second thought, he took my hand, leading me back toward the source of the commotion. The elegant atmosphere had morphed into a scene of startled guests, murmurs rising and falling like waves in a turbulent sea. I caught snippets of conversation as we pushed through the crowd, snippets that made my heart race—words like "fight" and "who threw that?"

We stepped into the ballroom just in time to see a waiter stumble, dropping a towering tray of champagne flutes that shattered across the polished floor like a cascade of glittering stars. The laughter and music had been abruptly silenced, and all eyes were now fixed on the chaos. I spotted the figure from earlier, still lingering in the shadows, watching with an inscrutable smile that chilled me to the bone.

"Looks like the party's taken a turn," Nathan murmured, tension radiating from him as he pulled me closer. "You okay?"

"More or less," I replied, my voice a whisper laced with nerves. "But we should go. This isn't just an accident."

His brow furrowed as he scanned the crowd, his protective instincts flaring. "I'm not leaving you alone, especially not with…" He trailed off, his gaze hardening as he focused back on the figure, who seemed to be slipping away.

"Who is that?" Nathan demanded, frustration creeping into his tone. "Are they connected to you?"

"More than I'd like to admit," I said, gritting my teeth. "But let's focus on what's happening here. I don't want to drag you into my mess."

"Too late for that," he shot back, a glimmer of defiance in his eyes that I found oddly comforting. "You're in this, so I'm in this."

I chuckled softly, grateful for his resolve even in the face of uncertainty. "And here I thought tonight would just be about dancing and bad jokes."

"Why do you think I dressed like this?" He gestured to his crisp suit with a playful grin. "I was fully prepared to sweep you off your feet and then back to the dance floor. Now I have to add 'fighting off your past' to my list of skills."

As the guests began to recover from the surprise, the atmosphere shifted from chaos to a burgeoning excitement. People whispered and laughed nervously, the glint of intrigue flickering in their eyes. I knew that if I didn't act quickly, the night could spiral into something far worse.

"Nathan," I said, my heart racing, "let's go after them. We need to know who they are and what they want."

His expression hardened, the laughter gone as he nodded firmly. "Lead the way, and I'll follow."

We maneuvered through the crowd, my heart pounding as I focused on the figure slipping through the side door. The lights from the gala glimmered behind us, and the air outside was cooler, a sharp contrast to the heat of the ballroom. The figure had vanished around the corner, but I could still feel the prickle of danger in the air, like a storm brewing just out of sight.

"What if they're not just here for you?" Nathan asked, his voice low and serious as we reached the edge of the building. "What if they're here for me too?"

"Let's hope they're not," I replied, a slight tremor of fear threading through my resolve. "I don't want you caught up in this because of me."

But Nathan didn't respond. Instead, he gestured toward a small alleyway, a narrow path lined with flickering lights and the soft sounds of laughter from behind the walls. My instincts screamed for caution, but something deeper urged me to follow. We stepped cautiously into the darkness, the world of the gala receding behind us, and in its place was the faint echo of something more sinister.

The alley was dim, the shadows heavy and thick, but there was a flicker of movement ahead—just enough to send a rush of adrenaline coursing through my veins. I reached for Nathan's hand, intertwining my fingers with his. It was a small gesture, but it felt monumental in that moment, grounding me as the uncertainty swirled around us.

As we rounded the corner, the sound of hurried footsteps echoed through the narrow space, and my heart raced. The figure was there, standing with their back to us, and for a brief moment, the air hung heavy with anticipation. The world seemed to pause, and I felt Nathan's grip tighten around my hand, his presence a comforting anchor.

"Who are you?" I called out, my voice steadier than I felt.

The figure turned, and recognition struck me like lightning. It was someone I had known long ago, a ghost from my past I never expected to see again. "You?" I breathed, astonished and terrified all at once.

"I didn't think you'd remember," the figure said, their voice smooth, laced with an eerie charm. "But you always were good at making an impression."

Nathan stepped forward protectively, positioning himself between me and this unexpected intruder. "What do you want?"

The figure's smile widened, an unsettling blend of familiarity and menace. "Oh, darling, I'm here for the show. And you two are right in the spotlight."

I felt the blood drain from my face, my heart racing as the reality of the situation settled in. Whatever game they were playing, I was caught in the middle, and the stakes were higher than I had anticipated.

With a sudden lurch, the figure lunged forward, and chaos erupted anew, propelling me into a whirlwind of uncertainty that threatened to consume us both.

The figure lunged at us with unexpected speed, their intentions cloaked in shadows and malice. Instinct kicked in, and I pulled Nathan back, creating a small barrier between us as I assessed the threat. My heart thundered in my chest, and I could feel the air thicken with tension, each moment stretched taut like a bowstring ready to snap.

"Stay behind me," Nathan commanded, his voice low and steady.

"Excuse me? I can take care of myself," I shot back, irritation mingling with fear. There was a fierce protectiveness in him that I both appreciated and resented.

The figure halted just short of us, their eyes gleaming with a mixture of recognition and amusement. "Oh, please. You both look like you stepped out of a fairy tale, blissfully unaware of the dark forces at play."

"Cut the theatrics," Nathan snapped, his stance wide and unyielding. "What do you want with her?"

The figure's laughter echoed down the alley, a sound that seemed out of place among the chaos of the gala. "You're both so adorably naive. It's not her I'm interested in; it's the secrets she keeps. Secrets that could unravel everything."

"Secrets? What are you talking about?" I asked, my voice barely above a whisper, a chill crawling up my spine.

"Oh, you know," they said, a smirk playing on their lips. "The kind that involve powerful people and whispered promises. You've been playing a dangerous game, haven't you? Dancing with fire and hoping not to get burned."

"I'm not afraid of you," I asserted, though my bravado felt thin and shaky.

"Ah, but fear isn't the only currency in this world. There are debts to settle, and trust me, you'll want to be on the right side of this one." The figure stepped forward, closing the distance, and the unmistakable glint of something sharp caught the light.

Nathan moved instinctively, pulling me back as the figure brandished a small knife, its blade shimmering ominously. "We don't need to resort to violence," he said, his voice calm but filled with an undertone of authority. "Let's talk this out."

"Oh, how quaint! Talking." The figure rolled their eyes dramatically. "But I've learned that words are often just a prelude to betrayal. Why waste time when we could cut to the chase?"

Without warning, they lunged forward, the knife aimed straight at Nathan. I gasped, adrenaline surging as I pushed him aside, my body colliding with theirs in a desperate attempt to intervene. The blade grazed my arm, a sharp sting blooming before the figure twisted away, caught off guard by my sudden move.

"Why don't you pick on someone your own size?" I retorted, though I was acutely aware of how small and fragile I felt in that moment.

"Foolish girl," they hissed, regaining their footing and narrowing their eyes. "This isn't a game you can win."

Nathan's arm slid around my waist, steadying me as he eyed the figure with renewed intensity. "Enough of this. If you have something to say, then say it. But don't think for a second that we'll let you leave here unscathed."

The figure laughed, a sound dripping with disdain. "You really think you have the upper hand here? You have no idea who you're dealing with. I'm merely the messenger."

"Messenger for who?" I pressed, frustration boiling beneath the surface. "If you have a point to make, just get to it. I don't have time for cryptic riddles."

With a dramatic flair, the figure leaned closer, their voice dropping to a conspiratorial whisper. "You think you can just brush the past under the rug? Your little dance here? It's all part of a larger story, one that you've been a part of whether you like it or not. You're in way over your head."

Before I could respond, Nathan stepped forward, defiance radiating from him. "We'll decide what we can handle. You don't scare us. But if you have a message, then deliver it and let us go."

The figure's smile was cold, devoid of warmth. "Oh, Nathan, you have no idea how amusing you are. I came here for her, but now I see the real potential lies with you."

"What the hell is that supposed to mean?" Nathan snapped, his patience fraying at the edges.

But the figure merely shrugged, feigning nonchalance. "Just know this: the game has changed, and the pieces are already moving. You're both pawns in a much larger scheme."

At that moment, I felt a shift in the air, an almost tangible weight pressing down on us as if the very fabric of reality was bending to accommodate the looming threat. The alleyway darkened, shadows creeping in as the figure stepped back, eyes glinting with something that resembled satisfaction.

"Let's see how long you can keep dancing around the truth," they said, and with that, they turned and melted into the shadows, leaving only the echo of their laughter hanging in the air.

I stared after them, the adrenaline still coursing through my veins, a mix of fear and confusion swirling in my chest. "What just happened?"

Nathan's expression was tight, jaw clenched as he turned to face me. "I think we've just been thrown into something much deeper than we anticipated."

"Great. Just what I wanted for tonight—a cryptic message and a stab at my arm." I winced, bringing my hand up to inspect the shallow cut that now marred my skin, a reminder of the chaos that had erupted so suddenly.

"Are you okay?" Nathan asked, his voice softening as he examined the cut, his fingers brushing against my skin, igniting a spark that was both reassuring and unnerving.

"I'll live," I replied, trying to play it off, though the tremor in my voice betrayed me. "But what does it all mean? What kind of secrets do they think I'm keeping?"

"More importantly, who sent them?" Nathan muttered, glancing down the alley, as if the shadows might reveal some hidden answer.

Before I could respond, a loud crash echoed from the gala, the sound cutting through the tension like a knife. My heart sank as I instinctively turned back toward the noise, dread pooling in my stomach.

"Something isn't right," Nathan said, the urgency in his voice matching my own growing sense of alarm. "We need to go back. Now."

As we hurried back toward the ballroom, the thrill of the night had shifted into something darker, a storm brewing just out of sight.

The laughter and music were replaced by frantic whispers and confusion as guests began to spill into the hallway, faces filled with fear.

I gripped Nathan's hand tightly, our previous levity replaced by a shared understanding that we were on the brink of something we could neither comprehend nor escape. Just as we reached the door to the ballroom, the lights flickered ominously, plunging us into darkness for a brief moment.

A scream pierced the air, shattering the fragile calm that had settled over us. We exchanged a glance, a silent acknowledgment that whatever was happening would change everything. The stakes had been raised, and we were caught in the eye of a gathering storm, one that threatened to sweep us away into chaos.

As the lights flickered back on, the scene before us was chaotic—a mix of confusion and fear, guests scrambling in all directions. I felt a chill race down my spine as I caught sight of the figure again, standing at the edge of the crowd, their eyes locked on me.

In that instant, the gravity of my reality sank in. The past was no longer just a memory; it was standing right in front of me, and it demanded to be reckoned with.

Chapter 8: Secrets Revealed

The gala had been a spectacle, a whirlwind of shimmering gowns and tailored suits, but now, standing in the quiet of my living room, it felt like a distant echo, a faded memory shadowed by the weight of secrets. The remnants of laughter and clinking glasses haunted me, each sound replaced by the heavy thud of my heart, still racing from the night's revelations. Nathan's brow furrowed as he stood across from me, the flickering candlelight casting shadows that danced between us, creating an illusion of distance that belied the intimacy of our conversation.

"What do you mean, notes?" he asked, his voice low and steady, drawing me back to the moment we had retreated from the chaos of the gala. I had shared with him the unsettling truth—the cryptic notes that had begun appearing in my mailbox, each one more ominous than the last, leaving me with a sense of dread I couldn't shake. I hadn't anticipated this would stir something in him, that the admission would transform our fragile alliance into something thicker, more complicated.

I could feel his gaze dissecting me, sifting through layers of bravado and vulnerability. "It's just... they're unsettling," I admitted, my voice barely above a whisper. "They talk about things—secrets, things I thought only I knew." My pulse quickened as I recalled the last note, the words etched in my mind like a curse: You think you know the truth, but I know more about you than you think.

Nathan stepped closer, the air thickening with the shared weight of our words. "Secrets can fester," he murmured, his eyes searching mine. "You don't have to carry this alone."

He stood there, a tall figure of comfort wrapped in the kind of understated strength that always pulled me in, but I couldn't let myself forget the history we shared. Once rivals in a world where ambition clashed with morality, we had found ourselves on opposing sides. Yet here he was, offering not just his understanding but something deeper—a connection that flickered like a flame, both illuminating and threatening to consume us.

"I don't know who's behind them," I said, forcing myself to breathe, to dispel the air of suspicion that hung around us like a storm cloud. "What if it's someone who really knows me? Someone I should be afraid of?"

His lips pressed into a line, a frown of contemplation gracing his features. "Maybe the real question is why they chose you." His voice was steady, a stark contrast to the whirlpool of emotions churning inside me. "You're strong. People don't usually target the strong unless they see a crack, a weakness."

My heart sank, a heaviness settling in my chest. "And what if I'm just... pretending? What if this strength is all a façade?"

In that moment, the distance between us narrowed, the air thick with unspoken truths. "We all have our shadows," he said, a warmth to his tone that beckoned me closer. "Even the strongest among us. It's how we handle those shadows that defines us."

I felt a pull, an undeniable magnetism that blurred the lines of our past. In the dim light, I caught glimpses of his own vulnerability—a hint of something unspoken in the furrow of his brow, the tightness of his jaw. "What about you?" I asked, emboldened by the moment. "What shadows do you carry?"

For a heartbeat, he hesitated, his gaze dropping as if he were weighing his words against the gravity of our connection. "I've made mistakes, things I wish I could undo. But I can't change the past, only how I face it now."

His honesty struck a chord within me, a note of familiarity that reverberated through my own tangled memories. "And facing it now means standing here with me?" I questioned, half in jest, half in earnest, as a smile danced on my lips, hoping to lighten the intensity of our moment.

He chuckled softly, the sound like a balm for the tension thick in the air. "Well, I certainly didn't expect to find myself comforting my rival in the middle of a secret war, but here we are."

A flicker of laughter bubbled up within me, momentarily dispelling the shadows that clung to my thoughts. "We might be rivals, but it seems we're also allies in this strange game."

"Strange doesn't begin to cover it," he replied, a hint of mischief glinting in his eyes. "But there's something to be said about a partnership built on mutual secrets. It makes the stakes higher, don't you think?"

"Yes, but what happens when the stakes get too high?" I countered, the weight of our conversation creeping back into my voice. "What if we lose ourselves in the process?"

He stepped even closer, the warmth of his presence enveloping me. "Then we find a way to bring each other back. But first, we need to figure out who's pulling the strings."

The resolve in his tone sent a shiver down my spine, igniting a flicker of hope. Together, we could navigate this murky landscape of threats and uncertainties, turning our fears into a formidable force. I reached for his hand, feeling the warmth radiate from his skin, anchoring me in a reality I had once believed was too chaotic to endure.

As the night deepened, we dove into the dark unknown, side by side, two unlikely partners in a dance of shadows and light. The gala's glamour faded into insignificance as the truth loomed larger than any deception. Each secret we uncovered stitched us together, weaving a bond that held the promise of protection and understanding. In that moment, I felt the stirrings of something more profound than rivalry—a connection forged in the fires of adversity, lighting the way through the darkness ahead.

As Nathan's hand enveloped mine, the warmth seeped into my skin, chasing away the chill that had settled deep within me. We stood there, suspended in a moment that felt both surreal and utterly necessary. I glanced around my living room, its familiar trinkets and warm hues suddenly feeling like an echo of a past I had nearly forgotten—a time when my biggest worry was the state of my plants and whether I had enough wine for a Friday night binge. Now, the room felt charged with something potent and uncharted.

"What's next?" Nathan asked, his voice low, almost a whisper, as if he feared the very air around us might eavesdrop. "Do you have any idea who might be behind the notes?"

I bit my lip, the taste of uncertainty bitter on my tongue. "I don't know. I thought I could handle this on my own, but now..." I trailed off, the thought of facing whatever threat lurked in the shadows too daunting to articulate.

He took a step closer, narrowing the space between us until I could see the flecks of gold in his hazel eyes. "Let's start by retracing your steps. Anyone who knows you well enough to write those notes would have to be close to your life, right?"

"Close," I echoed, my mind racing. "That narrows it down to a select few." I felt a knot form in my stomach as names flashed through my thoughts, friends who had become distant and acquaintances who had turned into ghosts of my past.

"What about that friend of yours?" Nathan asked, tilting his head slightly, curiosity woven into his tone. "Sarah, right? You mentioned her at the gala."

I chuckled softly, despite the tension curling in my gut. "Sarah could hardly find her way through a maze, let alone plot a conspiracy. No, if she's involved, it's because she's been swept up in something she doesn't understand."

"And if she's innocent?" Nathan countered, his brow arched, a playful smile tugging at his lips. "Maybe it's someone who pretended to be close while hiding in the shadows?"

"Or someone who knows my secrets all too well," I said, a sharp edge to my voice that I hadn't intended. The memory of my past mistakes hung in the air like smoke, blurring my vision. "There's plenty I've buried—things I'd rather forget."

"Things we've all buried," he replied, his expression softening. "But remember, you're not alone in this. I'm here, willing to dig through the dirt if it means keeping you safe."

The sincerity in his words struck me, unearthing a warmth that spread through my chest, yet the shadows of doubt still loomed. I released his hand, needing to step back, to breathe. "What do you get out of this, Nathan? Why do you care?"

He studied me for a long moment, his gaze unwavering. "Because I see something worth protecting," he said finally, each word deliberate, laced with conviction. "And maybe because I've been on the other side of that darkness myself."

"What do you mean?" I pressed, the intrigue weaving through my fear, drawing me back to him.

"My past isn't pretty," he said, voice steady but tinged with an undercurrent of pain. "I've had my own secrets, my own battles. But I learned that facing them is better than hiding in the shadows. I'd rather be your ally than a stranger."

The revelation hung between us like a fragile thread, and I wondered how many secrets lay buried beneath his facade. Before I could respond, the air shifted, heavy with the weight of our shared vulnerability. My heart quickened, not just with fear but with an unexpected exhilaration, a spark igniting in the depths of my uncertainty.

"Then let's be allies," I said, summoning the courage I didn't know I possessed. "Let's figure this out together."

He smiled then, a genuine expression that melted away some of the tension. "All right, but I'm going to need coffee and maybe some of your famed chocolate chip cookies. Those are essential for this kind of work."

I laughed, the sound lightening the atmosphere as I nodded toward the kitchen. "You drive a hard bargain, Nathan. I'll make sure to add a touch of desperation to the cookies to fuel our efforts."

"Perfect. Desperation always makes for the best recipes," he teased, falling into step beside me as we walked to the kitchen. As I prepped the coffee, I couldn't help but steal glances at him, the way he moved through my space as if he belonged there, a harmonious blend of past rivalry and newfound camaraderie.

The coffee brewed with an aromatic hiss, filling the room with the familiar scent that always anchored me. "You know, I never pictured us as partners in crime," I mused, trying to ease the weight of our earlier conversation. "More like frenemies navigating a battlefield of corporate politics."

"Life has a funny way of throwing us curveballs," he replied, leaning against the counter, his demeanor relaxed yet alert. "Who knows, maybe this is the beginning of a legendary partnership? Or at the very least, a thrilling misadventure."

"Legendary, huh? Bold of you to assume we'll survive this ordeal." I shot back, smirking as I poured steaming mugs, the rich aroma swirling around us like an unspoken promise.

"Survival is overrated," he grinned, lifting his mug in a mock toast. "What's important is that we take this journey together, all the while enjoying a few good cookies along the way."

"Agreed," I said, clinking my mug against his, warmth radiating through the ceramic and into my hands. Just then, my phone buzzed on the counter, slicing through the moment. My heart raced as I picked it up, scanning the screen. A notification flashed—an unknown number, a message that made my stomach drop.

I see you, and I know what you did.

The laughter faded as dread pooled in my gut, cold and heavy. Nathan's expression shifted as he watched me, the playful banter gone, replaced by an urgent tension. "What is it?"

"Just a... message," I managed, my voice trembling as I turned the screen toward him, the text glaring back at us, a haunting reminder of the danger lurking closer than I dared to admit.

His eyes darkened, filled with a mixture of concern and determination. "We need to take this seriously. Whoever it is, they're not just playing games anymore."

In that instant, the jovial atmosphere of our alliance morphed into something darker, more urgent. The thrill of adventure faded into the background, replaced by the stark reality that we were not just uncovering secrets; we were entangled in a web of threats, a game far more dangerous than I had ever anticipated.

The message sat on the screen like a loaded gun, its implications echoing through my mind as Nathan leaned closer, concern etching deeper lines across his brow. "What does it say?" he urged, his voice a low growl that sent a ripple of adrenaline coursing through me.

I handed him my phone, feeling exposed, vulnerable in a way I had never anticipated when we decided to work together. The words hung in the air like a thick fog, wrapping around us, obscuring the once warm light of our camaraderie. "It's just a message," I stammered, though the tremor in my voice betrayed me.

Nathan read it, his expression shifting as he absorbed the weight of those five simple words. "This isn't just a threat; it's a warning," he said, his voice steady but edged with urgency. "We need to figure out who this is before it escalates."

"Easier said than done," I shot back, annoyance prickling at my fear. "I don't have a clue where to start. My life isn't a crime novel; I can't just flip to the last chapter and see who the villain is."

He laughed, but it was humor tinged with a sharp edge, a recognition of the absurdity of our situation. "Maybe we could brainstorm. What are your secrets? I'm betting they're not all bad."

My stomach twisted. "Oh, please, let's not delve into my awkward phase of trying to impress people by baking too many cookies. That's not exactly riveting."

He grinned, clearly relishing the banter even as the situation grew tenser. "I'm all for cookie secrets. Let's start there."

"Very funny," I said, rolling my eyes. But I knew I had to shake off the heaviness pressing down on me. "Fine. Let's think this through. If someone knows my secrets, they might know about my past at work, my former colleagues. Anyone who knew me back then could have a motive."

Nathan nodded, his face serious again. "Then let's make a list. Who do you think might have a reason to target you?"

I leaned against the counter, considering the question, my mind racing. "There was Jenna, who got really upset when I left the team. But she wouldn't go this far, would she? Then there's Thomas—he always had a bit of a grudge against anyone who dared to outshine him. And, oh, let's not forget Mark, who I had a rather unpleasant breakup with."

"Ex-boyfriend drama," Nathan said, a hint of amusement breaking through his seriousness. "That's a classic plot twist."

"Funny, right?" I replied dryly, trying to ignore the tightening knot of anxiety. "But this is different. This isn't just about me. It's about someone with a vendetta. I could handle a petty argument; I'm not prepared for a stalker."

"Maybe it's someone from your past who feels wronged," Nathan suggested, his expression shifting back to focus. "Someone who believes they have a reason to come after you. But we can't draw conclusions without more information."

Just as I was about to respond, my phone vibrated again, this time a persistent buzzing that sent my heart racing. I picked it up hesitantly, my breath hitching as I recognized the number—the same unknown one from before. "It's them again," I breathed, feeling the thrill of fear coil tight in my chest.

Nathan's eyes locked onto mine, and I could see the resolve hardening in him. "Open it," he urged, his voice firm.

With a shaky finger, I tapped on the message. This time, it was a photo—blurry but unmistakable. It showed a dimly lit street corner outside my apartment, the angle tight and the figure hidden, but there was no mistaking the implication. Someone was watching me.

I nearly dropped the phone, my stomach turning at the thought. "What the hell? This is... this is too much!"

"Whoever this is is trying to intimidate you. We can't let them succeed," Nathan said, his voice low but steady, radiating a strength that cut through my panic. "We need to go out there and see if we can catch a glimpse of who it is."

"Are you insane?" I exclaimed, shaking my head vehemently. "You want to confront a potential stalker? That's a great way to end up as a headline in the local news!"

"Or it's a chance to take control of this situation," he countered, his gaze unwavering. "But we need to act fast. You can't let them have the upper hand."

I inhaled deeply, the weight of his words anchoring me as fear wrestled with a new kind of adrenaline. He was right; sitting here wouldn't help me. I needed to reclaim my narrative. "Fine. Let's do it," I said, determination hardening in my chest.

"Good. But first, we need to come up with a plan," Nathan said, a slight smile of approval crossing his face. "No wild adventures without some strategy."

"I'll grab my coat," I replied, moving swiftly to the hallway. The familiar wool felt like a suit of armor as I slipped it on, a layer of comfort amidst the chaos. My heart raced with each passing second as I joined him back in the living room, the urgency of the moment elevating the mundane into something electric.

Nathan checked his watch, then grabbed his keys. "Let's stick to the shadows. We'll keep a low profile and watch from a distance. If we see anything, we'll decide on our next move."

"Just like spies," I said, half-joking, half-serious. "How do you know you're not leading me into a trap?"

"Trust me, I know a thing or two about traps," he replied, his tone playful but with a hint of seriousness that sent a shiver down my spine.

We slipped out into the cool night air, the streetlamps casting soft glows against the pavement, transforming the ordinary into an almost cinematic scene. I felt a rush of exhilaration tinged with fear as we stepped into the unknown. Together, we moved with purpose, hearts pounding in sync, knowing that each shadow could hold the answer or a threat.

As we approached the corner captured in the photo, I held my breath, peering into the darkness. The world felt charged, alive with possibilities and dangers alike. I scanned the street, searching for anything out of the ordinary, anything that might give away the lurking presence.

Then, in the distance, I caught a flicker of movement—something dark, a figure slipping out of the shadows just as I turned to whisper to Nathan. My heart thundered in my chest as I nudged him, gesturing toward the alley.

"Do you see that?" I murmured, fear lacing my words.

He squinted into the darkness, his expression hardening. "Yes. Stay close to me."

We edged forward, moving stealthily as the figure began to turn, their features still obscured. My breath hitched, every instinct screaming for caution. Just as we were about to get closer, the figure froze, seeming to sense our presence.

"Run!" Nathan hissed, grabbing my arm and pulling me back into the shadows.

We bolted, hearts racing, the thrill of danger mingling with the adrenaline surging through our veins. The sound of footsteps echoed behind us, relentless and growing closer.

Suddenly, I felt a sharp pain as my foot caught on something, and I stumbled, hitting the ground hard. Nathan was at my side in an instant, concern etched across his features as he knelt beside me.

"Are you okay?"

"I'm fine," I managed, wincing as I pushed myself up. But as I glanced back, the figure loomed closer, their silhouette sharp against the moonlight, a stark reminder of the danger we faced.

In that moment, as Nathan helped me to my feet, I could feel the tension thickening around us, a palpable fear rising like smoke. I met his gaze, a silent understanding passing between us—this wasn't just about the notes anymore. Whatever was unfolding was more significant, more dangerous than we had ever imagined.

And as the figure stepped into the light, their face revealed, a chill shot through me. The world around us tilted, spinning into chaos as recognition crashed over me like a tidal wave, leaving only one chilling thought: this was far from over.

Chapter 9: Tides of Truth

The sun dipped low over Windward Bay, casting long shadows that danced across the quaint streets. I often thought the town wore its secrets like the evening fog that rolled in from the sea—thick, enveloping, and just heavy enough to obscure the truth. That evening, I found myself nestled among the weathered shelves of the local library, the scent of old paper mingling with the tang of salt in the air. Nathan was a few paces away, poring over a stack of books as if deciphering ancient scrolls, his brow furrowed in concentration. It was comforting to have him near, yet I could sense the tension simmering just beneath the surface of our shared glances, each one heavy with unspoken words.

As I leafed through the brittle pages of a faded newspaper, the brittle sound echoed in the stillness. There it was, buried beneath layers of yellowed ink—a small article that made my heart race. "Mysterious Disappearances Plague Windward Bay: A History of Fear." I could hardly breathe as the words leapt off the page, each syllable sending tendrils of dread spiraling through my thoughts. In a town that seemed so idyllic, the shadows whispered stories I was only beginning to comprehend.

"They vanished without a trace," I murmured, half to myself and half to Nathan, who had moved closer, drawn by my quiet intensity. The headline felt like a curse, a taunt. The details were scant but chilling—reports of families torn apart, loved ones searching for years, only to find empty echoes of lives once lived. My fingers trembled as I traced the faded ink.

"What did you find?" Nathan's voice was low and steady, grounding me in the chaos of my thoughts. He leaned in closer, the warmth of his presence wrapping around me like a protective cocoon.

I turned the page, revealing a crude sketch of a woman whose face held an air of sorrow that pierced my heart. "This woman," I whispered, "was one of the last to go missing, a young mother. It happened right around the time of the gala—the same time all of this... this madness began."

Nathan's expression shifted, a flicker of recognition sparking in his eyes. "You think there's a connection?"

"How can there not be? The gala brought so many strangers to town, and it feels like something awakened," I replied, the chill of realization settling deep in my bones. "What if we're being watched? What if we're next?"

"We need to be careful," Nathan said, his voice firm yet gentle, like the steady tide that ebbed and flowed with the moon. "But we can't let fear paralyze us. We have to uncover the truth, no matter how uncomfortable it might be."

As he spoke, his hand brushed against mine, a fleeting contact that sent a jolt of electricity through me. In that moment, the world outside faded—the unsettling headlines, the fear that loomed like storm clouds. It was just us, suspended in a breathless bubble of possibility, but I couldn't ignore the shadows lurking at the edges of my thoughts.

"What if this isn't just a series of unfortunate events?" I asked, the words escaping my lips before I could stop them. "What if there's something more sinister at play?"

Nathan's eyes narrowed slightly, contemplating my words. "What do you mean?"

"I mean, what if someone is orchestrating this? Using our past against us, drawing us into a trap?" The weight of my own history pressed heavily on me, suffocating. I had fought too hard to escape the chains of my past, only to find that it had a way of creeping back in.

He took a breath, a steadying inhale that steadied the chaos swirling within me. "We'll figure it out together. I promise."

I wanted to believe him, wanted to trust that we could face whatever was lurking in the shadows. Yet, doubts gnawed at my insides like a relentless tide. The more we uncovered, the more I felt the threads of my life unraveling, revealing a tapestry of intertwined destinies that might be far darker than I had ever imagined.

The air shifted as a door creaked open, and a gust of wind sent a shiver through the library. My pulse quickened, each heartbeat echoing the feeling of being watched. I turned instinctively, expecting to see someone slip in from the shadows, but the entrance was empty, the echoes of the past swirling in silence around us.

"We need to go," I said abruptly, the urgency in my voice startling even me. "We can come back, but right now, I need fresh air."

Nathan nodded, sensing the shift in my demeanor. As we stepped outside, the air was cool against my skin, invigorating yet heavy with unsaid words. The ocean whispered its secrets in the distance, crashing against the rocks like an impatient lover.

"What's the plan?" he asked, falling into step beside me as we walked.

I paused, looking out at the endless horizon where the sky kissed the sea. "We need to dig deeper, look for patterns in these disappearances. Someone has to know something—someone must have seen something."

"You're not alone in this," he reassured, his gaze steady on mine. "We'll find out who's behind this, even if we have to drag the truth out from the depths."

A shiver of hope flared within me, but it was quickly snuffed by the cold reality of our predicament. "You think so?"

"Absolutely." The conviction in his voice was a balm to my fears. "And I won't let you go through this alone."

With a nod, I felt a flicker of determination ignite. Together, we would confront whatever darkness awaited us. The sun dipped lower, casting golden hues over Windward Bay, but I couldn't shake the sense of impending storm clouds on the horizon, gathering their forces, ready to unleash their fury.

The following days passed in a blur of frantic research and hushed conversations. The once-familiar streets of Windward Bay took on an eerie quality, as if the very air was thick with secrets waiting to be uncovered. Every time Nathan and I crossed paths with the townsfolk, we exchanged furtive glances laden with meaning—conspiratorial, charged, as if we were members of a secret society tasked with unraveling a conspiracy that was far older and darker than we had ever imagined.

Nathan was unwavering in his determination, and his presence gave me courage I didn't know I had. He had become my confidant and, surprisingly, my anchor in a tempest of swirling emotions and burgeoning fears. I found myself entranced by his easy charm, the way his laughter felt like a balm against the growing weight of my worries. But beneath the surface, I could sense the growing tension between us, a current that crackled like electricity in the air, each brush of our fingers a promise and a peril wrapped in one.

One afternoon, we decided to take a break from the library's suffocating quiet, opting instead for the bustling café on the corner, its windows fogged from the warmth inside. The smell of freshly brewed coffee and baked goods enveloped us as we settled into a corner booth, the vibrant chatter of other patrons a pleasant distraction from our recent discoveries. I stirred my cappuccino, watching the foam swirl into intricate patterns as if the very act of creation could ease the tension in my chest.

"So," Nathan began, leaning back against the worn leather of the booth, a teasing smile tugging at his lips, "what's next on the agenda?

A daring escape from the library or a secret mission to unearth more of Windward Bay's illustrious past?"

I rolled my eyes, but my smile matched his. "How about we focus on something a little less dramatic? Like figuring out who keeps sending me these notes?" I held up the latest scrap of paper, its edges frayed, the ink still slightly damp from where I had hastily scrawled down the latest clue.

"Perhaps a series of friendly letters from a well-meaning ghost?" He quipped, his eyes sparkling with mischief.

I laughed, the sound genuine and bright, cutting through the tension like a warm knife through cold butter. "Right, because that's what I need—a ghost with a flair for cryptic poetry. No thanks."

As the laughter subsided, a familiar weight settled back over us. "What if the notes are a breadcrumb trail? Someone leading us to something, or away from it?"

Nathan's expression shifted, a shadow creeping across his features. "Or a warning," he said, his tone suddenly serious. "Someone wants us to stop digging."

The idea sent a chill skittering down my spine, yet I found myself leaning into the thrill of it all. "Well, I'm not one to back down from a challenge." My resolve felt as solid as the coffee mug in my hands. "And I have a feeling we're closer to uncovering something big."

Just as I finished speaking, the bell above the café door jingled, drawing my gaze. A woman stepped in, her dark hair cascading over her shoulders in thick waves, her demeanor exuding a confident air that instantly captured the attention of every patron in the room. She moved through the café with purpose, her heels clicking against the polished floor, the kind of sound that commanded attention without trying.

"Do you know her?" I asked, intrigued.

Nathan's brow furrowed slightly. "No, but she looks familiar. I might have seen her around town."

As she approached our table, I noticed her sharp blue eyes flickering between us, evaluating. "Excuse me," she said, her voice smooth yet commanding. "You're the ones looking into the past, aren't you? The disappearances?"

I exchanged a quick glance with Nathan, the sudden chill in the air thickening. "We might be," I replied cautiously. "And who might you be?"

"Name's Clara," she introduced herself, sliding into the booth across from us without waiting for an invitation. "I know a thing or two about the history of Windward Bay, and you might want to hear what I have to say."

"Do we have a choice?" Nathan shot back, his tone laced with skepticism.

Clara's lips curved into a knowing smile. "Smart boy. You do have a choice—keep digging blindly or listen to someone who can help."

I leaned in, curiosity piqued. "What do you know about the disappearances?"

"A lot more than I should," she replied, her gaze piercing. "You see, Windward Bay has always had its shadows. Some people prefer to keep the past buried, but others..." She leaned closer, her voice dropping to a conspiratorial whisper. "Others are desperate to bring it to light."

"What does that mean?" I pressed, my heart racing with a mix of apprehension and excitement.

Clara glanced around the café, ensuring no one else was eavesdropping. "Let's just say there are connections to those who went missing and people you might know."

Nathan and I exchanged looks, the weight of her words sinking in. "You can't drop a bomb like that and not elaborate," he insisted, his voice firm.

"Fine," Clara relented, her eyes flashing with a mix of annoyance and amusement. "I'll tell you what I know. But first, I need you to understand the risks involved. If you're going to pursue this, you might want to prepare for the consequences."

"Bring it on," I said, my resolve hardening. "I'm tired of living in fear of the past. If there's something to uncover, then let's uncover it."

Her laughter was soft, almost mocking. "You're a brave one. But bravery doesn't come without its price."

As she began to recount tales of the town's hidden history, the air around us thickened with a tension that was electric, each word pulling me deeper into a web of intrigue and danger I hadn't anticipated. I felt like I was stepping into a story much larger than myself, where every decision could lead to unexpected consequences. Yet, with Nathan at my side, the thrill of discovery was intoxicating, a balm against the fears that had been haunting me since the gala.

I leaned in closer, ready to unravel the threads of truth, even as shadows loomed ever closer, threatening to shroud the light of understanding.

Clara leaned back, her presence both commanding and unsettling as she spun tales of Windward Bay's shadowy past, her words dripping with intrigue. "The first disappearance happened just after the old lighthouse was abandoned," she said, her voice dropping to a conspiratorial whisper. "You know, that creepy place on the cliffs? It was rumored that the last keeper had gone mad before he vanished without a trace. No body, no clues, just a town left to wonder."

Nathan shifted in his seat, his eyes narrowing with suspicion. "And you believe the lighthouse has something to do with the recent events?"

Clara gave a slow nod, her expression serious. "It's not just the lighthouse. It's the stories that linger—the spirits of those who never made it home. Windward Bay has a way of keeping its secrets close. If you're digging too deep, you might stir up something best left undisturbed."

My heart raced at the thought. "Are you saying we could be in danger just for wanting to know the truth?"

"Danger? Oh, honey, it's not about wanting. It's about what you'll find when you look." Clara's eyes glinted with mischief and foreboding, a mixture that made me wary.

"I think we can handle whatever comes our way," I asserted, attempting to mask the uncertainty swirling within me. The atmosphere in the café shifted, the laughter and chatter fading into a muffled backdrop as I focused on Clara's piercing gaze.

"You don't know what you're asking for," she replied, her tone low, almost sympathetic. "Once you step onto that path, there's no turning back. The disappearances are just the beginning. There are others, things that have happened in this town that would chill you to the bone."

Nathan leaned forward, curiosity igniting in his eyes. "Like what?"

Clara hesitated, weighing her words as if choosing from a dangerous menu. "There were whispers of rituals, gatherings at the lighthouse under the cover of darkness—people from all walks of life. Some say they were looking for something, others say they were trying to bind something."

The idea of a hidden cult operating in our quaint little town made my skin crawl. "What were they trying to bind?"

"Let's just say, some stories tell of a darkness that was better left alone. But curiosity got the better of them, just like it has with you two." Clara's smile turned predatory, her confidence radiating like a beacon of warning.

"What's your angle in all this?" Nathan challenged, skepticism threading his words. "You seem awfully invested in our little expedition."

She chuckled, the sound sharp and unsettling. "I've seen too many people get caught up in the past, thinking they can handle it.

I'm just here to give you a friendly heads-up, or a nudge, depending on how you look at it. After all, someone has to keep an eye on the brave souls stirring the pot."

I felt a knot tighten in my stomach, the stakes suddenly feeling much higher. "So, what do we do now? Just sit and wait for something to happen?"

Clara leaned in closer, her voice a conspiratorial whisper. "If you're serious about this, you need to head to the lighthouse. Tonight."

"Tonight?" Nathan repeated, skepticism lacing his tone. "You expect us to just waltz in there without any backup?"

"Trust me," Clara said, the glint in her eye becoming almost predatory. "You won't be alone. I'll go with you."

I exchanged a look with Nathan, uncertainty coloring my expression. "And why should we trust you?"

"Because," she said, her voice dropping to a near growl, "if you don't go, you might never know the truth. And if you do, you might uncover something that could change everything."

An uneasy silence settled over us, the weight of Clara's words hanging in the air like a storm cloud ready to burst. I glanced out the window, the sun dipping lower on the horizon, casting an ominous glow over the town. The idea of the lighthouse—a structure wrapped in mystery and shadow—loomed large in my mind.

"What's the worst that could happen?" I murmured, half to myself.

Nathan's expression was cautious, yet resolute. "We need to be prepared. If we're going to do this, we have to go in with our eyes wide open."

"Fine," I agreed, adrenaline pumping through my veins, pushing the fear to the side. "Let's do it."

Clara grinned, a hint of something predatory lurking in her smile. "Good. I'll meet you at the lighthouse just after dark. Bring flashlights and something to defend yourselves—just in case."

A shiver ran down my spine at her words, but the thrill of the unknown ignited a fire in my heart. The café faded into the background as we exited, the cool evening air wrapping around us like a shroud.

As we walked toward the lighthouse, the streets felt emptier, the world around us darkening with each step. The sound of the ocean crashing against the rocks below provided a haunting backdrop, a reminder that beneath the surface, danger lurked.

"What are we getting ourselves into?" Nathan asked, glancing at me with concern.

"Something we should've done a long time ago," I replied, my voice steadier than I felt. "We can't let fear dictate our lives. We owe it to ourselves to uncover the truth, no matter how uncomfortable it might be."

The lighthouse loomed ahead, a dark silhouette against the twilight sky, its once-proud structure now shrouded in mystery. The air was thick with anticipation and dread, the wind whipping through the grass as we approached, each footfall echoing our resolve.

Once we reached the base, I turned to Nathan. "Are you ready for this?"

He nodded, determination etching lines on his face. "Together, right?"

"Always."

As Clara joined us, her presence both reassuring and unnerving, she gestured toward the entrance. "Let's go. The night is young, and we have secrets to unearth."

The door creaked open, revealing a narrow staircase spiraling upward into darkness. A sense of foreboding washed over me, the weight of what lay ahead pressing heavily on my chest.

With flashlights in hand, we stepped inside, the air thick with the smell of damp wood and salt. Shadows danced along the walls, and the wind howled through the gaps, as if warning us to turn back.

I took a deep breath, my heart racing with a mixture of fear and exhilaration. "No turning back now," I whispered, knowing that whatever awaited us at the top of those stairs would forever change the course of our lives.

Just as we ascended the first few steps, a low rumble echoed through the lighthouse, shaking the very foundation beneath our feet.

"What was that?" Nathan asked, his voice barely above a whisper.

Clara's eyes widened, the bravado slipping from her demeanor. "We need to hurry. Whatever is up there… it doesn't want us here."

The rumbling grew louder, accompanied by a sudden gust of wind that slammed the door shut behind us, trapping us in the darkness. My pulse quickened, a mix of fear and determination surging through me as we pressed onward, our flashlights flickering against the encroaching shadows.

And then, just as we reached the top of the staircase, the light from our flashlights illuminated an unexpected scene—a figure standing in the dim glow of the lantern, their back turned to us, shrouded in mystery.

"Who's there?" I called, my voice trembling slightly.

The figure turned slowly, revealing a familiar face etched with shadows, a smile curling on their lips that sent a wave of terror crashing through me.

The world around us spun, and in that moment, I knew that the truth we sought was closer than we had ever imagined—and far more dangerous.

Chapter 10: Echoes of the Past

The lighthouse loomed ahead, a sentinel of secrets and shattered hopes, its paint peeling like the memories of those who had vanished from our quaint little town. With each step I took on the craggy path, my heart raced, thudding against my ribcage as if trying to escape the weight of history pressing down upon us. The salty breeze tangled my hair, sending a chill spiraling through me, though whether it was the cold or the ominous presence of the lighthouse, I couldn't tell.

Nathan walked beside me, his brow furrowed in concentration. The man had a way of making the ordinary seem extraordinary; his voice held an irresistible gravity that pulled me closer, even when the shadows threatened to swallow us whole. "You really think those dreams mean something?" he asked, glancing sideways at me, his deep-set eyes glimmering with curiosity.

"They have to," I replied, trying to sound more certain than I felt. "They're vivid, Nathan. I can't shake the feeling that they're a warning or... maybe a clue." I pulled my jacket tighter around me, half from the chill in the air and half from the creeping sense of dread that followed us like a wayward ghost.

As we reached the lighthouse, its towering form cast an elongated shadow that swept across the jagged rocks. A scent of damp wood and seaweed filled the air, mingling with the faint smell of smoke that lingered from a distant bonfire. I stopped to catch my breath, trying to absorb the scene: the crashing waves, the rhythmic call of the gulls, and the soft hum of the wind. "This place is beautiful," I murmured, more to myself than to Nathan.

"Beautiful and terrifying," he said, stepping closer to the structure. "They say the lighthouse is haunted by the spirits of those who never returned." His voice dropped to a conspiratorial whisper, sending a shiver up my spine.

"What do you mean?" I asked, curiosity piqued despite the heavy blanket of unease settling over me.

"Fishermen, sailors, the ones who ignored the storm warnings. They say they wander these cliffs, searching for the families they left behind." Nathan looked up at the lighthouse, his expression a blend of fascination and fear. "Every time the light swings around, it's said to shine on the souls still looking for closure."

A gust of wind howled, as if in response, and I couldn't help but shudder. "Let's not keep them waiting, then," I said, masking my trepidation with bravado. I reached for the rusty doorknob, its surface cool against my palm, and pushed the door open with a creak that echoed like a groan.

Inside, the air was thick with dust, swirling in the narrow beams of light that filtered through grimy windows. The interior smelled of salt and neglect, with cobwebs draping the corners like heavy drapes. A staircase spiraled upward, worn steps beckoning us into the unknown. I glanced back at Nathan, who wore a half-smile that somehow managed to be both reassuring and mischievous.

"After you," he said, feigning an exaggerated bow that elicited a laugh from me, breaking the tension like glass shattering on the floor.

"Such a gentleman," I teased, stepping onto the first stair. It creaked ominously beneath my weight. "Just remember, if I trip and fall, I expect you to catch me."

"I'd never let you hit the ground," he replied, his tone low and serious.

With each step, the air grew heavier, as if it was saturated with memories too stubborn to fade. We reached the lantern room, and I was greeted by an expansive view of the tumultuous sea. Waves crashed against the rocks below, sending sprays of foam high into the air. "It's stunning," I breathed, leaning against the railing, momentarily mesmerized by the wild beauty outside.

But Nathan's gaze was fixed elsewhere. "Look," he said, pointing to a weathered chest tucked against the wall, almost camouflaged by shadows. "What do you think is in there?"

I stepped closer, curiosity piquing again. The chest bore the scars of time—its edges splintered and hinges rusted. "Only one way to find out," I said, glancing at him.

"Careful," he warned, his tone suddenly serious. "This could be more than just a treasure chest."

"Or it could be filled with forgotten love letters," I countered, lifting the lid with a groan. The sound reverberated through the room, and for a moment, the world outside faded into a distant roar. I peered inside, half expecting to find trinkets of some long-lost romance, but what I saw instead sent a chill straight to my bones.

The chest was filled with old, yellowed papers, their edges frayed and curling. I picked one up, and my heart dropped as I recognized the familiar scrawl—letters filled with desperation, pleading for help, and accounts of the storm that had claimed so many lives. "Nathan, these... these are letters from the people who disappeared."

His eyes widened, and he stepped closer, his breath catching in his throat. "What does it say?"

I scanned the fragile pages, and the words leaped off the paper, vibrant and painful. "They thought they were safe, that they could weather the storm." I glanced up, my voice trembling. "But they were wrong."

Suddenly, the lighthouse shuddered, a violent tremor running through the floorboards as if it were a living entity trying to warn us away. Nathan grabbed my arm, pulling me back as the lantern flickered ominously, casting eerie shadows across our faces.

"Maybe we should go," he suggested, his voice laced with urgency, but I couldn't move. The air crackled around us, heavy with unresolved tension, and the words of the letters echoed in my mind—warnings from the past that were now intertwining with our fate.

I felt an unshakeable pull toward the chest, an insistent whisper urging me to uncover more. "Wait," I said, shaking off his grip. "There's something here we need to find out."

Nathan hesitated but ultimately nodded, his eyes locked on mine, a silent agreement passing between us. Together, we would face whatever darkness lurked within the lighthouse, tethered by our shared determination to unearth the truth, no matter the cost.

As Nathan and I stood in the lantern room, the flickering light cast long, wavering shadows that played across the walls, mimicking the chaos of the stormy sea outside. The letters in the chest seemed to pulse with energy, their silent stories clawing at the edges of my consciousness. I carefully unfolded another, the crinkling paper whispering secrets long held captive. The words skated across my mind, a chilling reminder that the lives of those who had come before us were etched into the very fabric of this place.

"Listen to this," I said, holding the paper out for Nathan, who leaned in, his warm breath brushing against my arm. "It talks about a storm, how the waves were taller than the lighthouse itself, and they were warned to stay away. But they—"

"They didn't listen," he finished, his eyes darkening. "No one ever does, do they? There's something about human nature that craves confrontation."

I dropped the letter back into the chest, my heart heavy. "It's as if they were drawn here, like moths to a flame, hoping for safety that never came."

A shudder ran through me as I glanced around the room. The walls seemed to lean in, almost conspiratorial in their intimacy, holding secrets that had been waiting for someone to uncover them. My fingers brushed against a weathered map pinned to the wall. It showed the coastline and a series of Xs marking shipwrecks and lost souls. "Look at this," I said, gesturing for Nathan to join me. "These shipwrecks... they tell a story of their own."

He stepped closer, scanning the faded ink. "Every X represents someone who took the wrong turn, a choice made in desperation."

As if on cue, the wind howled, rattling the windows and sending a fresh wave of chill racing through the room. I glanced at Nathan, who seemed captivated yet uneasy, the gravity of our discoveries weighing on both of us. "Maybe we should check out one of these locations," I suggested, curiosity overtaking caution. "There could be more answers waiting for us."

"Or more ghosts," he replied, half-joking, but I could see the intrigue dancing in his eyes. "I don't know about you, but I'm not keen on adding to the local legends of lost souls."

"Let's hope it's just fishing nets and barnacles we find," I said, forcing a lightness into my voice as I stepped away from the map. "Unless you're secretly yearning to be a part of some folklore. Perhaps we can be the tragic love story of the lighthouse?"

"Tragic? We're not dead yet," he quipped, a teasing grin breaking through his initial seriousness. "But I have to admit, if we do find anything, I wouldn't mind having a good ghost story to tell at the pub later."

Laughter spilled from my lips, easing the tension that had coiled tightly around us. Nathan's ability to lighten the moment felt like a warm blanket on a cold night, drawing us closer even as the lighthouse continued to loom over us, a steadfast guardian of both light and shadow.

As the laughter faded, I felt the weight of the chest beside me, its contents still demanding our attention. "We need to finish reading these letters," I said, driven by a strange compulsion. "Each one seems like a piece of a puzzle."

"Let's do it," he said, moving back to the chest with purpose. "If we can figure out why they came here, maybe we can understand what's still haunting this place."

With a renewed sense of urgency, we sifted through the letters, trading off reading duties, our voices echoing in the empty room. Each letter unveiled more of the town's dark history: love lost, promises broken, and the weight of regret. One letter, particularly poignant, detailed a mother's frantic pleas to the lighthouse keeper to save her husband and son caught in the merciless waves.

"There's so much pain here," I whispered, my heart aching for those who had come before. "It's like their sorrow has seeped into the very walls."

"Perhaps that's why the lighthouse still stands," Nathan mused. "A testament to those who were lost. A warning to those who come after."

Just then, a loud crash echoed from below, shaking the lighthouse to its core. I jumped, clutching the edge of the chest as adrenaline surged through me. "What was that?"

"I don't know, but it sounded like it came from the lower levels," he said, his voice steady despite the uncertainty flashing in his eyes. "We should check it out."

"Of course we should," I replied, my heart racing. "What could possibly go wrong?"

"Optimism at its finest," Nathan shot back, a hint of amusement flickering through the tension.

Together, we descended the spiral staircase, our footsteps echoing in the hollow space. Each step felt like an invitation to danger, and the shadows danced menacingly around us as we moved further into the unknown. The air thickened, heavy with the scent of mildew and mystery, wrapping around us like a cloak.

When we reached the bottom, we found the door leading to the lower levels ajar, swinging gently on its hinges as if beckoning us in. I exchanged a wary glance with Nathan before stepping through the threshold. The darkness enveloped us, and the faint sound of dripping water echoed from somewhere in the depths.

"Do you hear that?" I asked, my voice barely above a whisper.

"Yeah, and it's not the comforting sound of rain," he replied, his expression serious.

Cautiously, we stepped inside, and as my eyes adjusted to the dim light, I could make out crumbling stone walls lined with rusted equipment. The air was thick with dampness, a stark contrast to the salty breeze outside.

"Looks like the old supply room," Nathan said, scanning the area. "They probably stored lanterns and emergency supplies here."

I moved deeper into the room, drawn to a large, tattered canvas. As I pulled it aside, I was met with a shocking sight: a row of photographs lined the wall, faces of people I had never met but whose expressions were steeped in desperation and longing.

"This is... disturbing," I breathed, stepping closer. Each image seemed to tell its own story, captured moments frozen in time, and yet all of them had the same haunting emptiness in their eyes.

"Who are they?" Nathan asked, his voice thick with disbelief.

"Maybe they're the lost ones," I suggested, scanning the names scrawled beneath each photograph. "They all have connections to the town. Look, here's one from the early 1900s."

As I read through the names, a creeping sensation crawled up my spine. "Nathan, we need to get out of here."

"Why? What's wrong?" he asked, concern etched across his features.

"Look at their faces," I urged, my heart pounding. "It's as if they're pleading for us to understand, to remember them. What if their stories are tied to ours?"

"I don't like this," he admitted, his voice low. "We should leave before we find something we can't unsee."

But before I could respond, the sound of footsteps echoed behind us. I froze, my breath hitching in my throat as I turned to face the source of the noise. The door creaked, the shadows shifting ominously, and suddenly, the air grew colder.

"Who's there?" Nathan called out, his voice firm yet edged with uncertainty.

Nothing answered but silence, thick and heavy, wrapping around us like a suffocating fog. My pulse quickened, a rhythm of fear that mirrored the storm outside. With the ghosts of the past swirling in the air, I couldn't shake the feeling that we were about to uncover something that would change everything.

The footsteps grew louder, reverberating through the damp air like a ghostly heartbeat. My instincts screamed for me to run, but something deeper held me rooted to the spot, tethered by the magnetic pull of the unknown. Nathan's grip tightened on my arm, his eyes wide with uncertainty as he shifted his stance, ready to face whatever emerged from the shadows.

"Maybe it's just the wind," I whispered, but the quaver in my voice betrayed my feigned bravado.

"Yeah, if the wind could walk and knock," he replied, his humor tinged with apprehension.

As the footsteps drew nearer, I felt a mix of excitement and dread unfurling in my chest. I couldn't help but wonder if we were on the brink of uncovering a truth that had long eluded this town—a truth that could be both illuminating and utterly terrifying.

Then the door swung open, and the dim light from the lantern room spilled into the darkness, casting a long shadow that stretched toward us. My breath caught as a figure stepped into view, silhouetted against the flickering glow.

"Who's there?" Nathan called again, his voice steadying as he shifted protectively in front of me.

A woman emerged from the shadows, her features obscured by a veil of darkness. "You shouldn't be here," she said, her voice soft yet insistent, echoing with the weight of countless warnings. "This place holds too many secrets."

I blinked, momentarily caught between disbelief and fascination. "Who are you?" I managed to ask, a spark of defiance igniting within me.

She stepped closer, and the light caught her face—pale, with high cheekbones and eyes that seemed to shimmer with the light of forgotten stars. "I am a keeper of their stories," she replied, her tone grave. "And you've awakened what should have remained undisturbed."

"Awakened?" Nathan echoed, glancing at me. "What do you mean?"

"The letters you found," she said, glancing at the chest as if it were a living entity. "They are more than just words; they are echoes of the past. Every name, every story is bound to this place, tied to the souls who never returned."

My heart raced as I processed her words. "You mean... they're still here? Their spirits?"

She nodded slowly, her gaze piercing through the darkness. "They linger, searching for the resolution that eluded them in life. But you," she said, pointing a slender finger at me, "you must tread carefully. Some truths can break a person."

I glanced at Nathan, uncertainty flickering in his eyes. "What kind of truths?" I asked, fear intertwining with a strange sense of urgency.

"Truths that reveal more than just history," she warned, her voice dropping to a whisper. "Some secrets are not meant to be uncovered, especially when they come with a price."

Nathan stepped closer, a protective barrier between me and the unknown. "What kind of price?" he demanded, his voice steady but with an underlying current of concern.

"The kind that takes what you love," she replied, her eyes narrowing. "The souls you've disturbed may not wish to be remembered. Their pain can manifest in unforeseen ways."

A silence fell, heavy and pregnant with possibility. I could feel the weight of her words, the ominous warning resonating deep within me. "But we have to know," I said, desperation creeping into my voice. "We can't just leave this place, not after what we've uncovered. These people deserve to be remembered."

The woman's expression softened, and for a moment, I thought I saw a flicker of compassion in her gaze. "You have a kind heart, but that kindness may lead you down a dark path. Do not underestimate their sorrow. It has teeth."

Before I could respond, the ground beneath us rumbled again, a deep, resounding growl that reverberated through the walls. I stumbled back, and Nathan steadied me, his face pale as he shot a look toward the door. "What was that?"

The woman's expression hardened. "It's too late. You've roused something. You must leave now."

"Wait!" I called out, a sudden panic rising within me. "We can't just walk away. Not when we're so close to the truth."

"The truth has a way of revealing itself, but it often comes at a cost." Her voice was urgent now, echoing with a sense of finality. "You need to go. Do not return."

"Why?" Nathan pressed, his brow furrowed in confusion and concern.

"Because the lighthouse does not take kindly to intruders," she warned, her voice trembling slightly. "And its guardians are awakening."

A cold draft swept through the room, extinguishing the lanterns in a swift, suffocating darkness. The shadows stretched and twisted, creeping closer, wrapping around us like serpents coiling for a strike. The air thickened with an oppressive weight, and I could feel something shifting, something ancient and powerful stirring just beyond the veil of our reality.

"Get out!" the woman shouted, her voice rising above the growing tumult.

Without thinking, Nathan grabbed my hand, and we bolted toward the door. I could hear the sound of the wind howling like a banshee outside, blending with the echoes of distant voices—anguished cries of the long-lost, rising in a crescendo that reverberated through the very core of the lighthouse.

We stumbled into the lantern room, gasping for breath, our hearts pounding in unison. I turned back to look for the woman, desperate to understand what was happening, but the room was empty, devoid of the presence that had only moments ago felt so real.

"Where did she go?" I asked, bewildered.

"Does it matter?" Nathan replied, urgency lacing his words. "We need to get out of here before whatever that was catches up to us."

As we raced down the staircase, the ground continued to quake beneath us, sending dust and debris raining from the ceiling like a macabre confetti. The shadows lengthened, grasping at our heels, and I felt an icy breath on the back of my neck—a reminder that the lighthouse wasn't just a structure; it was alive, a sentient entity that didn't take kindly to our intrusion.

"Nathan, hurry!" I shouted, scrambling down the final steps, my heart pounding in my ears.

We burst through the door, the storm outside crashing against us with a ferocity that almost knocked us off our feet. Rain whipped down like daggers, drenching us instantly, but we didn't stop; we sprinted across the rocky path, the lighthouse looming ominously behind us, its light swinging erratically like a sentinel in distress.

But as we reached the safety of the shore, a low, resonant voice echoed from the lighthouse, chilling me to the bone. "You will not escape that easily."

I stopped, the words wrapping around me like chains, paralyzing me with fear. I turned back toward the lighthouse, its structure darkening as if it were swallowing the light whole, and for a fleeting moment, I thought I saw faces in the windows—twisted, sorrowful, and pleading.

Nathan tugged at my arm. "We need to go. Now!"

But the storm had escalated, waves crashing violently against the rocks, and I could feel the weight of the lighthouse bearing down on us. Its very presence seemed to promise a reckoning that I couldn't ignore.

"Wait! We can't just leave!" I shouted, torn between the desire to run and the need to uncover the truth that had beckoned us into its depths.

Suddenly, a deafening roar erupted from the lighthouse, shaking the very ground beneath our feet. In that moment, I knew we were at the brink of something monumental. The past was clawing its way back into the present, and as I turned to Nathan, desperation etched in my heart, I realized that our journey was far from over.

The ground trembled once more, and as I stumbled, I caught a glimpse of something rising from the depths of the stormy sea—a figure breaking through the waves, reaching for us with a hand that glistened like salt and sorrow.

My breath caught, and just as I opened my mouth to scream, everything went black.

Chapter 11: A Dangerous Alliance

The scent of salt hung thick in the air, mingling with the musty aroma of aged paper and ink. Dust motes danced in the faint light filtering through the cracked windows of the lighthouse archives, casting an ethereal glow around us. As I reached for an ancient tome, my fingers brushed against Nathan's. A jolt of electricity surged through me, an unwelcome reminder of the chemistry we had been trying so hard to ignore. He looked up, his brow furrowed in concentration, and for a moment, the world outside faded into nothingness.

"You know," he said, his voice low and laced with a teasing undertone, "if we weren't in the middle of this dramatic sleuthing, I'd think we were filming a low-budget horror movie."

I smirked, flipping the book open to reveal a brittle page adorned with faded sketches of the town's founding families. "What? You think we're about to be attacked by ghostly relatives? Or perhaps a rabid raccoon?"

Nathan chuckled, the sound rich and warm, and I couldn't help but smile back. This was the man I had spent years competing against—over grades, awards, even fleeting glances from girls we both pretended not to care about. Now, here we were, bound together by the mysteries of this forsaken lighthouse, drawn deeper into each other's lives than I ever thought possible.

"Not a raccoon, but I wouldn't rule out a curse or two," he replied, leaning closer as he examined the drawings. His shoulder brushed against mine, igniting a flutter of something disconcerting in my chest.

"Curse or not, I think I prefer the idea of ghostly relatives," I shot back playfully, flipping another page to reveal a scrawled diary entry from a long-deceased lighthouse keeper. The words hinted at secrets buried deep within the town's history, darkened by betrayal and longing. I felt a thrill ripple through me, the pull of a story waiting to be unraveled, much like the threads of our own tangled past.

The air crackled with unspoken words, and the weight of our surroundings pressed in on us. The lighthouse had seen better days; the walls whispered stories of storms weathered and lives lived, much like the two of us navigating our own tempestuous relationship. I had always seen Nathan as a rival, a thorn in my side, but here, amid the crumbling relics, I began to see a man shaped by the same uncertainties I carried.

"Do you ever wonder why we're so drawn to this place?" I asked, my voice barely a whisper.

He glanced at me, his eyes reflecting a mixture of curiosity and vulnerability. "It's like the lighthouse is a magnet for lost souls," he mused. "Maybe we came here looking for answers, not just about the past, but about ourselves."

The intensity of his gaze made me shift uncomfortably, as if he could see straight through the carefully constructed walls I had built around my heart. With every moment we spent together, those walls began to crumble, revealing insecurities I had long buried under layers of bravado and ambition.

As the hours slipped by, we delved deeper into the archives, piecing together the fragmented history of the town and its inhabitants. Nathan uncovered a journal detailing the town's founding families, their alliances and betrayals intricately woven into the very fabric of our community. I discovered that his family's roots ran deeper than I ever imagined, tangled with mine in a web of shared history and hidden secrets.

"The Eldridges had a hand in everything back then," he said, his voice tinged with an edge of resentment. "Power, influence... and, apparently, a knack for creating enemies."

"Sounds like you know all about that," I replied, trying to lighten the mood, but the truth was undeniable. His family was intertwined with the very legacy of the town, and the weight of expectation pressed down on him like a heavy fog.

"What about you?" he countered, crossing his arms defensively. "You've always been the overachiever, the one with all the accolades. How do you deal with that kind of pressure?"

I paused, contemplating the years of hard work that had forged my identity. "I guess I bury myself in it. Success has always been my shield, my armor. But sometimes, I wonder what happens when that armor gets too heavy to carry."

Nathan's expression softened, his walls crumbling in tandem with mine. "Maybe we should lighten the load together."

The suggestion hung in the air between us, a delicate promise wrapped in shared vulnerability. Just as I was about to respond, the oppressive silence was shattered by the sound of footsteps echoing through the hallways of the lighthouse, sending a chill racing down my spine.

"Did you hear that?" I whispered, adrenaline surging through me as the realization that we were not alone in this place struck like a lightning bolt.

Nathan's eyes widened, and he quickly stood, glancing toward the door. "It's probably just the wind," he said, though his tone betrayed the uncertainty underlying his bravado.

I shook my head, the heaviness of dread settling in the pit of my stomach. "No, it sounded like... footsteps. Someone else is here."

Before we could move, the door creaked open, and the dim light from the hallway revealed a shadowy figure, partially obscured by the gloom. My heart raced as recognition set in, twisting my gut with a blend of fear and anger.

There stood Adam, my childhood friend turned distant memory, his expression one of cautious curiosity mixed with an unsettling

DARKFALL

tension. "I heard you two were digging up old ghosts," he said, his tone laced with sarcasm. "Looks like I wasn't wrong."

The air thickened with unspoken words, each of us teetering on the edge of a dangerous alliance forged in the shadows of our shared history. The fragile trust between Nathan and me now felt threatened, the walls we had built around our vulnerabilities challenged by the sudden reappearance of someone from my past.

Adam leaned against the doorframe, his presence instantly transforming the archive from a sanctuary of secrets into a battleground of old rivalries. The dim light caught the sharp angles of his face, highlighting the shadows beneath his eyes as if he hadn't slept in days. He was the last person I expected to see, the ghost of my childhood resurrected in a moment I had wished to keep buried.

"Nathan," he said, his gaze darting between us with the keen awareness of someone who sensed tension in the air, "I didn't realize you two were so... cozy."

Nathan straightened, his posture shifting from relaxed to rigid in an instant. "What are you doing here, Adam?" His voice held an edge, protective and wary, as if he were ready to defend not only his ground but the fragile truce that had been forming between us.

I opened my mouth to respond, but the words stuck in my throat, caught between surprise and irritation. "I could ask you the same thing," I managed, finally breaking the silence that had thickened around us. "What brings you to this decrepit lighthouse, Adam? Come to dig up more ghosts?"

His lips curled into a half-smile, though it lacked warmth. "Just looking for a little adventure. You know how it is in a town like this—endless secrets and all that." He stepped further into the room, the creaking floorboards announcing his arrival like an unwelcome herald. "And who better to hunt them down than the prodigal daughter and the town's golden boy?"

With every word, the air crackled, igniting the tension between us. Nathan's jaw tightened, a muscle flickering beneath the skin, while I felt the familiar stirrings of defiance and irritation bubble up. "If you've come to disrupt our work, I suggest you save your breath," I shot back, crossing my arms as if that could shield me from his invasive presence.

Adam shrugged, the casualness of his demeanor at odds with the intensity of the situation. "I'm not here to disrupt. Just curious about what you've unearthed. Maybe even willing to lend a hand. The town's history affects all of us, after all."

Nathan's gaze turned suspicious. "You? Lending a hand? Last time I checked, you were more interested in staying clear of anything resembling responsibility."

A hint of anger flickered across Adam's face, but he masked it with a smirk. "People change, Nathan. Or at least, they pretend to."

The unspoken words hung heavy between us. This was more than a simple reunion; it was a reawakening of the rivalries and unresolved issues that had long since simmered beneath the surface. Adam had always been the charming troublemaker, effortlessly drifting through life, while I had been the one who diligently studied, worked hard, and forged a reputation. Yet now, standing here, it was clear he was fishing for something beneath the surface, a vulnerability he thought he could exploit.

I took a step forward, my resolve solidifying. "If you want to help, you can start by staying out of our way. We're on the verge of something significant." The weight of my words hung in the air, an invitation and a warning wrapped into one.

Adam regarded me with a newfound respect, one that flickered and vanished like the ghostly shadows darting across the room. "Fine. I'll play nice. But if there's anything to be found in this crumbling relic, you'd want me on your side. I know the town's secrets as well as anyone."

Before I could respond, Nathan interjected, his voice steely. "And why should we trust you, Adam? Your 'help' comes with a history of selfish motives."

"Trust? That's rich coming from you," Adam shot back, the words laced with a challenge. "We're all playing our games, but you both can't deny that there's something bigger at play here."

I felt the pulse of tension between the three of us, a triangle of unresolved issues, deep-seated emotions, and hidden agendas. It was an intricate dance of loyalty and rivalry, each of us stepping cautiously around the other, unsure of the rhythm we were trying to establish.

Finally, I broke the standoff. "If we're going to get anywhere, we need to work together, whether we like it or not." My tone was firm, but beneath it lay a flicker of desperation. I understood all too well that in order to confront whatever threat lurked in the shadows, we would have to navigate our complex histories and weave a fragile alliance.

Nathan looked at me, a flash of understanding crossing his features. "All right. But this doesn't mean I trust you, Adam. It's a long way to go from enemies to allies."

Adam grinned, that infuriating charm resurfacing. "Oh, I wouldn't have it any other way. Nothing like a little competition to spice things up."

We began sifting through the archives again, the air thick with a new kind of energy—a mix of skepticism and reluctant camaraderie. The dusty pages were filled with tales of tragedy and triumph, secrets that could upend our understanding of the town. As we flipped through the brittle pages, I could feel the layers of history weaving around us, pulling us into a narrative much larger than ourselves.

"Look at this," Nathan said, his voice sharp with excitement. He pointed to a faded photograph, the edges tattered, depicting a group of solemn faces against the backdrop of the lighthouse, a lighthouse that seemed to loom larger in its past than in its current state. "This was taken when the town was first founded. Do you recognize anyone?"

I leaned closer, squinting at the faces. "Those eyes… they remind me of someone I know."

Adam moved beside me, his curiosity piqued. "You think it's one of your ancestors?"

"Maybe," I said, my heart racing. "Or perhaps one of yours."

The words lingered in the air, wrapping us in the unease of the unknown. I could sense Nathan's tension beside me, a solid wall of apprehension. Whatever history we had with Adam was complicated, and now, in the midst of secrets and suspicions, we were all drawing closer to a truth that could unravel everything we thought we knew.

Just then, the air shifted, and a draft swept through the room, ruffling the pages and sending a shiver down my spine. I glanced toward the entrance, half-expecting to see a shadow lingering just beyond the threshold. The feeling of being watched tightened the knot in my stomach, and I exchanged a glance with Nathan.

"Did you feel that?" I asked, my voice barely above a whisper.

"Yeah," he replied, eyes narrowed. "I don't think we're alone."

The atmosphere thickened with unease, the specter of our unknown stalker creeping into our consciousness once more. The connection we had begun to build now felt fragile, strained by the weight of our pasts and the uncertainty of our future. But I knew one thing: together, we had to confront whatever darkness lay ahead, for the safety of our town and our growing alliance.

The air felt charged as Nathan and I exchanged glances, our earlier moment of connection now fraught with the weight of unspoken fears. Adam, leaning against the archive table, glanced between us, an amused grin tugging at his lips, as if he reveled in the tension that crackled like static electricity. I could almost hear his thoughts: this was his chance to assert himself, to reclaim some of the attention that Nathan and I seemed to monopolize in this labyrinth of history and secrets.

"Let's not forget why we're here," Adam said, his tone playfully dramatic. "You two are playing at amateur sleuths while I've got a treasure trove of dirt on this town to share. Aren't you dying to know how it all connects?"

Nathan shot him a skeptical look, folding his arms. "And why would you want to share that information? What's in it for you?"

"Ever heard of collaboration?" Adam quipped, feigning innocence. "We could uncover some juicy stories that'll shake this town to its core. Not to mention, it could be quite the thrill ride. Just imagine—"

"Thrill ride? Is that what you call digging through old papers?" I interjected, shaking my head at him. "If you're after a thrill, I'd suggest a theme park instead of a crumbling lighthouse."

"Touché," Adam conceded, raising an eyebrow. "But old papers can lead to new adventures, can't they? Secrets waiting to be exposed. Isn't that what we're all after?"

I could see it in Nathan's eyes; he wanted to push Adam away, to keep our focus narrow, but I felt the creeping allure of what Adam was proposing. There was something intoxicating about the idea of a treasure hunt—a hidden history lurking just beneath the surface, waiting for us to uncover it.

"All right," I said, surprising even myself with my own boldness. "Let's hear what you've got. But if it leads to more trouble, I'm holding you responsible, Adam."

His grin widened, a glint of mischief dancing in his eyes. "Fair enough. But I think you'll find it's more fun when trouble's involved."

As we returned our focus to the archives, Adam leaned in, flipping through the pages with an eagerness that caught my attention. "Here's something interesting." He held up a brittle sheet, the ink faded but still legible. "This mentions an old meeting of the founding families—ones that Nathan's might have been a part of."

"Let me see that," Nathan said, leaning closer to Adam, tension still simmering beneath his surface. I watched as the two of them compared notes, each trying to claim the upper hand in this unholy alliance we had formed. The competition felt strangely exhilarating, pushing me to the edge of my own comfort zone.

The deeper we delved into the records, the more I felt the history of the town wrap around us like a cloak—thick, suffocating, but somehow protective. "Did you know that there were accusations of betrayal among the families?" I pointed out, my voice dropping as I read about a supposed scandal that had nearly torn the town apart. "This suggests a conspiracy. Maybe the stories of curses and secrets aren't just tales meant to scare children after all."

"Of course not," Adam chimed in, "every town has its skeletons. It's just a matter of digging them out of the closet."

"I'd rather dig them out of a lighthouse," Nathan remarked dryly, but I caught the hint of a smile playing on his lips.

As laughter bubbled up, a sudden noise shattered our moment. The sound of a heavy thump echoed through the archive, reverberating off the stone walls. We froze, the levity of the moment evaporating as quickly as it had arrived.

"Did you hear that?" I whispered, glancing nervously toward the door, which now felt like a portal to a realm I wasn't ready to face.

Nathan nodded, his expression serious. "Yeah, it came from outside."

Adam shifted on his feet, the bravado from moments earlier replaced by uncertainty. "Shouldn't we check it out?"

"Check it out?" I repeated incredulously. "You mean walk out there and greet whatever might be lurking in the dark? Brilliant idea."

"Oh, come on," Nathan said, a steely resolve creeping into his voice. "We can't ignore it. If there's someone out there, we need to know if they're a threat."

"Or if they're just another ghost looking for attention," I muttered, but I could feel my heart quickening, a primal instinct to flee mingling with an undeniable curiosity to confront whatever lay beyond.

With a nod of agreement, we made our way toward the door. Each step felt heavy, as if the air thickened with anticipation and dread. Nathan reached for the door handle, and for a split second, I could see his hesitation mirrored in Adam's eyes.

As Nathan pulled the door open, the gust of wind swept through, sending a chill down my spine and whipping my hair around my face. "I'll go first," he declared, stepping out into the gloom.

I followed closely behind, Adam falling in step beside me. The night had deepened, casting long shadows that danced along the ground, taunting us with their obscured shapes. The lighthouse loomed above us, its beacon unlit, a sentinel guarding secrets long forgotten.

"What exactly are we looking for?" I whispered, scanning the darkness. "A killer? A rogue raccoon?"

"Focus," Nathan said sharply, but the concern in his voice belied his bravado. "We need to see what that noise was about."

We moved slowly, hearts racing, adrenaline surging through our veins. Suddenly, the ground shifted beneath us—a heavy footfall, then another, echoing from the path leading to the cliffs.

"There!" Adam pointed, his voice barely above a whisper.

We squinted into the inky darkness, where a figure emerged from the shadows, just beyond the reach of the lighthouse's fading light. The silhouette was tall and imposing, a haunting reminder of the dangers that had lurked at the edge of our small town for far too long.

"Who's there?" Nathan called, his voice steady despite the tension coiling in the air.

The figure paused, then stepped forward, revealing a familiar face shrouded in the darkness. My breath caught in my throat as recognition washed over me—along with a wave of disbelief.

"Looks like you've all been busy," the figure said, a smirk playing on their lips, eyes glinting with a dangerous light.

In that moment, time seemed to freeze, the weight of unanswered questions hanging heavy in the air. We stood on the precipice of revelation, the stakes higher than ever, but before I could utter a word, the ground beneath us trembled, and a low rumble echoed through the lighthouse, shaking the very foundation of our world.

"What is happening?" I shouted, panic gripping me as the earth shook violently.

The figure's expression shifted from smug satisfaction to alarm. "Run!" they shouted, but it was too late.

A blinding flash erupted behind us, illuminating the night, and as the lighthouse began to crumble, I felt my feet slip from beneath me, plunging into darkness. My heart raced, a chaotic drumbeat in my ears, as everything I knew spiraled into chaos. In the midst of the disaster, a chilling realization dawned: this alliance, fraught with tension and uncertainty, might be the only thing standing between us and total ruin.

Chapter 12: The Heart of the Storm

The storm battered Windward Bay with a ferocity that felt almost personal, as if the heavens themselves were responding to the turmoil churning within me. I had always loved the sea, with its rhythmic tides and eternal whispers, but tonight, it was an unruly beast, thrashing against the rocky shore as rain lashed against the windows of the lighthouse. I had sought solace in this aged sentinel, a place that had watched over countless storms, and now I found myself ensnared in one far more chaotic than any the lighthouse had weathered before.

Nathan stood beside me, his silhouette framed by the flickering light of the lantern. His expression flickered between concern and something deeper, something that sent tremors through my heart. The air around us was thick with electricity, charged not just from the tempest outside but from the unspoken words that hovered like ghosts in the corners of the room. He reached for my hand, his fingers brushing against mine with a tentative intimacy that ignited a fire in my chest. I glanced up, our eyes locking in a moment that stretched infinitely, where the world outside faded into the background, and it was just us—two souls drawn together by the raging storm.

"Do you think the lighthouse can withstand this?" he asked, his voice low and steady, cutting through the howling wind. It was a question with more layers than he likely intended, an inquiry that spoke not just of the structure but of our own precarious footing in this unpredictable storm of feelings.

I chuckled softly, the sound rising to compete with the tumult outside. "If this lighthouse can survive the likes of me, it can handle anything." I offered a wry smile, my heart thudding in my chest, both from the tempest outside and the awareness of his proximity.

We were too close, yet it felt as if we were dancing on the edge of something exhilarating and terrifying.

His lips quirked into a smile, a flash of warmth in the cold, damp air that surrounded us. "Well, I certainly hope you aren't the reason we're about to become a shipwreck." The banter between us felt effortless, yet laden with an intensity that crackled like the lightning outside. As I watched him, the storm raging on, I could see his walls slowly crumbling, revealing the raw vulnerability beneath. It was an intoxicating glimpse, one that made my heart ache with the promise of connection.

But then, as if nature itself was throwing us a challenge, a loud crash reverberated through the lighthouse, shaking the very foundations beneath our feet. My heart leaped into my throat, fear slicing through the moment. Nathan's gaze darted towards the door, his posture tense. "What was that?"

"Probably just the sea trying to remind us of its power," I said, attempting to keep my voice light, though I could feel the shadows of worry creeping in. Still, there was a thrill in the air, a daring call to abandon caution. I stepped closer, the distance between us diminishing further, until our breaths mingled in the charged atmosphere.

"Or maybe it's the universe trying to keep us from getting too comfortable," he said, his voice a low rumble. He took a step forward, pulling me closer until the warmth of his body enveloped me, drowning out the chill from the storm. "What do you think?"

I couldn't help but grin, a wicked glint lighting my eyes. "I think the universe should be careful, because I refuse to back down from a little challenge."

The air between us thickened, and suddenly, in that flickering light, with the storm as our backdrop, everything shifted. Nathan's gaze bore into mine, his lips parted slightly as if searching for words that danced just out of reach. I leaned in, an undeniable magnetism pulling us together, the storm's fury mirrored in the tempest of emotions crashing inside me. And then, without another thought, I closed the space, my lips meeting his in a kiss that felt as if it could silence the storm itself.

For a heartbeat, the world fell away. The rain, the wind, the crashing waves—they faded into a distant roar, leaving only the warmth of his mouth against mine, the taste of salt and something sweet. It was reckless and wild, the kind of kiss that made everything else seem trivial, as if the storm had become a mere background to our own personal tempest. His hands tangled in my hair, pulling me deeper into the moment, and I lost myself entirely, surrendering to the force of what was unfolding.

But just as abruptly as it had begun, the moment shattered. A blinding flash of lightning illuminated the room, followed by another bone-rattling crash, louder this time, jolting us back to reality. I broke the kiss, breathless and wide-eyed, and the warmth of the moment was replaced by a cold dash of reality.

"We should check that," Nathan said, his voice a mix of urgency and concern, drawing back as he stepped towards the door, the intimacy between us swiftly morphing into a shared mission. I could see the hesitation in his eyes, the desire mingled with caution. The connection we'd forged was still hanging in the air, but the storm outside demanded our attention, pulling us back from the brink.

"Right," I replied, my voice shaky as I followed him, my heart still racing from what had just transpired. The storm was relentless, and we had to face whatever chaos awaited us outside. I didn't know what lay ahead, but the kiss lingered on my lips, an echo of our momentary alliance, and I was determined to face whatever came next—together.

As Nathan pushed open the heavy door, a wall of wind slammed against us, almost knocking us back into the warm embrace of the lighthouse. The howling gale carried the salty scent of the sea, mingling with the sharpness of rain-soaked earth and the unmistakable hint of adventure. I shivered, not just from the chill, but from the jolt of adrenaline coursing through my veins. The storm was alive, a raging beast that had unleashed its fury upon Windward Bay, and here we were, two unlikely heroes at the precipice of chaos.

"Hold on tight," Nathan shouted over the roar, his voice barely audible as he stepped out onto the narrow, winding path that led around the lighthouse. I gripped the doorframe for a moment, watching him as he leaned against the wind, his body taut and determined. In that moment, he looked less like a man battling the elements and more like a warrior, ready to face whatever challenge lay ahead. There was an undeniable allure to his bravery that drew me out of my shelter, a pull I couldn't resist.

"Didn't anyone tell you it's dangerous to stand out in a storm?" I teased, stepping forward and taking his hand, grounding myself against the ferocity of the winds. He shot me a sidelong glance, an amused glint in his eyes.

"Who doesn't love a little danger?" he quipped back, the corner of his mouth lifting in a smirk. "Besides, I think we're well past that point, don't you?"

We moved cautiously, inching our way toward the edge of the cliff. The world around us was a chaotic whirl of water and wind, each wave crashing against the rocks with a violence that echoed my own tumultuous thoughts. What had started as a fleeting connection inside the lighthouse now felt monumental, the kiss sparking a flame I had never expected to ignite. The reality of our situation pressed heavily on me, a reminder that the storm outside was nothing compared to the tempest of feelings brewing within.

As we reached a vantage point, the scene before us was breathtaking and terrifying all at once. The sea roared, its waves rising higher than I had ever seen, crashing against the cliffs like an ancient giant throwing a tantrum. Each surge of water seemed to scream its own story, and for a moment, I felt small, utterly insignificant against the might of nature. Nathan's grip tightened around my hand, anchoring me as I took in the spectacle.

"Isn't it beautiful?" I asked, my voice soft as I turned to him. The way the lightning split the sky, illuminating the turbulent waters, felt like a work of art, raw and primal.

"Beautiful and deadly," he replied, his brow furrowing as he scanned the horizon. "We should head back inside. It's not safe out here." The humor in his voice had faded, replaced by a seriousness that sent a chill down my spine.

"Agreed, but just give me one moment," I said, reluctant to leave this wild beauty behind. I let go of his hand for just a second, stepping closer to the edge of the cliff. The wind whipped my hair around my face, and I laughed, the sound lost in the storm. "This is exhilarating!"

But as I peered down into the depths below, my exhilaration faded, replaced by a sense of foreboding. The jagged rocks looked almost hungry, gnashing at the waves as they crashed against them. I turned back to Nathan, ready to retreat, but my heart sank as I saw his expression shift to one of alarm.

"Emma!" he shouted, his voice slicing through the wind. Before I could comprehend the urgency in his tone, a massive wave surged forward, propelled by the storm's relentless energy. My instincts kicked in, and I stumbled back, but the ground beneath me gave way. I felt myself teetering, a moment of weightlessness that shattered my heart in the instant I realized I was falling.

"Emma!" Nathan lunged, his hand reaching out, fingertips grazing mine as I fell back, the world around me spinning in a whirl of panic and darkness. But just as quickly, he grabbed my wrist, his grip solid and sure, pulling me back from the brink.

We crashed onto the rocky path, breathless and wide-eyed. Nathan pinned me against the ground, his face inches from mine, and for a heartbeat, time seemed to still. "Are you okay?" he asked, his voice thick with concern. I could feel the warmth of his breath against my cheek, and the intensity of his gaze held me captive.

"I think I might have forgotten how to breathe," I managed to say, my heart racing not just from the fear but from the closeness of his body against mine. The moment was electric, a current that sparked between us, igniting everything I had been trying to ignore.

"Maybe you should focus on that," he replied, the corners of his mouth twitching up in a smile, despite the gravity of the situation. "Breathing first, and then we can discuss our next great adventure."

With a shaky laugh, I rolled to my side, brushing the dirt off my clothes, my heart still pounding. "You know, I think my 'next great adventure' involves being much more careful around cliffs."

"Let's stick to solid ground for a while, then," he said, standing and offering me a hand. As I took it, his warmth enveloped me, grounding me amid the chaos swirling both outside and within.

We retreated back into the lighthouse, the storm still raging, but the tension had shifted between us. There was an intimacy now, a thread binding us together in a way that felt both exhilarating and terrifying. I caught a glimpse of the flickering lantern light behind us, casting long shadows on the walls, as if even the lighthouse recognized the change in the air.

As we stepped back inside, the howling wind became a distant murmur, replaced by the soft glow of the lanterns, flickering like the hopes we held for what lay ahead. "We should probably secure the door," I suggested, still feeling the remnants of adrenaline surging through my veins.

"Right," Nathan nodded, and as we moved together, it felt as if we were weaving a tapestry, each action binding us closer, each glance shared deepening the connection. The world outside might have been a raging storm, but inside, something new was blossoming—a fragile hope, daring to take root in the midst of chaos.

We secured the heavy door, the wind howling like a banshee outside, and I felt an odd mix of safety and confinement enveloping us. The room was dim, illuminated only by the flickering light of the lanterns, which cast dancing shadows on the weathered walls. Nathan's presence beside me felt as solid as the lighthouse itself, yet the air crackled with unspoken words and tension, creating an electric atmosphere that pulsed between us.

"What do you think is going to happen next?" I asked, attempting to cut through the thick silence. My heart still raced from our close call, but beneath the surface, curiosity bubbled. It was a question I wanted answered, not just about the storm, but about us, this uncharted territory we found ourselves navigating.

Nathan's eyes danced with mischief, a spark of playfulness cutting through the gravity of the moment. "Well, I could make a wild guess involving us being swept away into a romantic adventure on the high seas, but I'm not sure how much of that involves me rowing the boat while you yell at me about proper technique."

I laughed, the sound breaking the tension that had gripped us. "I can assure you, I'd only yell if you were doing it wrong. I'd probably be busy admiring the view."

His grin widened, the warmth of his expression lighting up the room. "And what view might that be? The treacherous waves crashing against the rocks or the fearlessly charming sailor attempting to keep us alive?"

"Definitely the latter," I shot back, feeling a rush of boldness as I closed the distance between us. The familiar flutter in my chest returned, the one I had tried to dismiss but now surged with clarity. "But only if that sailor knows how to fix a boat, because I can't swim."

"Noted," he said, his voice softening, and suddenly, the lightheartedness shifted. "But I might need a little help with the whole saving-you-from-a-storm thing. You know, teamwork and all that."

"Teamwork, huh? I can handle that," I replied, allowing myself to lean closer, the space between us shrinking once more. The moment was delicate, a fragile thread that felt as if it could snap at any second. Just then, the wind shrieked outside, rattling the windowpanes, reminding us of the chaos we had momentarily forgotten.

I glanced out at the raging storm, the dark waves rising ominously against the cliffs. "We should probably focus on making sure this place holds up," I said, forcing myself to step back. "After all, we're not quite ready to become sea legends just yet."

Nathan nodded, his playful demeanor shifting into one of determination. "Right. Let's secure the windows." As we moved together, working in tandem to check each pane, I couldn't shake the sense that this was more than just a storm. It felt as if the world outside was a reflection of everything happening inside me—a whirlwind of uncertainty, passion, and the undeniable need to protect what we were building.

With each window we fortified, the intimacy between us deepened, the shared purpose weaving a bond that felt stronger than any words could express. "You know," I said, testing the waters of conversation, "I've never been good at waiting for things to happen. I prefer to take action."

He paused, leaning against the frame of the window, his eyes thoughtful. "And what if taking action leads you to places you never expected?"

"Like this?" I gestured between us, my heart thudding in my chest. "Is that what you mean?"

"Exactly. Sometimes, the scariest paths are the most rewarding." His gaze bore into mine, and I felt the weight of his words settle in the air around us, thick with possibilities. "But they can also be unpredictable."

I considered his words, a sense of foreboding creeping in. "You think we're making a mistake? Trying to navigate this storm... this connection?"

"No," he replied firmly, and his honesty washed over me like a balm. "But I do think we need to be prepared for whatever comes next. Both outside and in here." He pointed between us, his gesture intimate and yet somehow daunting.

Before I could respond, the ground beneath us trembled. A low rumble echoed through the lighthouse, and the lanterns flickered ominously. "Did you feel that?" I asked, my heart skipping a beat.

"Yeah," Nathan said, his voice steady despite the tension tightening around us. "Stay here. I'll check it out."

"Like I'm going to let you go off on your own during a storm? I'm not that foolish," I countered, matching his seriousness with my own. The thought of being separated from him, even for a moment, felt wrong, as if the world outside would swallow him whole.

"Then let's stick together," he said, taking my hand once more, and together we stepped away from the safety of the lantern light into the deeper shadows of the lighthouse.

As we moved cautiously through the winding stairs, the wind howled louder, wrapping around us like a living thing, and the storm seemed to unleash its fury anew. Every creak of the structure felt alive, a reminder that we were trapped in a vessel of wood and stone, battling against the elements.

Just as we reached the landing, another crash reverberated through the walls, more violent than before. A sense of urgency pulled at me, my instincts screaming for caution. "Nathan, we should really—"

Before I could finish, the window nearby shattered with a deafening roar, the glass exploding outward like shrapnel. I ducked instinctively, pulling Nathan down with me as the wind howled into the room, fierce and unforgiving.

"What the hell!" he yelled, his voice barely audible over the chaos. I felt him tense beside me, the warmth of his body grounding me against the storm's wrath.

"Get back!" I shouted, struggling against the force of the wind trying to drag us both outside. The room swirled with debris, the tempest clawing at the walls, a reminder that we were teetering on the edge of something far more dangerous than either of us had anticipated.

As we scrambled for cover, something caught my eye—a shadow lurking just beyond the broken window, shifting with the wind. My heart dropped, a cold fear washing over me. "Nathan, there's something out there!"

He turned to me, his expression a mix of concern and confusion. "What do you mean?"

"I don't know, but we're not alone!" I gasped, adrenaline coursing through my veins. The shadow moved again, and a chill ran down my spine.

Just then, a figure emerged from the storm, a silhouette outlined against the chaos, and my breath caught in my throat. It was too dark to see clearly, but the shape was unmistakable, advancing towards the lighthouse with a purpose that sent my heart racing.

"Emma, we need to move!" Nathan shouted, pulling me away from the window as the figure stepped into the flickering light, revealing a face I never expected to see. A face that held secrets darker than the storm itself, and just like that, everything I thought I knew began to unravel.

Chapter 13: Shadows in the Wind

The storm's aftermath left the town in a disarray of branches and debris, a stark contrast to the vibrant blooms of spring that had graced our streets just days before. Each gust of wind now seemed to carry whispers of the past, rustling through the remnants of fallen leaves and crumpled papers, while the skies wept soft, dreary tears. Nathan stood beside me at the edge of my porch, his gaze scanning the horizon as if he could see the shadows lurking just beyond the edges of our small community. The air crackled with electricity, charged with both the remnants of the storm and the unspoken tension that hung between us.

"Do you think it's safe to go out?" I asked, unable to keep the tremor from my voice. The notes had arrived like clockwork, each one more sinister than the last, their jagged edges like the fractured pieces of my resolve.

Nathan turned to me, his expression a mix of determination and concern, and I felt my heart swell with both fear and admiration. "We can't let them intimidate us, Emma. We'll face whatever this is together." The weight of his words wrapped around me like a warm blanket, yet I couldn't shake the chill that ran down my spine.

The sun struggled to peek through the clouds, casting an ethereal light across the puddles that dotted the street. I nodded, swallowing my anxiety. We had become allies in this storm—he, with his unyielding strength, and I, with my fierce spirit. There was a strength in our unity, a promise that we wouldn't let the darkness engulf us.

Together, we walked toward the town library, a crumbling relic of architecture that seemed to sigh with the weight of its own history. The wooden doors creaked as we entered, and the musty smell of old pages enveloped us, a familiar comfort amid the chaos. My fingers brushed over the spines of books, each a silent witness to the stories and secrets that lay within.

"We need to find something—anything—that can help us make sense of the notes," I said, my voice barely a whisper against the hush of the library. Nathan nodded, his brows furrowed in concentration as he led us to the back, where the history section beckoned with its promise of untold tales.

As we delved into dusty volumes and brittle newspapers, I felt the weight of every unturned page pressing against my chest. The town's history was rich with tragedy and triumph, but beneath the surface, I sensed a darkness that whispered of betrayal. Nathan and I exchanged glances, each filled with unspoken questions, the kind that lingered just out of reach.

Then, nestled between two thick tomes, I spotted an article, its headline faded but familiar: Mysterious Disappearances in Maple Grove. My heart raced as I skimmed the text, recounting stories of townsfolk who had vanished without a trace over the decades, their names now mere ghosts haunting the pages. I felt Nathan shift beside me, his presence grounding me as I read aloud.

"'The local authorities dismissed these cases as mere coincidence, but a pattern emerged—those who got too close to uncovering the town's secrets found themselves in peril.'" I looked up, my voice trembling with the weight of the revelation. "Do you think... do you think this is connected?"

Nathan's jaw tightened as he leaned closer, studying the faded words. "It's possible. If someone doesn't want us to uncover the truth, they might resort to intimidation."

A chill raced through me, as if the very walls of the library were closing in, suffocating the air around us. "But why us? We're just trying to figure this out. Why would anyone go to such lengths?"

"Because they know we're getting close," Nathan replied, his voice low, almost a growl. "And maybe because they see you as a threat."

His words lingered in the air, heavy with implication. I swallowed hard, grappling with the idea that I could be seen as a threat. The thought was both terrifying and oddly empowering.

As the afternoon wore on, the storm clouds dissipated, leaving behind a stark blue sky. We emerged from the library, the sunlight blinding after the dimness of our research. I could almost feel the warmth washing over me, a balm against the anxiety simmering beneath my skin. But that comfort was short-lived as I spotted something on the ground—a crumpled piece of paper, its edges frayed.

Nathan bent down to retrieve it, his brow furrowing as he unfolded the note. I felt my breath hitch in my throat as I read the scrawled words: Leave Nathan. He's a part of the darkness you can't escape.

"Emma," Nathan said, his voice low and serious. "This is getting dangerous. We can't keep ignoring the threat."

But I refused to let fear dictate my choices. "I'm not leaving," I stated, my voice steady. "Not now, not ever. I'm not running from something that wants to consume us. We're in this together."

The resolve in my voice seemed to strengthen the bond between us, and for a brief moment, the world around us faded away. It was just Nathan and me, standing on the precipice of something greater than ourselves, ready to face the shadows that threatened to tear us apart.

"Then let's find out what this darkness is," he replied, a fierce glint in his eyes. I could feel the rush of adrenaline, a surge of purpose igniting within me. We would uncover the secrets buried beneath our town, no matter the cost, and in doing so, we would forge a connection stronger than any threat that dared to come our way.

The shadows danced in the periphery, but they wouldn't claim us. We were ready to confront whatever lay ahead, armed with determination and a bond that no darkness could extinguish.

The warmth of the afternoon sun began to wrap around us like a comforting embrace, but I couldn't shake the chill that had settled deep in my bones. As Nathan and I walked through the town, I could feel the eyes of the past watching us, an invisible audience lingering in the shadows. Each step felt like a deliberate act of defiance against the unseen threat that had plagued my thoughts for too long. The world was vibrant and alive, yet a dark undercurrent flowed just beneath the surface, stirring a sense of urgency that propelled us forward.

"Do you think we should tell someone about the notes?" I asked, my voice low, as if uttering the words aloud might summon some lurking danger. "Maybe the sheriff? He'd want to know someone's messing with us."

Nathan's brow furrowed, a sign of his careful consideration. "And tell him what? That we've got an anonymous stalker who sends us creepy notes? It sounds a little ridiculous when you put it that way."

"Right, but we can't just ignore it," I insisted, frustration bubbling to the surface. "This isn't a game, Nathan. Someone wants to hurt us."

"I know," he said, his voice steady but edged with concern. "But I don't want to escalate things unless we have to. Let's figure out who's behind this first."

The resolve in his eyes ignited a flicker of hope within me. With Nathan at my side, I felt emboldened, like a knight on a quest against an unseen dragon. Our search for answers had become a shared mission, a thread that wove us closer together amidst the chaos.

As we strolled past the quaint shops lining Main Street, the familiar smells of baked goods and fresh coffee wafted through the air. My stomach growled in protest, reminding me that I hadn't eaten since breakfast. "How about we grab a bite at The Maple Leaf? I could use a slice of that famous pie for some much-needed fuel."

Nathan smiled, the corners of his mouth lifting slightly. "Only if you promise not to share your pie with any lurking shadows."

We pushed open the door to the café, and the bell above jingled cheerfully, momentarily lifting the heaviness that hung over us. The interior was a charming blend of rustic wood and pastel colors, with the comforting hum of conversation surrounding us. I scanned the room for a familiar face and spotted Mrs. Jenkins behind the counter, her white apron dusted with flour. She was the embodiment of warmth and small-town hospitality, and I could always count on her for an extra scoop of kindness.

"Emma! Nathan!" she exclaimed, her voice bright as she wiped her hands on her apron. "It's so lovely to see you both! What can I get you today?"

"Just some coffee and a slice of that famous pie," I replied, settling into a cozy booth by the window. "Something to fortify us for a little adventure."

"Adventure? You two are always up to something. Just promise me you won't get into any trouble." She raised an eyebrow, a teasing glint in her eye.

I couldn't help but chuckle. "No trouble, just... detective work."

As Mrs. Jenkins prepared our order, I leaned closer to Nathan, my voice barely above a whisper. "Do you think she knows something? About the notes? She's been around forever; she might have heard something."

"Could be," he mused, glancing toward the counter. "But if she knows anything, she's not showing it."

Moments later, she returned with our coffee and a generous slice of pie, its golden crust glistening in the sunlight. "You two are going to love this," she said, placing it in front of me with a flourish. "A slice of summer, right here in fall!"

As I took my first bite, the sweet, tangy flavor burst on my tongue, a reminder that even in the darkest of times, there were moments of joy. "This is amazing," I declared, savoring every crumb. "I don't think I could ever get tired of this."

Nathan watched me with a mixture of amusement and admiration. "You're not half bad at finding bright spots in the darkness," he said, raising his coffee cup in a mock toast. "To pie and perseverance."

"To pie and perseverance!" I echoed, clinking my cup against his.

As we relished our moment of respite, I couldn't shake the feeling that something was off. The café buzzed with laughter and chatter, but my mind was fixated on the looming threat outside, the notes lurking in the shadows. What if someone was watching us, waiting for the right moment to strike?

"I can't shake the feeling that we're being watched," I admitted, setting down my fork. "What if our mystery goes deeper than we thought? What if it's connected to something more sinister?"

Nathan's expression turned serious, the playful glint in his eye replaced by steely determination. "Then we dig deeper. We follow the breadcrumbs until we find the source. Whatever it is, it won't stand a chance against us."

His words ignited a fire within me. The adrenaline surged through my veins, urging me to act. "What if we start by asking around? The townsfolk might have stories about the disappearances or the notes. There's always someone who knows something, right?"

"Good idea," he agreed, finishing his coffee. "Let's hit the pavement after we're done here. We'll go from shop to shop, ask some questions. The more people know we're on the case, the harder it'll be for whoever's behind this to operate in the shadows."

As I finished the last bite of my pie, the sweetness lingered, but it felt like a fleeting moment in the face of our impending confrontation with darkness. I couldn't ignore the gnawing anxiety in my gut, nor the flickering shadows that seemed to dart just out of sight. I had to believe that our combined strength would guide us through whatever lay ahead.

After settling the bill, we stepped back into the sun, which now bathed the street in a warm, golden glow. "Where to first?" I asked, my heart racing with anticipation.

"Let's check in with Tom at the hardware store. He's been around forever, and he's got an ear for gossip," Nathan suggested, leading the way down the street.

As we walked, I felt the weight of the world lift ever so slightly, buoyed by the promise of new leads and the camaraderie we shared. Yet the sense of urgency never quite left me; the unknown still loomed, waiting to unveil its mysteries. Together, we were determined to confront whatever shadows threatened to upend our lives, one question at a time.

The hardware store stood like a weathered sentinel at the end of the street, its red paint peeling away like memories long forgotten. As we approached, the familiar scent of sawdust and fresh paint wafted through the door, mingling with the nostalgic sound of tools clinking and clattering in the background. Tom, the store's owner, was a portly man with a shock of white hair and a penchant for gossip that was only rivaled by his love for a good fishing tale.

"Emma! Nathan! Come on in!" he bellowed from behind the counter, where he was sorting through a chaotic assortment of nails and screws. "What brings you two in today? Planning a home improvement project? I've got just the thing for you." His eyes twinkled with mischief, hinting at the endless supply of oddball gadgets he always seemed to have on hand.

"Actually, we're on a bit of a... fact-finding mission," I said, exchanging a glance with Nathan. "You know how rumors fly in this town. We were hoping you might have heard something about some unusual happenings lately. Maybe even about the old disappearances?"

Tom leaned back, his expression shifting to one of concern. "Ah, those. They're like ghosts that refuse to be buried. Folks don't like to talk about it. Bad juju, you know?" He leaned closer, lowering his voice conspiratorially. "But I've heard things. Things that make the hair on the back of your neck stand up."

Nathan crossed his arms, leaning forward. "What kind of things? We're not afraid of a little spooky talk."

"Yeah, well, you should be," Tom replied, a grin playing on his lips despite the ominous tone. "There was a rumor about a group that met in the woods just outside of town—a secret society of sorts. People say they were involved in some shady business, all hush-hush. And you know what they say: where there's smoke, there's fire."

My heart raced at the mention of a secret society. "Do you know what they were up to?"

"Not much, just that they were obsessed with the town's history. They thought they could harness some sort of power from the old stories. Weird stuff. A few people who got too close ended up leaving town in a hurry—never came back." He straightened, shaking his head as if shaking off a bad memory. "Best to leave that one alone."

But I could feel the pieces of a puzzle clicking together in my mind. "And you think this could be connected to the notes? To what's happening now?"

Tom shrugged, but his eyes reflected a flicker of concern. "Might be. Or it might just be a bunch of old wives' tales. You know how people can get when they're bored. Still, I'd be careful if I were you two. Curiosity has a way of leading you down dark paths."

"Thanks for the warning, Tom," Nathan said, a thoughtful frown creasing his brow. "We'll be sure to keep our eyes peeled."

As we left the store, the warm glow of the afternoon sun seemed to be overshadowed by a growing sense of dread. The weight of Tom's words lingered like smoke in the air. "A secret society?" I mused aloud, my mind racing with possibilities. "What kind of power could they be after? And why would they want to silence anyone who got too close?"

"Sounds like we're not the only ones poking around where we shouldn't," Nathan replied, glancing around as if the very trees might be eavesdropping on our conversation. "Maybe we should check out the woods he mentioned. See if we can find any signs of this group. It might give us a clue."

I nodded, the adrenaline thrumming through me at the thought of venturing into the unknown. "Let's do it. The sooner we figure this out, the safer we'll be."

The path leading to the woods was shrouded in a mixture of sunlight and shadows, the trees towering like ancient guardians, their branches whispering secrets with every rustle of the leaves. The atmosphere felt charged, electric, as if the very earth beneath us was alive with anticipation.

As we walked deeper into the woods, the sounds of the town faded, replaced by the soft crunch of leaves underfoot and the occasional chirp of a hidden bird. "You know," I said, trying to lighten the mood, "if we find a group of witches sacrificing goats or something, I'm officially out. I draw the line at goat blood."

Nathan chuckled, his laughter cutting through the tension. "What's the matter? Afraid you'd have to take a turn as the high priestess?"

I rolled my eyes. "Please, the only sacrifice I'm willing to make is to my love for pie."

"Fair enough. Just promise me if we stumble into a coven, you won't try to charm them with baked goods." He smiled, but I could see the concern in his eyes.

The deeper we ventured, the more the atmosphere shifted. The sunlight grew dimmer, filtered through the thick canopy of leaves above, and an unsettling stillness enveloped us. A sense of urgency hung in the air, palpable and oppressive.

Suddenly, we stumbled upon a clearing, the ground littered with remnants of what appeared to be an old campfire. The stones were cold, but the smell of ash lingered, heavy and suffocating. Scattered around were a few faded, weathered pieces of fabric, and a set of crude symbols etched into the ground that sent a chill racing up my spine.

"What do you think this was?" I whispered, kneeling down to inspect the symbols more closely. They were jagged and uneven, resembling an amalgamation of ancient runes and modern graffiti. It felt wrong, like an intrusion upon something sacred.

"I don't know," Nathan replied, his voice barely above a murmur as he studied the surroundings. "But it looks like we're onto something."

Before I could respond, a rustling from the bushes nearby made us both jump. "Did you hear that?" I asked, my pulse quickening.

"Yeah," he replied, his gaze fixed on the source of the noise. "Stay behind me."

With a trembling breath, I nodded, my heart pounding in my chest. Nathan stepped forward, the tension in the air thickening around us. The rustling intensified, and my instincts screamed that we weren't alone.

Just then, a figure emerged from the shadows, cloaked in a dark hood, their face obscured. The atmosphere shifted in an instant, the air heavy with foreboding. "You shouldn't have come here," the figure warned, their voice low and gravelly, sending shivers down my spine.

I instinctively stepped closer to Nathan, my heart racing as the figure took a step forward. "Who are you?" I demanded, trying to sound braver than I felt.

"Leave this place. You have no idea what you're meddling with," the figure hissed, their eyes glinting with an unsettling intensity.

In that moment, the shadows seemed to close in around us, and the weight of their warning hung in the air, suffocating. My mind raced, trapped between the instinct to flee and the burning desire to uncover the truth. But before I could speak, the figure lunged toward us, and the world around us erupted into chaos.

Chapter 14: The Unraveling

The air in Windward Bay felt charged, as if the very atmosphere held its breath, bracing for the inevitable. I stood at the edge of the old pier, the wooden planks creaking beneath my feet, an echo of my rising anxiety. The salty breeze tousled my hair, mingling with the scent of damp earth and seaweed, a nostalgic reminder of childhood summers spent exploring tide pools and sailing makeshift boats on the shimmering water. But today, nostalgia was eclipsed by a sense of foreboding. I could feel the weight of my past pressing down, a specter that had lingered just out of sight but was now stepping into the light, demanding acknowledgment.

My heart raced as I turned to face the person approaching. It was Clara, a familiar figure from my youth, though the years had softened her sharp edges and replaced youthful bravado with a wary elegance. She wore a sundress that fluttered like butterfly wings in the wind, but there was a storm brewing in her eyes that hinted at unspoken words. "There you are," she said, a hint of reproach in her voice. "I thought I'd find you here, staring at the waves like they hold the answers."

I swallowed hard, trying to shake off the weight of her gaze. "I'm not staring at the waves. Just...thinking." It was a weak deflection, but I wasn't ready to share the tumult inside me.

Clara stepped closer, her expression shifting from curiosity to something more serious. "You can't avoid it forever, you know. The past has a way of catching up. It's like a shadow—you can run, but it'll follow." Her voice held a tremor, as if she were speaking from experience.

"What do you know about it?" I snapped, the words escaping before I could tame them. The sharpness of my tone cut through the air, a defensive barrier against the encroaching memories.

"Enough," she replied quietly, her gaze steady. "Enough to know that you're not the only one who's suffered because of it." The silence stretched between us, heavy with unspoken truths and the weight of shared history.

Before I could respond, a familiar presence enveloped me like a comforting blanket. Nathan arrived, his tall frame and easy smile a welcome sight amid the emotional tempest. "Hey, what's going on here?" he asked, his eyes darting between us, concern knitting his brow.

"Nothing I can't handle," I said, the automatic reply sounding feeble even to my ears. Nathan's mere presence ignited a flicker of warmth within me, grounding me in the storm swirling around us.

Clara studied him, her lips twisting into a knowing smile. "Just a stroll down memory lane, Nathan. Nothing too dramatic." She was toying with the truth, a dangerous game I wasn't ready to play.

"Right," he said, his skepticism barely concealed. "I'll just take your word for it." He leaned in closer, lowering his voice so only I could hear. "Are you okay? You seem...off."

"Just a blast from the past," I replied, my voice barely a whisper. I couldn't meet his gaze, the intensity of his concern unraveling the carefully knotted facade I had built around my heart.

Clara broke in, her voice brightening with false cheer. "Well, I should be going. Just wanted to check in, make sure you weren't planning any clandestine meetings with old ghosts." With a conspiratorial wink, she turned to leave, the air between us thick with unresolved tension.

As she walked away, I could feel Nathan's scrutiny burning into my side. "You need to tell me what that was about," he insisted, his tone shifting from gentle to firm.

"I just need some space to think," I said, my frustration bubbling beneath the surface. "This whole situation is...complicated."

"Complicated doesn't even begin to cover it," he countered, crossing his arms. "You're not in this alone, you know. Let me help."

His offer was a lifeline, yet I felt a sudden swell of guilt. I had always prided myself on being independent, but the way he looked at me, his eyes filled with a mix of concern and something deeper, made me question if I could truly shoulder this burden alone.

Before I could respond, a flicker of movement caught my eye—a figure lurking in the shadows of the nearby alleyway, half-hidden by the flickering streetlamp. My breath caught in my throat as I squinted into the gloom, trying to decipher whether my mind was playing tricks on me. But the figure remained, a dark silhouette against the backdrop of my world that suddenly felt much smaller and more dangerous.

"Did you see that?" I whispered, my heart pounding against my ribcage like a caged bird desperate to escape.

"What?" Nathan asked, turning sharply toward the alley, his instincts kicking in.

"There's someone there." I pointed, feeling the adrenaline spike within me.

He stepped forward, shielding me behind him, his posture protective yet ready to confront whatever shadow loomed in the darkness. "Stay close. I'll check it out."

"No!" I protested, grabbing his arm. "It could be dangerous."

"Or it could be nothing. But we won't know unless we look." The determination in his voice left no room for argument.

I hesitated, torn between the instinct to flee and the desire to understand what was unfolding around me. I could feel my pulse quicken, each beat echoing the mounting tension that gripped the bay. With a reluctant nod, I stepped closer to Nathan, knowing that the shadows might not hold the comfort I craved but the uncertainty was suffocating.

Together, we moved toward the alley, each step fueled by a mixture of fear and resolve. The night had thickened, the air heavy with secrets and unspoken words, the kind that could shatter everything if left unaddressed. In that moment, I realized that the unraveling had begun, and there was no turning back.

The alley was steeped in shadow, a forgotten stretch of cobblestone that had likely witnessed more than its fair share of whispered secrets and hurried escapes. I glanced at Nathan, his silhouette framed by the dim light spilling from the streetlamp above, the lines of his jaw set in determination. My heart raced, fueled by the juxtaposition of fear and a thrill I couldn't quite place. What could possibly be hiding in the dark?

As we stepped cautiously forward, the figure emerged from the depths, a flicker of movement that quickly materialized into a woman. Her face was obscured by a hood, the fabric draping around her like a shroud. I instinctively squeezed Nathan's arm, the warmth of his skin grounding me against the rising tide of apprehension.

"Who are you?" Nathan called out, his voice steady yet low, like a warning to the shadows.

The woman paused, her posture stiffening as if weighing her options. "I didn't mean to startle you," she said, her voice smooth but edged with something I couldn't quite define. "I'm just... looking for someone."

"Looking for someone?" I echoed, my curiosity piqued despite the apprehension curling in my stomach. "Who?"

She hesitated, glancing back as if the shadows themselves might betray her. "Someone connected to your past, I believe."

Nathan and I exchanged glances, a silent agreement passing between us. "And why should we trust you?" he challenged, stepping slightly in front of me, the protector once more.

"Because," she replied, lowering her hood just enough for a sliver of moonlight to catch her features, illuminating a face that was both familiar and foreign. "Because I know things about your father."

The words landed like a stone in a still pond, rippling out into the depths of my thoughts. "My father?" I stammered, my mind racing to reconcile the past I had buried with the present unfurling before me. "What do you know about him?"

"Everything and nothing," she said cryptically, her eyes narrowing. "I know he was involved in something... bigger than anyone in Windward Bay could imagine. And you, you've been drawn back here for a reason."

Nathan's grip on my arm tightened, his body tense beside me. "What are you implying?"

"I'm not implying anything," she shot back, her patience wearing thin. "I'm telling you that the threads connecting you to him are fraying, unraveling. And if you don't act soon, you might lose not just the connection but your very sense of self."

The air crackled with tension, and the world around us faded, the reality of our surroundings slipping away like sand through an hourglass. "What do you mean by that?" I pressed, urgency driving my words. "What's happening? Who's behind this?"

"Someone wants to keep the past buried," she replied, her gaze shifting, suddenly wary. "And they'll do anything to protect their secrets, even if it means threatening you. You're a threat to them."

"Threat?" My voice came out as a whisper, a chilling realization crawling up my spine. "What do you mean?"

But before she could answer, a loud crash echoed from the street, reverberating through the alley and shattering the fragile tension that had gripped us. The woman flinched, her eyes darting toward the sound, panic flickering across her features. "I have to go," she said abruptly, her tone turning urgent. "They're coming."

"Wait!" I reached out, but she had already melted back into the darkness, the shadows swallowing her whole.

"What the hell just happened?" Nathan demanded, turning to me, the storm brewing in his eyes mirroring my own chaos.

"I... I don't know. I just—" I faltered, grappling with the fragments of her words. "My father? What could he possibly be involved in that would threaten us now?"

"First, let's get out of here," Nathan urged, his voice firm, slicing through the fog of confusion that enveloped me. "We can figure this out somewhere safe."

Reluctantly, I nodded, the urgency of the moment pushing us both forward. As we retraced our steps back to the street, the bright lights felt like a refuge, a beacon cutting through the night's ominous shroud. But the echo of her warning lingered, a haunting melody in the back of my mind.

The town felt different now, each corner potentially concealing a hidden danger, each passerby a possible ally or foe. "Do you think she was telling the truth?" I asked, my voice barely above a whisper. "About my dad?"

"Truth is subjective," Nathan replied, his eyes scanning the street as if trying to pierce through the fabric of uncertainty. "But we need to dig deeper. If your father's involved in something shady, it could explain a lot about why you came back here."

"Great," I muttered, sarcasm dripping from my words. "Just what I need—more family drama."

"Hey, I'm here with you," he reassured, a softening in his tone as he caught my gaze. "We'll figure this out together, I promise."

The sincerity in his voice sent a ripple of warmth through me, the depth of his support stirring emotions I hadn't fully acknowledged. We were on a precipice, teetering between safety and chaos, and I was desperate to cling to the one thing that felt solid.

We walked in silence for a few moments, the world bustling around us, oblivious to the tumult brewing just beneath the surface. The faint sound of laughter echoed from a nearby café, a vibrant reminder of life continuing despite the shadows lurking at the edges of our reality.

"What now?" I asked, breaking the silence.

"We need to gather more information," Nathan said, his expression thoughtful. "There's got to be something in your father's past that can explain all of this. Do you have any old journals or papers? Anything that could give us a clue?"

I nodded slowly, recalling the box of keepsakes tucked away in my attic—old photos, letters, and the remnants of a life that felt like a distant memory. "I think I might have something."

"Then let's head to your place," he said, determination flooding his voice. "We'll sift through it together."

As we made our way home, the weight of the unknown pressed down on me, but it was tempered by the steady presence of Nathan beside me. Whatever lay ahead, I knew I couldn't face it alone. The shadows were closing in, but together, perhaps we could shine a light on the secrets that threatened to unravel not just my past, but our future as well.

The path to my home was familiar yet shrouded in an unfamiliar haze. Each step felt heavier than the last, weighed down by the lingering unease that now accompanied me like a shadow. I glanced at Nathan, who walked beside me, his expression a mix of concentration and resolve. The way the streetlights illuminated his features, casting gentle shadows across his face, made my heart ache with something I couldn't quite name.

"Do you think she'll come back?" I asked, trying to sound nonchalant, though the tremor in my voice betrayed me. "That woman with the hood? The one who knew my dad?"

"Maybe," Nathan replied, his tone thoughtful. "But if she does, we'll be ready. We just need to stick together."

"Right," I nodded, the words tasting like a half-hearted mantra. "Together." But the thought of facing more revelations about my father and the secrets that enveloped him sent a shiver down my spine. What if this was just the beginning?

As we reached my house, the old wood creaked underfoot, the familiar scent of musty books and lingering cedar enveloping me like a comforting blanket. Yet, the shadows in the corners seemed to stretch longer than usual, an unsettling reminder of the turmoil brewing just beneath the surface. I led Nathan inside, and the door clicked shut behind us with a definitive finality.

"Where's that box?" I asked, my voice bouncing off the walls, as if seeking solace in the echoes. I headed toward the attic, the dust motes dancing in the slanted light filtering through the small window, casting an ethereal glow over the cluttered space.

"Up here," I muttered, pulling down the ladder with a decisive tug. As I climbed, I felt Nathan's presence just behind me, a solid anchor in a world that had begun to tilt. The attic was a treasure trove of memories, filled with the remnants of my childhood— old toys, books with cracked spines, and the box of keepsakes that held fragments of my family history.

"Wow, it looks like a time capsule in here," Nathan remarked, stepping into the space and glancing around. "What's the story behind all this?"

I rummaged through the chaos, my hands brushing against a dusty teddy bear that had long since lost its stuffing. "Just... memories. Some of it is mine, some belonged to my dad. It's all jumbled together."

His gaze softened as he watched me sift through the mementos. "You know, you don't have to go through this alone. I mean it. If it gets too heavy, I'm right here."

The sincerity in his voice tugged at my heartstrings, and for a fleeting moment, the weight of our current situation lifted. "I appreciate that. It's just—this whole thing with my dad feels like a puzzle I'm not sure I want to solve."

"Then let's take it one piece at a time," he suggested, a small smile breaking through the tension. "For now, let's see what you've got in that box."

I finally located the battered cardboard box, its corners frayed and edges soft with age. Setting it down, I opened the lid with a soft creak, revealing a trove of memories that flickered before my eyes. Old photographs of my father, younger and somehow more carefree, stared back at me. In one, he was laughing, his arms wrapped around my mother, both of them radiant and alive in a way I had never seen them before.

"Wow," Nathan breathed, leaning in closer. "You look just like him."

"Except for the smiling part," I quipped, my heart heavy with nostalgia. "I didn't inherit that gene."

As we shuffled through the photographs, we uncovered letters, brittle and yellowed with age. "What's this?" Nathan asked, holding up a neatly folded piece of paper.

"Probably just old love letters," I replied, a hint of bitterness creeping into my voice. "My mom and dad had a tumultuous relationship."

"Want to read it?" He held it out, curiosity dancing in his eyes.

With a reluctant sigh, I took the letter and unfolded it, my heart racing as I scanned the elegant script. "Dearest Claire," it began, the words flowing smoothly like honey. I read aloud, the words evoking a haunting resonance: "I will always cherish you, despite the storms that may come."

Nathan's eyes were fixed on me, his expression a mixture of intrigue and concern. "What's the date?"

I scanned the page. "It's from... twenty years ago?" I looked up, confusion etched on my face. "That doesn't make sense. They divorced before I was even born."

"Then something must have happened between then and now," he suggested, leaning closer. "Keep going."

I continued reading, the words weaving a narrative that felt both familiar and foreign. "You are my anchor in this turbulent world, my reason to fight against the darkness. But I fear..." I paused, my breath catching in my throat. "I fear that my past will catch up to us, and I may not be strong enough to face it."

"What past?" Nathan pressed, urgency creeping into his voice.

"I don't know," I admitted, frustration bubbling beneath the surface. "But this is more than just a letter. There's something bigger at play, something my dad has hidden from me."

The attic felt stifling, as if the air itself was thick with the secrets trapped within these walls. I folded the letter back, trembling with both anticipation and dread. "We need to keep looking."

As I rummaged deeper into the box, I unearthed a small, leather-bound journal. It was worn, the edges frayed, and as I flipped it open, the ink smudged in places, the handwriting shaky but familiar. "It's my father's journal," I whispered, my heart pounding.

"Do you want to read it?" Nathan's voice was low, almost reverent.

"Let's see if there's anything useful," I said, thumbing through the pages. There were scattered entries, but one stood out, a passage written in a hurried scrawl: "The consequences of my past decisions are coming home to roost. I cannot protect them forever. I must face the truth, no matter the cost."

"Truth about what?" I muttered to myself, the unease rising like bile in my throat. "What were you involved in?"

Just then, a loud bang echoed from downstairs, rattling the attic and sending a jolt of adrenaline coursing through my veins. Nathan and I exchanged wide-eyed glances, the realization sinking in that our sanctuary had been invaded.

"What was that?" I breathed, my heart racing.

"I don't know, but we should check it out," he said, a protective instinct flaring in his eyes.

As we descended the ladder, my mind raced with possibilities, fear gnawing at my insides. Could it be the woman from the alley? Had she returned, or was it someone worse?

We crept through the darkened rooms, the quiet of the house amplifying every creak and groan. The thudding noise came again, louder this time, reverberating through the walls. I glanced at Nathan, his jaw set in determination.

"Stay close," he whispered, his voice steady.

We reached the living room, the air thick with tension. Suddenly, the front door swung open with a force that rattled the frame, revealing a shadowed figure standing just beyond the threshold, half-hidden by the night.

"Are you ready to uncover the truth?" the figure called out, their voice laced with an unsettling familiarity.

My breath hitched, the recognition clawing at the back of my mind. "You?" I whispered, dread pooling in my stomach.

The figure stepped into the light, and the realization struck me like a lightning bolt—everything I thought I knew was about to be shattered.

Chapter 15: A Descent into Darkness

I crouched low, the damp, musty air swirling around me as I fumbled with the flickering flashlight, its beam illuminating the crumbling walls of the underground chamber. The light danced erratically across the uneven stone, casting eerie shadows that seemed to whisper secrets of the past. Nathan was close behind me, his presence a reassuring weight in the oppressive darkness. We had stumbled upon this hidden passage while searching for answers, and the air was thick with anticipation. What lay ahead felt like an unraveling tapestry of dread, woven tightly with threads of history and loss.

As I moved further into the chamber, I stepped over a rusted chain that lay abandoned on the ground, a forgotten remnant of some long-ago restraint. My heart raced, a frantic drum echoing in my chest. The walls bore the marks of time, etched with names and symbols that whispered of those who had once walked these cold, stone corridors. I felt as if I were intruding on a sacred space, a graveyard of memories that had been buried far too deep. Nathan's breath was steady behind me, and the warmth of his body contrasted sharply with the chill that clung to the air. It was a reminder that, even here, in this shadowy underworld, I was not alone.

We rounded a corner, and my flashlight landed on a collection of photographs pinned to a weathered corkboard. They were black-and-white images, faded and curling at the edges. Each face stared back at me, eyes filled with a mixture of hope and despair. I took a step closer, my fingers brushing against the glass that separated us from their silent pleas. In one photograph, a young girl held a doll, her smile bright against the somber backdrop of the lighthouse. Beside her, a couple stood with arms around each other, their faces radiating a joy that felt painfully out of place in this forgotten place. It struck me then that these were not just relics; they were lives—stories abruptly halted, souls unmoored.

"What do you think happened to them?" Nathan's voice cut through the silence, low and reverent.

I turned to him, my heart heavy. "I don't know, but whatever it was, it left a mark on this town. They disappeared without a trace." My voice trembled slightly, betraying the unease that coiled tightly in my stomach. The chamber felt like a tomb, a mausoleum filled with echoes of the past. I swallowed hard, forcing myself to maintain composure. "We need to find out more."

Nathan nodded, and together we moved deeper into the chamber. The air grew colder, more oppressive, as if the very walls were closing in on us. My flashlight flickered, casting long shadows that flickered like ghosts around us. I felt the presence of the lost, their sorrow wrapping around me like a shroud. It was a suffocating reminder that we were not just searching for answers; we were also walking among the remnants of lives that had been extinguished, consumed by the darkness that surrounded us.

I spotted a wooden table against the far wall, littered with old papers and a few more photographs. My fingers brushed against the yellowed pages, and I hesitated. Among the scattered artifacts, a journal lay open, its pages frayed and delicate. I could feel Nathan's eyes on me, urging me silently to delve into the past. With a deep breath, I approached it, my heart racing as I leaned closer, the scent of mildew and age rising up to meet me.

The journal belonged to a woman named Clara, her script a flowing elegance that belied the terror captured within her words. As I began to read, my heart sank further with each line. She wrote of strange occurrences in the town, of shadows lurking just beyond sight, and of the inexplicable fear that gripped the residents. "They vanish without a trace," she had penned, "like mist evaporating at dawn. Each day brings new whispers of those we've lost, and the lighthouse looms ever larger, a beacon of our despair."

I could feel Nathan tense beside me as I read aloud, the weight of Clara's words heavy in the air. "She describes a fear that grips the townsfolk," I murmured, my voice barely above a whisper. "A growing dread that something is watching."

"We've felt that, haven't we?" Nathan replied, his gaze fixed on the pages. "Like something is lurking just out of sight, waiting for the right moment to strike."

I nodded, my mind racing with the implications of her writings. "What if the lighthouse is more than just a relic? What if it's a gateway to whatever took them?" The thought sent chills racing down my spine, a visceral reminder of the danger that loomed.

As I turned the pages, Clara's tone shifted. Her handwriting grew frantic, letters scrawled with urgency. "They are coming for me. I hear their voices in the night, feel their presence creeping ever closer. I cannot stay. I must leave this place before it consumes me as it has consumed the others." My breath hitched, the reality of her fate dawning on me.

I could feel Nathan's hand brush against mine, grounding me in the chaos of emotion swirling around us. "We have to find a way to stop this," he said, determination flooding his voice. "We can't let whatever this is take anyone else."

I met his gaze, and in that moment, something shifted. We were no longer just two people exploring the past; we were allies, bound by a shared purpose. The gravity of our discovery weighed heavily on us, but so did the flicker of hope ignited by the possibility of change. I could feel the fire of resolve igniting within me, pushing away the fear that threatened to consume us both. Together, we would face whatever darkness awaited us, armed with the knowledge of those who had come before.

The air grew thicker with each passing moment, the weight of Clara's words lingering like smoke in my lungs. I closed the journal gently, as if I were shutting away the souls of those who had once inhabited this place. Nathan's expression mirrored my own turmoil, a mix of determination and anxiety that spoke volumes without the need for words.

"Where do we even start?" he asked, glancing around the dim chamber as if the shadows might reveal some hidden clue.

"Clara mentioned something about a 'darkness' in her journal," I replied, my mind racing through the fragments of her narrative. "What if it's tied to the lighthouse itself? It feels like it's been watching us, doesn't it?"

"Like a creepy sentinel," Nathan quipped, attempting to lighten the mood. "Great. Just what I wanted in a vacation destination—an ominous lighthouse with a penchant for psychological warfare."

A nervous laugh escaped me. "We should at least take a look at the top. Maybe there's something up there that can help us."

With a shared glance, we turned toward the narrow staircase that spiraled upward, each step creaking underfoot, echoing the uncertainty brewing in our minds. The air felt cooler as we ascended, the oppressive weight of history pressing down harder with each twist of the stairwell. The walls seemed to close in, adorned with peeling paint that hinted at countless storms weathered, both outside and within.

Emerging at the top, I pushed the door open to a room dominated by dust and disuse. Sunlight streamed through the cracked windows, illuminating motes that danced like ghosts in the shafts of light. I stepped forward, my heart racing with a mix of excitement and trepidation. The lanterns were old but still clung to a sense of grandeur, and at the center of the room stood the enormous lens of the lighthouse, its glass prisms catching the light and fracturing it into a kaleidoscope of colors.

"Wow," Nathan breathed, his eyes widening. "It's stunning."

"It is," I agreed, drawn closer to the glass. As I examined it, I noticed something strange—scratches etched into the surface. My fingers traced the grooves, each line a whisper of the past. "These look fresh. Like someone's been here recently."

Nathan moved beside me, his brow furrowing. "Or something."

A chill ran down my spine, and I glanced toward the door, half-expecting a shadow to appear. "Let's see if there's a way to access the light mechanism. Maybe it holds more secrets."

We moved cautiously, exploring the small room. My hands brushed against the brass levers and polished wood of the operating station. Just as I was about to pull one of the levers, I heard a soft sound—a scuffle, perhaps a footstep from behind us.

I whirled around, my heart pounding. "Did you hear that?"

Nathan's expression sharpened. "Yeah. It came from downstairs."

"Great, just what we need. A friendly ghost." I tried to inject humor into my voice, but it came out more strained than I intended.

"Let's check it out," he said, his tone all business now.

We descended the staircase, every step resonating in the quiet, each creak a warning of what might be waiting for us. My mind raced with thoughts of Clara and the others. Had they heard the same sounds? Had they known they were being watched?

As we reached the bottom, the air grew thick again, the kind of weight that made it hard to breathe. The chamber felt more alive, as if the shadows had deepened and were now watching us with a malevolent intent. The photographs seemed to shift in the corner of my vision, their eyes following our every move.

"What if it's the same thing that took them?" I whispered, a tremor of fear lacing my words. "What if it's still here, waiting for us to let our guard down?"

Nathan grabbed my hand, a gesture of both comfort and strength. "We'll face it together, whatever it is." His grip was firm, grounding me in the midst of the uncertainty swirling around us.

As we ventured deeper into the chamber, I caught sight of something unusual—a faint glow emanating from a stack of debris in the corner. Intrigued, we moved closer, the light revealing a small, ornate box partially buried under the rubble. Its surface was etched with intricate patterns that gleamed even in the dimness.

"Do you think it's safe to open it?" Nathan asked, his eyes darting around as if expecting something to leap out at us.

"Safe? Probably not," I replied, biting my lip. "But we need to know."

With a shared breath, I reached for the box, my fingers trembling slightly. The moment I lifted it, the light seemed to flicker around us, and a low hum vibrated in the air, as if the chamber itself was alive with anticipation. I hesitated, glancing at Nathan, whose eyes were wide with curiosity and fear.

"Okay, on the count of three?" he suggested, his voice low but steady.

"One... two... three!"

We opened the box together, the lid creaking as if protesting its release from slumber. Inside lay a collection of small trinkets: a tarnished locket, a worn compass, and a slip of parchment that fluttered slightly in the cool breeze wafting through the chamber.

I picked up the parchment, my heart racing as I unfolded it. The words were hastily scrawled, as if written in a panic. "The lighthouse holds the key. Beware the darkness that waits within. Trust no one."

My breath caught in my throat. "This is bad, Nathan. We need to leave."

But as I looked up, the air shifted again, heavier now, charged with an unnameable tension. The shadows around us thickened, coiling tighter like a serpent ready to strike. I felt the familiar sensation of being watched, the prickling unease crawling along my skin.

"Let's go," Nathan urged, pulling me toward the exit.

But just as we turned, a figure emerged from the shadows, cloaked in darkness, eyes glinting with an unnatural light. My heart raced, a visceral fear clawing at my throat. It was as if all the horror of the past had materialized into flesh and bone, and we stood frozen, caught in a moment where time seemed to stretch infinitely, both a warning and a harbinger of what was to come.

The figure loomed before us, obscured in shadows, its presence a grotesque mockery of all that was sacred in this place. My heart thudded in my chest, a wild rhythm that echoed the panic swirling within me. I stole a glance at Nathan, his face pale but resolute, a flicker of determination igniting in his eyes. Whatever stood before us was the embodiment of our darkest fears, and yet, I could not help but feel a strange pull, as if this being had been waiting for us all along.

"What do you want?" I called out, my voice steadying against the rush of adrenaline. It felt foolish to confront the unknown, yet there was something liberating about demanding answers. The air thickened with tension, and for a moment, the world seemed to hold its breath.

The shadow shifted, revealing a face partially obscured by a hood. "You seek the truth, but the truth demands a price," it rasped, the voice like gravel grinding against stone. Each word felt like a stone dropped into still water, sending ripples of dread cascading through the chamber.

"Truth? Price?" I echoed, a mixture of defiance and fear surging within me. "What do you mean?"

With a sweeping motion, the figure gestured toward the remnants of the chamber, the photographs, the journal, the artifacts that whispered of lives lost. "Those who perished here left pieces of themselves behind. Only by understanding their pain can you hope to escape your own."

Nathan stepped closer to me, his hand gripping mine tightly. "We're not afraid of the past. We want to help."

The figure's laughter echoed through the chamber, hollow and chilling. "Help? You cannot help what you do not understand. The darkness consumes everything, and it will consume you too if you linger here."

"Why do you keep saying that?" I demanded, frustration flaring up like a match in the dark. "We're not here to be victims! We're here to find answers!"

A silence fell, thick and suffocating. The figure seemed to contemplate my words, the air vibrating with an energy that felt alive. "Very well. But know this: the past is not as easily buried as you might hope. Its roots run deep, and they will ensnare you."

Suddenly, the ground beneath us trembled, a low rumble that vibrated through the walls and rattled the artifacts. The figure straightened, and in that moment, I caught a glimpse of its eyes—dark, swirling voids that spoke of anguish and despair. A warning shot across my mind, and I realized that whatever this entity was, it had been shaped by the same darkness that had swallowed the town whole.

"Run!" Nathan shouted, pulling me toward the staircase as the tremors intensified, sending debris cascading from above. The shadows seemed to reach for us, clawing at my ankles, urging me to stay, to succumb to the fear that threatened to overwhelm.

We stumbled backward, the ancient wood creaking ominously underfoot as we raced toward the narrow stairs. I glanced back, the figure now standing still, watching us with an unsettling calm as if the chaos swirling around us was of little concern.

"What is it doing?" I gasped, trying to keep pace with Nathan. "Why isn't it following?"

"It's playing with us," Nathan replied, his voice tense but steady. "It wants us to feel powerless. We can't give it that satisfaction."

The exit felt miles away as we barreled down the stairs, shadows darting in the corners of my vision, taunting us. The air thickened with each step, a palpable weight that pressed against my chest, squeezing the breath from my lungs. I couldn't shake the feeling that we were being drawn deeper into its web, that our every movement was anticipated, calculated.

We burst through the door into the chamber below, only to find the atmosphere charged with a raw energy. The glow from the box illuminated our path, casting distorted shadows that danced across the walls like mocking phantoms.

"Do we go back?" I asked, my voice breathless. "We can't just leave everything behind."

Nathan hesitated, glancing at the artifacts strewn across the floor. "We need to take the journal and the box. Whatever is in there might be the key to understanding what we're facing."

"Are you sure?" I bit my lip, torn between the urgency of escape and the need for answers.

"We can't leave without knowing how to fight this thing," he replied firmly, already crouching down to gather the journal and the ornate box.

As I moved to help him, the ground quaked again, this time more violently, the walls trembling as if they might cave in. My instincts screamed for us to flee, but the urge to uncover the truth pulled me back, deeper into the chaos.

"Let's go!" I urged, clutching the journal tightly as Nathan secured the box. We turned, racing toward the staircase, but as we reached the bottom step, the door slammed shut with a resounding boom, locking us in.

I spun around, panic flooding my veins. "What the hell?"

"Stay calm," Nathan said, but the tremor in his voice betrayed his own fear. "There has to be another way out."

My mind raced. The energy in the room crackled, and the shadows thickened, coiling around us like snakes ready to strike. I pressed my back against the door, testing it, but it wouldn't budge. "We need light," I said desperately. "Maybe we can—"

Before I could finish, the figure appeared again, emerging from the shadows like a nightmare made flesh. "You cannot escape the truth," it declared, its voice a low rumble that vibrated through my bones. "And you cannot escape me."

The darkness seemed to swirl, closing in on us from all sides, and I felt the air grow cold as I locked eyes with Nathan, a silent agreement passing between us. We were trapped, but we wouldn't go down without a fight.

In a heartbeat, I knew we had to confront whatever this darkness was—whether it was a part of our reality or a manifestation of our fears. It was time to take a stand, and as I drew a shaky breath, the weight of the journal in my hands felt like a lifeline—a reminder that the truth was worth fighting for, no matter the cost. But before we could act, the shadows surged, and the world around us began to blur, the very fabric of reality unraveling as we stood on the precipice of an abyss, the darkness ready to consume us whole.

Chapter 16: The Final Confrontation

The soft glow of dawn filtered through the cracked blinds of my cluttered apartment, casting slanted shadows across the chaotic jumble of notebooks, crumpled papers, and half-finished mugs of coffee that had become my life. My heart raced in tune with the rhythm of my thoughts, a cacophony of fears and hopes merging into a singular determination. I no longer wanted to be the timid observer, forever lurking in the corners of my own existence. No, today was different. Today, I was ready to step into the spotlight, to confront the puppeteer behind the notes that had haunted me.

Nathan stood across the room, his presence a reassuring anchor in the swirling tide of anxiety that threatened to engulf me. His dark hair tousled, a shadow of stubble framing his jaw, he looked more like a rugged hero from a film than the quiet guy I had initially dismissed. But beneath that facade lay a sharp mind and a fierce loyalty that had slowly unwrapped my heart like the petals of a reluctant flower. He had become my partner in this twisted game, each day bringing us closer to a truth neither of us fully understood.

"Are you ready?" he asked, his voice a deep rumble, the question laced with both concern and excitement. The world outside was waking up, the sounds of the bay mingling with the distant calls of seabirds, but in that moment, it was just us—two souls poised on the precipice of a storm.

I inhaled deeply, the scent of salt and adventure mingling with the mustiness of my surroundings. "As ready as I'll ever be," I replied, forcing a confident smile even as my stomach twisted in knots. We had crafted a meticulous plan, a carefully laid trap designed to draw out the enigmatic figure lurking behind the notes, but the uncertainty of what lay ahead was a wild beast clawing at my insides.

With a shared nod, we gathered our gear—flashlights, my trusty voice recorder, and a few essential supplies we thought might come in handy. The key to our success rested in the shadows of Windward Bay, where the coastal paths meandered like serpents, leading us toward the heart of the mystery. We knew that this confrontation could shatter the delicate balance of our lives, but the thought of the truth finally surfacing invigorated me, a sweet nectar that drowned out the bitterness of fear.

As we stepped outside, the crisp morning air embraced us, refreshing and invigorating. The streets were mostly empty, the early risers still cocooned in their blankets, blissfully unaware of the brewing tempest. Nathan and I made our way toward the cliffs, the salty breeze tousling our hair, invigorating our spirits as we approached the edge of the bay. The sunlight sparkled on the water's surface, transforming it into a tapestry of diamonds, a stark contrast to the darkness we were about to unearth.

"Do you think they'll show?" Nathan asked, his tone casual, but I could see the tightness in his jaw, the way his fingers twitched at his sides. I understood that he shared my doubts, the fear that our efforts might lead to nothing but empty air.

"They have to," I replied, my voice steadier than I felt. "They've been watching us for too long. This is our moment." The words felt like a talisman, empowering me to push through the self-doubt that clawed at my confidence.

As we neared our destination, a secluded cove where the cliffs rose dramatically from the shore, the atmosphere shifted. The air was thick with anticipation, every sound amplified—the soft lapping of waves against the rocks, the rustle of leaves in the wind. Each step brought us closer to the unknown, and with it, the electrifying thrill of the hunt.

We arrived at the designated spot, a small, weathered wooden bench that overlooked the churning sea. It had been our meeting point for weeks, a place where we had exchanged ideas and shared our fears, but now it felt like a stage set for a showdown. I could feel the weight of the moment pressing down on us, and I glanced at Nathan, his eyes locked on the horizon as if trying to pierce the veil of mystery shrouding our foe.

"Remember, we stick to the plan," he said, his tone serious. "If anything goes sideways—"

"I know," I interrupted, my heart racing with a mix of excitement and dread. "We'll retreat, regroup. But we won't run away this time. I refuse to be scared anymore."

He met my gaze, a flicker of admiration lighting up his eyes. "You're braver than you think, you know that?"

Before I could respond, a rustle from the underbrush startled us both. My heart leaped into my throat as I turned to see a shadowy figure emerging from the trees, the sunlight dancing off the contours of a face I recognized all too well.

"Surprise, surprise," a voice dripped with mockery, pulling a smirk from my lips. "I didn't think you'd have the guts to show up."

The figure stepped closer, revealing a familiar, unnerving smile—one I had seen far too many times in the notes that had haunted my every thought. The chill that ran down my spine had nothing to do with the sea breeze. This was the moment we had prepared for, but nothing could truly brace me for the reality of standing face-to-face with the architect of my torment.

"Welcome to the grand unveiling," I said, my voice steadier than I felt, an unexpected confidence surging within me as I confronted the very essence of my fears.

The figure stepped into the light, the remnants of twilight casting a soft glow around them, illuminating a face that had haunted my thoughts. It was Alex, the person I once considered a friend, a confidant. Now, standing before me, they embodied the very embodiment of betrayal. The tension hung thick in the air, crackling like the static before a storm. I could hardly believe this was the same person who had shared laughs over coffee and whispered secrets under the stars.

"Did you really think I wouldn't find you?" Alex purred, their voice a silken thread woven with disdain. The glimmer of mischief in their eyes sent an involuntary shiver down my spine, a prelude to the chaos they promised to unleash.

"Honestly, I hoped you'd be too busy with your knitting or whatever it is you do," I shot back, my words sharper than intended, a thin veneer of bravado covering the unease bubbling beneath the surface. Nathan shifted beside me, the tension radiating from him palpable.

"Cute," Alex replied, unfazed by my attempt at humor. "But we both know this isn't a game anymore." The air was electric, and the world around us faded into a blur. The weight of unspoken words hovered like storm clouds, dark and ominous.

"Why, Alex? Why all of this?" I gestured wildly, encompassing not just the notes, the fear, but the very essence of our shattered friendship. Memories of our laughter felt like echoes from a distant past, now tainted by their betrayal.

Alex chuckled, a sound devoid of warmth, and for a moment, it felt like we were both transported back to simpler times, before everything spiraled into chaos. "You really don't see it, do you? The thrill of it all. Watching you scramble, piecing together clues like a jigsaw puzzle, all the while thinking you were the one in control."

I swallowed hard, feeling the burn of anger mix with confusion. "This isn't thrilling; it's cruel. You've turned my life into a living nightmare."

"Oh, sweet girl," they said, leaning in, their expression a twisted combination of pity and delight. "You misunderstand. It's not about you. It's about me. It always has been."

A chill ran down my spine as I tried to wrap my mind around their words. It felt like I was speaking to a stranger dressed in familiar clothing. "You think this is about you?" I laughed, though the sound was brittle, echoing hollowly in the space between us. "You're delusional if you think this is anything but pathetic."

"Pathetic?" Alex's eyes flared with something—was it rage or hurt? "You think you're the first person to stand against me? This is about proving I'm not just a shadow, not just the friend sitting in the background."

Nathan took a step forward, his posture protective. "You've crossed a line, Alex. This has gone too far. It's time to end this."

"Oh, brave Nathan, always trying to be the hero." Alex's voice dripped with sarcasm, and for a brief moment, I felt the weight of their disdain directed not just at me, but at the very foundation of our relationship. "But heroes don't save the day; they just make the villain's story that much more interesting."

"Enough with the theatrics," I snapped, my patience wearing thin. "What do you want? What's the endgame here?"

"To watch you squirm, of course," Alex said, a smirk dancing across their lips. "To watch you become the person I always knew you could be—strong, resilient. Just not in the way you want."

There was something almost poetic in their madness, a darkness that twisted my gut. "You want me to become a villain?"

"No, darling, I want you to understand that life isn't as clear-cut as you think. You're naïve if you believe everyone plays by the rules. Sometimes, you have to break a few to get what you want."

"I won't be a pawn in your game," I shot back, my heart pounding with resolve.

"Ah, but you already are." Alex stepped back, the shadows of the cove swallowing their form momentarily before stepping back into the light. "You don't even realize it yet. This is bigger than just us, it's about the town, the secrets buried beneath the waves of Windward Bay."

My pulse quickened, the realization that I was standing at the edge of something monumental. "What do you mean?"

"Let's just say, Windward Bay has its ghosts, and I intend to resurrect a few," Alex replied, a wicked glint in their eye. "And you, my dear, will be right at the heart of it."

I felt Nathan's hand slip into mine, his warmth grounding me in a reality that threatened to spin out of control. "We can stop this, Alex. Whatever it is you're planning—"

"Stop?" Alex interjected, laughter ringing like shattered glass. "Oh, Nathan, you truly have no idea. This is just the beginning."

The weight of their words pressed down on me like an anchor, pulling me deeper into a sea of uncertainty. I couldn't let fear dictate my choices any longer; I had to confront the storm head-on. "We know your game, Alex. We won't let you manipulate us any longer."

For a moment, the air thickened with silence, an unspoken challenge hanging between us like a taut string ready to snap. Then Alex shrugged, a dismissive gesture that belied the intensity of the situation. "If you think you can stop me, go ahead. But remember, every action has consequences, and you might not like the outcome."

Before I could respond, Alex turned, fading into the shadows of the trees, leaving behind a palpable tension that made the hair on the back of my neck stand on end. I stared after them, the adrenaline surging through me, each heartbeat a drum echoing my resolve.

"What now?" Nathan asked, his voice low and steady, an anchor in the storm swirling within me.

I turned to him, my expression a mixture of determination and defiance. "We dig deeper. If Alex thinks they can threaten us, they have another thing coming. We're not finished yet."

The sunlight dipped lower, casting long shadows across the path as we prepared to chase the truth. Each step forward felt like a promise, a pledge to unravel the mystery and reclaim the narrative of our lives. I could almost taste the salt in the air mingling with anticipation, the world stretching out before us like an uncharted map filled with secrets waiting to be discovered.

The cove was eerily quiet, as if the world was holding its breath, waiting for the next act in this unsettling drama. Nathan and I stood at the precipice, both literally and metaphorically, our eyes trained on the spot where Alex had vanished into the underbrush. The tension crackled in the air, a palpable energy that had me teetering between dread and exhilaration. I could feel my heart thudding in my chest, a relentless reminder that the stakes were higher than ever.

"Okay, so they've dropped their little hints, but we know what they're after," Nathan said, breaking the silence with a tone that was both steady and urgent. "We can't let this go unanswered. It's time to dig into Windward Bay's secrets."

I turned to him, a mix of determination and fear swirling inside me. "Do you think we can trust what they said? About the town having secrets?"

He took a step closer, his intensity matching the brewing storm around us. "I don't think they were lying, but I also don't think we can rely on anything they say. We need to investigate on our own terms."

With that, we began to walk along the rocky shore, the rhythm of the waves a comforting backdrop to our escalating anxiety. Each step felt heavy with purpose, the thrill of uncovering hidden truths urging me onward. My mind raced as I considered the possibilities: Alex's words hinted at something deeper, something that could turn our entire understanding of Windward Bay upside down.

"Did you notice how they spoke about the ghosts?" I mused, feeling a shiver of excitement at the thought. "What if there's more to this town's history than we've been told?"

Nathan nodded, his brow furrowing. "You mean the kind of history that's been swept under the rug? If that's true, it might explain why they're so fixated on dragging us into it."

As we rounded a bend, the cliffs rose sharply, towering above us like ancient sentinels. I could feel the weight of their presence, a stark reminder that the landscape held stories long forgotten. "If we're going to confront whatever this is, we need to start at the beginning," I said, squinting against the sun reflecting off the water. "Let's head to the library. Maybe we can uncover something in the archives."

Nathan flashed me a grin, the corners of his mouth lifting in a way that made my heart flutter. "I'm all in for a little sleuthing. Just promise not to get us kicked out this time."

"Only if you don't accidentally set anything on fire," I teased back, my spirit buoyed by the light banter. It was moments like these, even amidst the chaos, that reminded me how we had become a team, two halves of a whole navigating a treacherous path.

The library loomed ahead, its façade a mixture of aged brick and ivy, a relic of the town's storied past. As we entered, the familiar scent of aged paper and polished wood enveloped us, a comforting embrace amidst the uncertainty. I loved this place, with its countless shelves filled with stories waiting to be unearthed.

We made our way to the local history section, the quiet hum of the library a stark contrast to the tempest of emotions swirling within me. As I sifted through the neatly arranged volumes, my fingers brushed against a spine embossed with gold lettering. It was a collection of Windward Bay's history, an intriguing lead. I pulled it out and flipped through the pages, scanning for anything that might hint at the secrets Alex alluded to.

"Anything good?" Nathan asked, leaning over my shoulder, his warmth radiating as he studied the pages with me.

"Not yet," I replied, biting my lip in concentration. "But there's a lot here. It's like piecing together a puzzle—wait." I paused, my heart skipping a beat. There, nestled among the entries about the town's founding and its maritime history, was a mention of an old estate that had burned down decades ago. "This fire... it was said to have destroyed everything. But what if there were things that survived?"

"Like secrets?" Nathan leaned closer, his breath warm against my ear. "Maybe that's where we need to start digging."

My mind raced with possibilities. "If there's any chance that Alex is linked to this estate, we need to find out more. There could be evidence—something that ties everything together."

Just then, a sound broke the hushed atmosphere, a sharp thud echoing from the back of the library. We both turned, instinctively moving toward the source, curiosity piqued. The shadows lengthened as we navigated through the aisles, the dim light casting an ethereal glow around us.

"Hello?" Nathan called out, his voice cutting through the silence.

No response came, only the faint rustle of pages turning somewhere in the depths of the library. I glanced at Nathan, a question unspoken passing between us. We were no longer just searching for clues; we were stepping deeper into a mystery that was fast becoming far more dangerous than we anticipated.

As we reached the back, the air turned colder, a shiver racing down my spine. An old reading room sat empty, except for a single table illuminated by a flickering lamp, the light casting eerie shadows across the room. On the table lay a notebook, its pages fluttering slightly as if touched by an unseen hand.

"Who would leave a notebook here?" I whispered, glancing around warily. "This doesn't feel right."

"Let's see what it says," Nathan urged, his tone low but firm, a mix of intrigue and caution.

I reached for the notebook, the leather cover cool against my fingertips. As I opened it, my breath caught in my throat. The pages were filled with familiar handwriting—the scrawls and loops unmistakably belonging to Alex.

"This can't be…" My voice trailed off as I flipped through the pages, each entry revealing a twisted narrative of obsession, secrets, and connections that seemed to bind Alex to the very fabric of Windward Bay's hidden past.

"We need to take this with us," Nathan said, his voice urgent, but I hesitated, a nagging feeling creeping up my spine. "It's evidence. It could help us understand what they're really after."

Before I could respond, the library doors swung open with a force that sent a tremor through the room. The figure who stepped inside was cloaked in shadow, the sudden rush of wind extinguishing the flickering lamp. Darkness enveloped us, and I could barely make out the shape moving closer.

"Looking for something?" The voice was cold and familiar, slicing through the tension like a knife.

I glanced at Nathan, fear mingling with adrenaline, our previous bravado extinguished by the palpable danger now confronting us. "Alex," I breathed, and the shadows danced ominously, as if the very air held its breath, waiting for the climax of this unrelenting tale.

Chapter 17: A Whisper of Fear

The salty breeze swept through the lighthouse window, carrying with it the tang of the ocean and the whisper of secrets yet to be uncovered. As I peered out into the inky depths of Windward Bay, the moon hung like a watchful eye, its silver light dancing on the water's surface, creating a shimmering path that seemed to lead into the unknown. Nathan leaned against the weathered railing beside me, his presence a sturdy anchor against the storm brewing within my heart. The lighthouse, a beacon of hope and a prison of memories, stood resolutely against the encroaching darkness, but I knew that hope had its limits, and dread had a way of gnawing at the edges of even the most steadfast resolve.

"Do you ever think about what will happen if we fail?" I asked, breaking the silence that stretched between us like an unspoken pact. My voice felt small against the vastness of the night, but the question hung heavy in the air, its weight palpable. Nathan turned to me, his eyes reflecting the uncertainty I felt.

"Every day," he admitted, his tone low and serious. "But we can't let fear dictate our actions. We have to trust our instincts, and more importantly, we have to trust each other." He squeezed my hand, and a surge of warmth spread through me, a reminder of the bond we had forged amid chaos. Yet the comforting gesture could not dispel the shadow of doubt that loomed over my thoughts like a thundercloud waiting to burst.

The townsfolk of Windward Bay had grown restless, their once jubilant spirits dulled by the threat that loomed over us. Rumors swirled like the tide—whispers of a figure in the shadows, a dark force that threatened to unravel the very fabric of our lives. Each passing day brought new tales of strange occurrences: lights flickering ominously in the dead of night, the sudden disappearance of beloved pets, and a pervasive feeling that something sinister lurked just out of sight.

"It's like we're living in a horror story," I mused, trying to lighten the mood, but my words fell flat. The weight of reality pressed down on us, making it hard to breathe, let alone joke.

"Maybe we are," Nathan replied with a wry smile, his eyes glinting with mischief despite the tension in the air. "But every horror story has a hero, right?"

"Hero, or just two idiots who decided to poke the bear?" I shot back, unable to suppress a chuckle.

"Potato, potahto," he said with a playful shrug, though I could see the flicker of seriousness in his gaze. "We'll find a way through this. Together."

The sincerity of his words struck a chord deep within me, but the gnawing anxiety still clung to my mind. I glanced at the old clock on the wall, its hands ticking steadily toward midnight. Time felt like a relentless tide, pulling us toward an inevitable confrontation.

As the clock chimed, a sudden gust of wind rattled the shutters, and the sound of crashing waves echoed in the distance. Nathan's expression shifted; I could see the gears turning in his mind, the weight of responsibility heavy on his shoulders. "It's time," he said, his voice steady yet laced with urgency.

Together, we descended the narrow, spiraling staircase, each step echoing like the beat of a war drum in my chest. The air was thick with the scent of salt and impending rain, and as we reached the ground floor, I felt a chill sweep through the room.

"Are you ready?" Nathan asked, his eyes searching mine for reassurance.

"I don't know if I'll ever be ready," I replied honestly, my stomach a knot of dread and determination. "But we can't back down now."

The night air was crisp as we stepped outside, the moon now shrouded in a veil of clouds. The world felt muted, as if holding its breath in anticipation of what was to come. We moved toward the town square, our footsteps quiet on the cobblestones, the faint hum of tension palpable in the night.

"I wish we had more time," I whispered, the enormity of the situation weighing heavily on my heart.

"Time's a luxury we don't have," Nathan replied, his tone firm yet softening as he glanced back at me. "But what we do have is each other."

Our journey to the square was laden with memories, both sweet and bitter. I recalled the laughter that had once echoed through the streets, the warmth of summer nights spent under the stars, and the promise of a future that now felt just out of reach.

As we approached the center of town, the flickering lights of the streetlamps cast eerie shadows that danced like specters against the cobblestones. The gathering crowd murmured restlessly, eyes darting in the dark, each person a thread woven into the fabric of our shared anxiety.

Then, from the depths of the shadows, a figure emerged—a silhouette that sent a ripple of fear coursing through the crowd. Gasps filled the air as recognition dawned, and the tension escalated to a fever pitch. I felt Nathan's hand tighten around mine, the warmth grounding me as adrenaline surged through my veins.

In that moment, I realized that fear could be a double-edged sword; it could paralyze or galvanize. And as the figure stepped into the light, the world around us held its breath, waiting to see what would unfold.

The figure stepped fully into the glow of the streetlamp, revealing a familiar face twisted in a mask of anger and fear. It was Anna, someone I had known since childhood, a friend turned adversary in this spiraling tale of betrayal and mystery. Her hair, once a golden halo of sunshine, now hung in disarray, darkened by shadows that clung to her like a second skin. The crowd gasped collectively, their murmurs intensifying, a low hum of anxiety rising as if the air itself were trying to escape the palpable tension.

"Anna!" I called out, my voice slicing through the tension like a knife. "What are you doing here?" I couldn't help but feel a rush of conflicting emotions—concern, anger, confusion. How had she become part of this turmoil?

She looked up, her eyes glistening with unshed tears that reflected the moonlight, creating a hauntingly beautiful but unsettling image. "You don't understand! You have to listen to me!" she shouted, her voice trembling but insistent. The way she clutched her arms around herself made her seem smaller, vulnerable in a way I had never seen before.

"Listen to what?" Nathan's voice was low and cautious, his grip on my hand unwavering. "You've been behind all of this, haven't you?"

"Not by choice!" she shot back, taking a step forward, her defiance mingling with desperation. "I'm in over my head, and I need your help! They're coming for us, for all of us!"

A murmur rippled through the crowd. Whispers of fear and uncertainty floated through the air like ghosts. I could feel my heart pounding in my chest, the kind of fear that wraps around your throat and constricts your breathing. Yet, despite the chaos of emotions, a spark of loyalty flickered within me. I had to hear her out.

"Who's coming for us?" I asked, stepping slightly away from Nathan, creating a small space between us, signaling my intent to confront this head-on. The crowd shifted uneasily, curiosity mixed with dread as they waited for answers.

"The Society," Anna spat out the words like venom, her face contorting with disdain. "You have no idea what you're dealing with! They're not just a group of people; they're a web of power and deceit that stretches farther than you can imagine. They don't play fair. And they've set their sights on Windward Bay."

The tension thickened like fog, wrapping around me, stifling my thoughts. I exchanged a glance with Nathan, who seemed equally stunned. "Why should we trust you?" he asked, his voice steady but laced with skepticism.

"Because I'm here, aren't I?" she retorted, her expression softening momentarily. "I've seen what they can do, and I know how to stop them. But we have to act fast. They're coming tonight."

I inhaled sharply, the reality of her words striking like a bolt of lightning. "How do you know this?"

"Because they were watching me. I overheard them discussing you two, how they plan to eliminate the threat you pose." Her eyes darted nervously around the square, as if she expected shadows to spring to life. "And they're closer than you think."

The crowd's murmur intensified, panic brewing as people began to turn away, their instincts urging them to flee from danger. But I felt rooted in place, caught in the swirling currents of doubt and urgency. "If we're going to confront this, we need a plan," I stated, my mind racing. "What do you suggest?"

Anna hesitated, a flicker of fear crossing her face as she considered her next words. "We need to lure them out. They'll be looking for you, and if we can create a diversion—"

"Hold on," Nathan interrupted, his voice firm. "You want us to put ourselves in the line of fire? We're not just pawns in this game."

"I'm not asking you to be pawns," Anna replied, her voice tinged with desperation. "But if we don't take control, they will. We have to fight back."

The determination in her voice sparked something within me, a flicker of hope amidst the darkness. I turned to Nathan, seeking his reassurance. "What do you think?"

He looked contemplative, his brow furrowing as he weighed the options. "We don't have much choice. If they're truly coming for us, then we can't just hide. We have to be proactive."

"Fine," Anna said, a glimmer of relief washing over her. "Meet me at the old wharf in an hour. I have a plan, but we need to move fast. I'll gather what we need, but you have to trust me."

"What if it's a trap?" Nathan asked, skepticism lacing his words.

"Then we'll be ready for them," I countered, my heart racing at the thought of diving headfirst into danger. "We can't afford to be paralyzed by fear. We need to act."

As the crowd began to disperse, fear trickling into the streets like a rising tide, I could feel a sense of urgency building within me. "Stay together," I called out to the remaining onlookers. "We're stronger as a community. We can't let them tear us apart!"

The atmosphere shifted, determination igniting within the hearts of those still gathered. Conversations sparked back to life, voices raised in agreement. I glanced at Nathan, who nodded in silent accord, the shared resolve between us solidifying like iron.

"Let's do this," I said, feeling the weight of our decision settle over us, a cloak of responsibility. The stakes had never felt higher, but I could see in Nathan's eyes that we were no longer mere players in someone else's game. We were fighters, ready to reclaim our narrative, our lives, and the very soul of Windward Bay.

As we moved toward the wharf, I felt a rush of adrenaline, an invigorating blend of fear and anticipation. We would face whatever was coming together, ready to rewrite our story in the face of darkness, the flickering hope of dawn just beyond the horizon.

The old wharf loomed ahead, its weathered planks creaking underfoot as the waves lapped against the pier with a rhythmic, almost mocking cadence. The moon, now a thin crescent, offered little light, casting a silver sheen over the rotting wood, while shadows slithered in the corners, whispering secrets only the night could understand. The air smelled of brine and moss, a pungent reminder of the ocean's dominance over this forsaken corner of the world. I could almost feel the history embedded in the timbers—tales of fishermen's laughter, heartbreak, and the ever-present dance with danger.

"Why do I feel like we're about to walk into a scene from a bad thriller?" Nathan quipped, breaking the tension as he adjusted his grip on the makeshift weapon we had scavenged—an old rusted pipe that now felt like our lifeline.

"Maybe because we are," I shot back, trying to muster some courage amid the shivers that danced down my spine. "But at least we're not the ones wearing matching outfits and running from the killer. We've got a plan."

"Right, a plan," he said, his tone teasing but his eyes serious as they scanned the darkness. "I just hope Anna knows what she's doing. She's not exactly the poster child for reliability."

"Hey, neither are we, but look at us now," I replied, my voice steadying as determination surged within me. "We're in this together, right? Whatever happens, we'll handle it."

"Together," he echoed, the word hanging in the air like a spell.

Just then, Anna appeared from the shadows, her silhouette sharp against the faint light. She was panting slightly, her expression a mixture of urgency and fear. "You made it," she said, relief flooding her voice as she hurried toward us. "We don't have much time."

"What's the plan?" I asked, my heart racing as the weight of the moment settled upon us like a heavy shroud.

Anna's eyes darted to the water, then back to us. "I've set a distraction at the other end of the wharf. A fire. It'll draw their attention, but we need to move quickly before they realize it's a ruse."

"Isn't that a little extreme?" Nathan asked, skepticism creeping into his tone.

"Not as extreme as what they plan to do to us," Anna countered, her voice rising. "They're ruthless. You have no idea the lengths they'll go to protect their secrets."

"What kind of secrets?" I pressed, the question slipping from my lips before I could think.

"Things that could ruin lives, including ours," she replied, her tone grave. "But right now, we need to focus on keeping ourselves alive."

The urgency in her voice sent a shiver of adrenaline through me. "Let's do it," I said, feeling the pulse of determination quicken in my veins. We were on the precipice of something monumental, a chance to reclaim our lives from the shadows that threatened to engulf us.

As we moved toward the end of the wharf, the wooden boards creaked ominously beneath our feet, echoing the silent fears we all harbored. "So, what do we do when they arrive?" Nathan asked, glancing over his shoulder as if expecting danger to leap out from behind the shadows.

"We wait," Anna replied, her voice low. "And we strike when the moment is right."

The tension crackled in the air like static electricity, amplifying the sound of our breathing and the soft lapping of the waves. I stole a glance at Nathan, his face etched with determination yet shadowed by doubt. "You okay?" I whispered, my heart aching to soothe his worries.

"Just thinking," he replied, a smirk breaking through his tension. "About how I'm pretty sure this was not how I planned to spend my evening."

"Me neither," I said, allowing a small laugh to escape, an effort to lighten the atmosphere as much as to ease my own nerves. "I was thinking more along the lines of popcorn and a movie, not standing on a rotting wharf waiting for God-knows-what."

"Now you're making me hungry," he teased, the flicker of humor in his eyes a welcome reprieve from the encroaching dread.

Suddenly, the distant sound of engines roared to life, breaking through our moment of levity. The noise sent a shudder through the air, and I felt the knot of fear tighten within me. "They're here," Anna whispered, her face paling as she turned toward the sound.

"Get ready," Nathan said, his voice low and steady, the joking demeanor vanishing in an instant as adrenaline surged. We positioned ourselves behind a stack of crates, their sharp edges digging into my skin as I peered through the gaps, straining to catch a glimpse of our approaching adversaries.

From the darkness emerged silhouettes, a group of men clad in dark clothing, their movements deliberate and calculated. My heart raced as I tried to make sense of the scene unfolding before us. The air crackled with tension as they fanned out, searching the area, their eyes glinting with malice.

"There's too many of them," I murmured, dread pooling in my stomach.

"Stick to the plan," Anna urged, her voice barely above a whisper. "We need to draw them away from here."

The men paused, their whispers rising and falling like the tide, an unsettling murmur that sent shivers down my spine. I felt the world around me shrink, the shadows deepening, wrapping us in their cold embrace.

Then, as if on cue, a burst of flame ignited at the far end of the wharf, sending a plume of orange and yellow skyward. The fire roared to life, illuminating the dark water and casting flickering shadows across the faces of our enemies.

"Now!" Anna shouted, her voice cutting through the chaos as we sprang into action.

We dashed from our hiding spot, adrenaline propelling us forward as we sprinted toward the fire. Behind us, the men were shouting, their voices rising in alarm as they rushed to assess the new threat.

"Stick together!" Nathan shouted, his voice rising above the chaos as we darted toward the blaze, desperate to create a distraction that would buy us precious seconds.

But as we reached the flames, a realization washed over me—our plan was working, but the fire wasn't the only danger lurking in the darkness. From the periphery, a figure emerged, eyes glinting with a predatory hunger. My heart sank as recognition struck like lightning.

"Anna!" I screamed, just as the figure lunged forward, a dark blur against the backdrop of fire and chaos, reaching for her with an intensity that froze the breath in my lungs.

Time seemed to slow as I watched, horror-stricken, the world around me fading into a blur. Would we make it out alive, or would this night end in tragedy? The answer hung in the air, suspended like the smoke curling into the night, as the flames danced and the shadows deepened, leaving us on the brink of an unknown fate.

Chapter 18: The Game Begins

The ocean whispered secrets as the waves lapped against the shore, a rhythmic lullaby that both calmed and stirred my insides. Each gust of wind carried the brine of salt, a tangy reminder of the stakes at play. The darkness wrapped around us like an old friend, shielding our intentions while heightening our senses. Nathan's presence beside me was a tether, a steady pulse against the unknown chaos that lay ahead. I stole a glance at him, his brow furrowed with concentration, the sharp angles of his face defined against the soft glow of the moon. There was a wildness in his eyes that mirrored my own—a mix of bravery and uncertainty that made my heart race.

We were cloaked in shadows, two conspirators in a game far larger than either of us had anticipated. The plan had taken shape over the past weeks, each late-night conversation morphing into whispered strategies, each step calculated yet tinged with a reckless hope. The beach, usually a sanctuary of warmth and laughter, had transformed into a stage for our confrontation. It was here that we would confront the ghost of our shared anxiety, the figure whose cryptic notes had haunted us, darkening our idyllic town like an unwelcome storm cloud.

As we crouched behind a cluster of jagged rocks, I could feel the cool grit of the sand beneath my palms, grounding me in the moment. My heart pounded a frantic rhythm as I scanned the treeline, each rustle of leaves igniting my nerves. What if we were wrong? What if this was all for nothing? Nathan's hand brushed mine, a reassuring squeeze that bolstered my resolve. We had to believe we were doing the right thing; the safety of Windward Bay depended on it.

The night seemed to hold its breath, a stillness settling over the landscape as time stretched. Then, just as my anxiety threatened to consume me, a figure emerged from the shadows. Cloaked in darkness, they stepped into the moonlight, their features obscured but the stance familiar. My breath caught in my throat as recognition slammed into me like a wave crashing against the shore. It was someone I'd seen often, someone who had woven themselves into the fabric of our lives in ways I hadn't considered until now.

"Nathan," I whispered, urgency lacing my voice. "It's... it's—"

"I know," he replied, his tone low and tense. The air was electric between us, a palpable charge that felt both exhilarating and terrifying.

The figure paused, scanning the beach as if they could sense our presence lurking in the shadows. I felt as if I'd been plunged into ice water, the shock of realization making my limbs tremble. How had we not seen it before? The signs had been there, subtle yet unmistakable. This was the person whose laughter rang through the town square, whose kindness masked a deeper darkness. The thrill of unearthing the truth was quickly overshadowed by the chilling implications of their actions.

"Why are you doing this?" Nathan's voice broke through the stillness, firm yet laced with confusion. It hung in the air like a question mark, taunting and challenging all at once.

The figure turned, the moonlight catching their features, revealing the set of their jaw, the determination etched into their brow. "You don't understand," they said, their voice low but steady. "You think this is just about the notes? It's so much more."

My heart raced, torn between disbelief and a morbid curiosity. "What do you mean?" I challenged, stepping out from behind the rocks, emboldened by my rising anger. "What could possibly justify this?"

They laughed—a sharp, mirthless sound that echoed against the backdrop of the ocean. "You're all so naïve. You think you're living in some quaint little town, untouched by the chaos of the world. But you're wrong. This place is teetering on the edge, and I'm the only one who sees it."

I exchanged a glance with Nathan, his brow raised in skepticism, a mirror of my own disbelief. "And you thought stalking us would somehow help?" he countered, voice steady. "You think this is going to save Windward Bay?"

"Don't you see?" The figure stepped closer, the moonlight revealing the glint of something metallic in their hand. "You need to wake up! The world is not as safe as you think. These notes were a warning, a wake-up call. I thought you'd understand."

With every word, the tension escalated, crackling through the air like electricity. The truth hung heavily around us, each revelation unraveling the tidy narrative I'd clung to about our lives. Nathan took a step forward, his body poised protectively between me and the threat. "You've crossed a line," he stated firmly, an edge of anger lacing his voice. "This isn't just a game anymore. You need to stop."

I felt my heart race with adrenaline, the stakes soaring higher than ever. What had started as a quest for answers was now spiraling into something much darker, much more complex. The figure's eyes burned with an intensity that both fascinated and terrified me, the passion behind their motives both admirable and twisted.

"You don't get to decide how I respond to this world," they spat, their voice dripping with disdain. "I'm here to show you the truth, whether you like it or not."

The atmosphere thickened with tension, and I realized we were standing on a precipice, teetering between understanding and danger. The waves crashed against the shore, a backdrop to the storm brewing within us. Nathan's protective stance only fueled my resolve; I wouldn't let fear dictate my actions. The confrontation was far from over, and as the moon hung high above us, I prepared to dive deeper into the dark waters of betrayal and revelation.

With the air thickening between us like an approaching storm, the figure stepped closer, the shadows dancing around them as if they were part of the dark fabric of the night itself. My pulse quickened, the tension palpable, each heartbeat a reminder of how fragile our reality had become. I could see their eyes now, glinting in the moonlight, a mix of desperation and fervor that sent a shiver down my spine. This wasn't just a confrontation; it was the unraveling of everything I thought I knew.

"You think you're heroes, don't you?" they sneered, the corners of their mouth twisting into a mockery of a smile. "Brave defenders of a quaint little town. But what happens when the monsters lurking in the shadows are people you trust?"

Trust. The word echoed painfully in my mind, a familiar dagger that pierced through the comfortable layers of our lives. I glanced at Nathan, his jaw clenched tight, the muscles there taut like a coiled spring. "This isn't a game," he said, the authority in his voice barely masking the underlying concern. "You need to stop this before it goes too far."

"Far?" the figure scoffed, taking a bold step forward. "You have no idea what far looks like. This is merely the beginning. The world out there is crumbling, and you're all too busy playing pretend." Their eyes darted between us, searching for any sign of weakness. "You think ignorance is bliss? I'm offering you a glimpse of the truth."

I felt the urge to step back, to retreat into the comfort of denial, but the fire in my belly urged me to stand my ground. "Truth? Is that what this is about?" I challenged, my voice steady despite the tremors of fear threatening to surface. "Your twisted version of the truth? You don't have to do this."

"You don't understand," they insisted, their voice rising with fervor. "The notes were warnings! I've seen what lurks beneath the surface of this town, the darkness festering in every corner. I wanted to show you—make you see the reality we're all living in."

"What reality?" Nathan shot back. "You're scaring people! You think instilling fear is going to wake us up? All you're doing is pushing us further into our shells."

"You're too comfortable!" They pointed a finger at us, and for a brief moment, I saw a flicker of vulnerability behind their rage. "Look at you, standing here all brave and defiant. You don't know what it means to fight for your survival."

My heart raced, caught in the crossfire of emotion. "What happened to you?" I asked, my voice softer, almost pleading. "Why are you doing this to yourself? To us?"

The figure paused, their façade slipping just enough for me to see the cracks beneath the anger. "You think I wanted this? You think I wanted to become this—this person, this monster? But when you see the world for what it truly is, you either fight or you fade away. I chose to fight."

The conviction in their voice was almost persuasive, and for a moment, I found myself teetering on the brink of empathy. What pain had led them to this dark path? But the fear they'd instilled in our community, the chaos that had seeped into the lives of my friends and neighbors, was a cost too high to ignore.

"That doesn't justify your actions," I said, determination sharpening my resolve. "You can't force us to see things your way by terrorizing us. We need to stand together, not let fear drive us apart."

Their expression shifted, a brief flicker of doubt flashing across their face. "Together? But you're too naïve to understand what's coming. I've seen it—the shadows creeping closer. You're still stuck in your perfect little world. Just wait until it comes crashing down."

"I'd rather face the truth alongside my friends and family than cower in fear behind threats and intimidation," Nathan interjected, his voice steady and resolute. "You may think you're saving us, but all you're doing is pushing us away."

With that, the figure's facade finally cracked, their bravado melting into something raw and unsettling. "You think you're so different, don't you? But you'll see. One day, you'll wish you had listened."

Silence enveloped us, heavy with unspoken words. I felt a shift in the atmosphere, as if the world had taken a collective breath, waiting for what would happen next. In that moment of stillness, the air shimmered with tension, and I knew we had reached a crossroads.

"Let's just walk away from this," I proposed, desperation creeping into my voice. "You don't have to do this. We can find a better way to talk about what you're feeling. No more notes, no more stalking. Just... let's find a way to be honest."

But the figure shook their head, a sad smile ghosting across their lips. "You're not ready for this conversation. Not yet." They turned away, ready to vanish back into the shadows, but then paused, glancing over their shoulder. "Remember, I tried to help you. When the storm hits, don't say I didn't warn you."

And just like that, they disappeared into the trees, leaving us standing on the beach, breathless and bewildered. The sound of the waves crashing against the shore was the only thing breaking the silence, a reminder that life continued even as our worlds felt irrevocably altered.

"What just happened?" I finally breathed, the weight of the encounter pressing down on my shoulders. Nathan turned to me, his expression a mix of disbelief and concern. "We didn't just face them, we got a glimpse into something much darker. This isn't over, is it?"

"No," I replied, my voice shaking but resolute. "I have a feeling this is just the beginning." The uncertainty loomed ahead like a storm cloud, but I knew one thing for sure—we had to uncover the truth behind the fear that had gripped Windward Bay. Together.

The moonlight cast eerie shadows on the sand, turning the beach into a surreal landscape that felt both familiar and foreign. I could still hear the echo of the figure's parting words ringing in my ears, a haunting refrain that clung to the night air like a ghost. As Nathan and I stood there, the weight of our encounter settled over us like a dense fog, thickening the already tense atmosphere.

"Did we really just let them walk away?" Nathan's voice broke through my spiraling thoughts, his brow furrowed with concern. "I mean, it's not like they were just going to have a change of heart after this."

"I know," I replied, shaking my head as I tried to dispel the lingering unease. "But what could we have done? They were beyond reason. It was like talking to a wall." My heart ached at the thought of how lost they seemed, trapped in their own spiraling fear and delusion.

Nathan ran a hand through his hair, frustration radiating off him like heat from a fire. "We can't let this slide. If they think they can intimidate us, they'll only escalate things. This is about more than just notes now; it's about control."

A chill ran down my spine, the implications of his words heavy. Control. That was the core of it, wasn't it? The figure wanted to wield power, not just over me but over everyone in Windward Bay. "We need to figure out what's going on in their head. Maybe there's something we can use to help them see reason."

"Or maybe they'll drag us into their chaos," Nathan countered, his tone sharper than intended. "It's risky to play the savior when they're holding all the cards." His eyes searched mine, a storm of emotions flickering across his face. I could see his concern mirrored in the depths of my own uncertainty.

"Then what do we do?" I asked, desperation creeping into my voice. "We can't just wait for them to strike again. We need to stay proactive." My resolve hardened, fueled by the adrenaline still coursing through me.

Nathan sighed, his expression softening as he leaned against a weathered boulder. "You're right. We can't be paralyzed by fear. But we need a plan—something we can control."

Just then, a distant sound cut through the air—a crack of branches snapping, accompanied by the unmistakable crunch of footsteps on gravel. My heart leapt into my throat. "Did you hear that?" I whispered, dread pooling in my stomach.

"Yeah," he muttered, his eyes narrowing as he focused on the treeline. "It could be them."

With no time to spare, we ducked behind the boulder, our breaths shallow, each inhalation mingling with the salty scent of the sea. The footsteps grew closer, heavy and deliberate. I could almost feel the tension radiating from Nathan, a taut bowstring ready to snap.

"Whoever it is, they're coming this way," he murmured, a note of urgency lacing his words. "Get ready."

I clenched my fists, the cold bite of fear mingling with the thrill of anticipation. Just as the figure broke through the trees, I caught my breath—the silhouette was familiar but different. It was Sam, our friend from the diner, her face illuminated by the moonlight. Relief washed over me like a cool tide, but it was quickly replaced by confusion.

"Sam?" I called out, stepping cautiously from behind the boulder. "What are you doing here?"

She froze, her wide eyes reflecting the moon's glow, but I could see the glimmer of fear behind them. "I... I thought I heard something," she stammered, her voice barely above a whisper. "I came to see if you were okay."

"Why would you think something's wrong?" Nathan interjected, his tone a mix of suspicion and concern.

Sam shifted her weight nervously, glancing over her shoulder as if expecting someone else to emerge from the darkness. "You guys have been acting weird since those notes started showing up. I thought maybe I could help."

I exchanged a glance with Nathan, and something clicked into place—a realization that made my stomach twist. "You've been worried about us?" I asked, my voice softening. "Why didn't you say anything sooner?"

"Because," she replied, her gaze dropping to the sand, "I didn't want to pry. I thought you could handle it. But then I saw you two sneaking out at night, and I knew something was up. I just had this feeling—like you were in danger."

Nathan stepped closer, his expression softening. "We're okay, but it's getting complicated, Sam. There's someone out there—someone we thought we could trust. It's like they've woven themselves into our lives, and now they're... trying to control everything."

Her eyes widened, fear and confusion battling for dominance on her face. "Control? What do you mean?"

I hesitated, unsure how much to reveal. "They think they're saving us by scaring us. It's all very twisted."

"Twisted doesn't even begin to describe it," Nathan added, his voice laced with anger. "They've made it personal, and we can't ignore it anymore."

A flicker of determination sparked in Sam's eyes. "Then let's do something about it. We can't let them win."

Before I could respond, a rustling noise came from the treeline, drawing our attention. My heart sank as I saw a shadow moving just beyond the line of trees. It was too large, too menacing to be anything innocent.

"Nathan, get down!" I shouted, instinctively pushing Sam behind me as I braced for whatever was coming.

The shadow emerged into the light, revealing not one figure, but three—each cloaked in darkness, faces obscured. My heart raced as I took in their threatening stance, each of them armed with a glint of something sharp in their hands.

"This is just the beginning," one of them said, their voice gravelly, echoing the very threats we had been grappling with for weeks.

Panic surged through me as I realized the stakes had escalated far beyond what I had anticipated. We weren't just dealing with one misguided individual; we were facing a trio, their intentions shrouded in darkness and malice.

"Run!" Nathan shouted, his voice cutting through the air like a lifeline.

But before we could move, the lead figure lunged forward, brandishing their weapon, and I felt a rush of adrenaline mixed with sheer terror. Time slowed, and as I looked into their eyes, I realized something chilling. They weren't just there to scare us—they had come to finish what they started.

Chapter 19: The Face of Betrayal

The shock of the revelation crashed over me like a tidal wave, threatening to pull me under. I stood frozen, my breath hitching as the world around me spun with disbelief. Before me was a face I once greeted with warmth and camaraderie, now twisted with malice, eyes glinting like shards of glass in the dim light of the abandoned warehouse. The shadows loomed large, and my mind raced, seeking refuge in memories of laughter shared, secrets whispered. But now, those memories felt tainted, the joy snuffed out by betrayal.

"You didn't really think I'd let you win, did you?" They stepped closer, the acrid scent of betrayal hanging heavy in the air. The familiarity of their voice sent a shiver down my spine, a cruel reminder of how trust can morph into something dark and unrecognizable. The fluorescent bulbs flickered above us, casting an eerie glow that danced across their features, illuminating the contempt etched into their brow. I glanced at Nathan, his jaw clenched, the tension radiating from him palpable, an unspoken agreement that we would face this together.

The heart of the town pulsed in the background, a distant reminder of the life we had fought to protect. My mind flooded with questions: How had I missed the signs? Had the warmth of friendship blinded me to the simmering resentment that lay just beneath the surface? Their lips curled into a sardonic smile, as if they could read my thoughts, and that made my stomach churn. I could almost hear the echo of our shared laughter ringing hollow in the cavernous space, replaced by a silence that screamed of unresolved conflict.

"You've always been the golden child," they continued, voice dripping with sarcasm. "Always the hero. But what happens when the hero falls? When the town turns its back on you, just like it did me?" Their words sliced through the air, each syllable a reminder of the fragile line between ally and adversary. My heart raced as I pieced together the fragments of their narrative—one of a person discarded, overlooked, desperate for acknowledgment. In their eyes, I saw not just hatred but an aching loneliness, an emptiness that demanded to be filled, no matter the cost.

"I didn't cast you aside," I said, my voice steadier than I felt. "You chose to walk away." My statement hung in the air, heavy with unresolved tensions, and their expression flickered for a moment—was it regret, or perhaps vulnerability? I wanted to reach out, to bridge the chasm that had formed between us, but the distance felt insurmountable, thick with anger and pain.

A bitter laugh escaped their lips, harsh and raw. "You think this is about you? This is about reclaiming my life, my dignity, stripped away by the very people you hold dear." Their body language shifted, tension rippling through them like the quivering surface of a disturbed pond. "You can't even begin to understand the cost of your so-called heroism. You stand on your pedestal, and here I am, the forgotten one."

Nathan shifted beside me, a silent sentinel. The air crackled with unspoken words, a storm brewing just beneath the surface. "What do you want?" he asked, his voice low and measured, the kind of steadiness I found both comforting and alarming. This was no mere confrontation; this was a reckoning. I could sense the turning of the tide, the moment where words could become weapons.

Their gaze flickered between us, and I felt a mix of dread and determination well up inside me. "What I want," they said slowly, savoring the words, "is for everyone to see the truth. You are not the savior of this town; you're its greatest illusion." I could feel my heart pounding in my chest, the weight of their accusation hanging like a heavy fog. But I also felt the fire of my own conviction rising, urging me to challenge this twisted narrative.

"You think tearing me down will rebuild you?" I retorted, anger igniting the embers of courage within me. "This isn't a game of thrones. There are no winners in this kind of destruction. You're only tearing yourself apart." The truth of those words resonated in my core, grounding me as their expression flickered with uncertainty.

For a brief moment, the mask slipped. I could see the cracks in their façade, the vulnerability lurking just beneath the surface. But then it was gone, replaced by a steely resolve that chilled me to the bone. "You don't understand the game you're playing. You've made me your enemy, and I intend to make you feel the consequences."

My grip tightened around Nathan's arm, the warmth of his presence anchoring me in this storm of chaos. Together, we faced this enemy, our resolve intertwining like roots of an ancient tree, deep and unyielding. The battle ahead would be one of wills, a clash of ideals, and I was determined not to let fear dictate my response.

"Whatever you think you can achieve," Nathan said, stepping forward, his voice low and fierce, "you're wrong. We won't let you harm this town, or anyone in it. You think you're a puppet master, but in the end, you're just a marionette tangled in your own strings." The conviction in his voice rippled through me, a shared strength that stoked the flames of defiance.

The tension thickened, an electric charge hanging in the air as we stood ready to confront the darkness that threatened to engulf us. The shadows around us felt alive, eager to consume the light of hope we clung to. I knew we were in for a fight—not just against a person we once trusted, but against the very essence of betrayal that sought to undermine everything we believed in. As I looked into Nathan's eyes, I saw not just a partner in battle but a reflection of my own resolve. Together, we would face this storm, ready to reclaim our narrative, and ensure that our truth would emerge unscathed from the wreckage.

The atmosphere around us crackled with tension, a taut string ready to snap at any moment. My heart hammered in my chest, each beat a reminder of the stakes we faced. The flickering lights above cast our faces in stark relief, illuminating the sharp angles of betrayal etched into our foe's features. I took a deep breath, gathering my thoughts as Nathan shifted his weight, a silent signal that he was ready for whatever came next.

"Is this your big plan, then?" I challenged, forcing my voice to stay steady despite the adrenaline coursing through my veins. "To expose me? To turn everyone against me? News flash: it's not exactly groundbreaking." The words felt heavy with irony, but I pushed on, fueled by a mixture of anger and the desperate need to reclaim the narrative. "You think they'll rally around you just because you've got a vendetta? This isn't some soap opera; this is real life."

Their lips curled into a sneer, but I noticed a flicker of uncertainty behind their bravado. "Oh, but you underestimate the power of perception," they retorted, their voice dripping with disdain. "People will believe what they want to believe. And all I have to do is plant the right seeds of doubt. You'll be the villain in this story, and I'll be the hero who was wronged."

A wry laugh escaped me. "Is that really how you see yourself? A hero? Because right now, you're just a sad footnote in a story that's way bigger than you." The defiance in my voice surprised me, a flame igniting in my chest. I had faced tough moments before, but never had the stakes felt this personal, this raw.

Nathan stepped closer, his shoulder brushing against mine. "You're not the first person to think they can rewrite history," he said, a calm confidence radiating from him. "But let me tell you something: the truth has a way of surfacing, no matter how deep you bury it." I could feel his strength beside me, grounding me as I braced for the fallout.

"Spare me the lecture," they spat, hands clenching at their sides, as if readying for an attack. "You think you've got this all figured out, but you're just a pawn in my game. You and your precious town—you're nothing without me."

"Funny, because it seems to me you're the one desperate for attention." I shot back, feeling emboldened. "A town isn't built on a single person's glory; it's a tapestry of everyone's stories. And right now, you're just trying to tear it apart because you can't stand being on the outside looking in."

For a moment, I could see the inner turmoil playing out on their face, the flicker of regret battling with resentment. But before I could process it further, they lunged forward, the movement sharp and sudden. My instincts kicked in; I sidestepped, grabbing Nathan's arm as we evaded the oncoming chaos. "This isn't just a conversation anymore," I muttered, adrenaline surging through me. "We need to get out of here."

The enemy's laughter echoed off the cold, damp walls, sending shivers down my spine. "Run if you want! But the truth is coming for you. You can't escape what you've done." Their voice was a haunting melody, lingering in the air as they closed the distance again, their intent clear.

With a shared glance, Nathan and I dashed deeper into the warehouse, the shadows swallowing us whole. Our footsteps echoed against the concrete floor, a desperate rhythm of escape. The layout of the place was labyrinthine, filled with crates and machinery that seemed to conspire against us. I could hear their footsteps behind us, the sound of fury and determination chasing us like a predator to its prey.

"Do you know where you're going?" Nathan asked, his voice steady despite the urgency. I could sense the tension in his body, the way his muscles coiled like a spring, ready to unleash.

"Not a clue," I admitted, my heart racing not just from fear, but also from a fierce determination to outsmart our pursuer. "But I refuse to be cornered like a rat. We need to find something—anything—that can help us turn this around."

As we ducked behind a stack of crates, I peered through the gaps, trying to gauge our enemy's movements. They prowled the space, a wolf hunting its prey, their expression twisted into a mask of fury and frustration. The bitterness radiating from them was palpable, an aura that threatened to suffocate.

"Did you think you were the only one with plans?" they called out, voice echoing through the empty space. "You're nothing without your precious friends! You're just a girl with delusions of grandeur, playing the role of the hero in a story where you don't belong."

"Wow, someone needs a hug," I shot back, trying to mask my fear with humor. "You're right about one thing: I'm not alone. I've got Nathan, and he's not about to let you turn me into your punching bag."

Nathan shifted slightly, his focus unbroken, but I could feel the tension ripple between us, a reminder that we were both fighting for more than just survival. We were fighting for our home, for the people who believed in us, and for the very essence of who we were.

"Enough with the theatrics!" our foe yelled, exasperation coloring their voice. "You think you're so clever, but you'll regret underestimating me. I will expose you for what you really are—a fraud, a liar, a hollow shell."

With a surge of adrenaline, I pushed back against the fear threatening to drown me. "I'm not a fraud," I called out, my voice steady now, carrying the weight of my truth. "I've fought for this town. I've put in the work, built relationships, and faced my own demons. You may think you know me, but you've only seen what I've allowed you to see."

The truth hung between us, heavy and undeniable. In that moment, I realized that while our adversary was consumed by their desire for revenge, I was driven by something far greater—a commitment to the people and the place I loved. And as long as I held onto that, no amount of venomous words could diminish my resolve.

Nathan nodded subtly, and together we pushed from our hiding spot, determined to turn the tide of this confrontation. We might be outnumbered in a sense, but together we would forge a path through the darkness, reclaiming the narrative one moment at a time.

As I prepared to move forward, my pulse quickened, each beat a reminder that this moment was a precipice, and I could feel the gravity of the situation pulling me in different directions. Nathan and I stood shoulder to shoulder, an unspoken promise binding us together. The air was thick with the scent of metal and dust, the warehouse an echo of forgotten ambitions and twisted intentions. Every sound—the creak of wood, the scuttling of something unseen—seemed amplified, underscoring the urgency of our predicament.

Our opponent, fueled by rage, paced like a caged animal, their movements erratic yet calculated. "You're so blinded by your little fairy tale," they spat, their voice a venomous whisper that curled around us. "You think you're the protagonist, the brave knight saving the day. But you're just a little girl playing dress-up in a world far beyond your grasp."

"Cute try, but I'm more of a warrior than a damsel," I shot back, surprising even myself with the heat in my words. "And you're more of a villain than you realize. Heroes and villains are defined by their choices, and right now, your choice is to be the bitter specter haunting the edges of my story."

Their expression shifted, confusion mingling with rage. "You really believe you can turn this around, don't you? This town is nothing without me. You've all painted me as the monster, but the truth is I'm merely a reflection of what you've created."

"Or what you've chosen to become," Nathan interjected, stepping forward. "You're not a monster because you've been wronged; you're a monster because you've chosen to harm others rather than confront your own pain." His voice was calm, steady—a lifeline in the tumultuous waters swirling around us.

They halted, taken aback by his audacity. "You think you understand me? You think you know my story?" There was a tremor in their voice now, a crack that hinted at the fragility beneath their bravado. "You're just kids playing a game that's far more dangerous than you realize."

"Then why don't you enlighten us?" I challenged, daring to step closer. "If we're just players in your twisted version of reality, what's your endgame? What do you really want?"

A tense silence settled over the room as they hesitated, a flicker of something indecipherable passing through their eyes—was it regret or perhaps a fleeting glimpse of vulnerability? Then, with a sharp intake of breath, they resumed their bravado, masking the brief crack in their armor. "I want them all to see! To witness the truth! You think you can just waltz in here with your shiny ideals and save the day? Newsflash: this isn't a fairytale, and I'm no simple villain."

I could feel Nathan's hand subtly squeeze mine, a silent reminder of our unity. "Then show us the truth," I urged, my voice steady, cutting through the tension like a blade. "Let's see what you really have to offer."

Their laughter was cold, hollow. "Oh, you're going to see more than you bargained for, my dear." The words dripped with malice, and I couldn't help but shiver at the threat hanging in the air. "But it won't be a revelation that frees you; it will be a reckoning."

Before I could respond, the lights overhead flickered ominously, plunging the space into brief darkness. The sudden shift in ambiance was palpable, like the world holding its breath, waiting for something inevitable. As the lights returned, I noticed a shadow darting behind one of the crates—a fleeting figure slipping through the gloom, unseen but undeniably present.

"Did you see that?" I whispered, panic clawing at my throat. "We're not alone."

The realization settled over us like a shroud, and Nathan's expression hardened. "We need to move," he said, his tone shifting to one of urgency. "We can't let them use this against us."

But before we could decide on a direction, the familiar face of betrayal twisted into a grin. "Ah, but you're mistaken. I'm never truly alone." Their voice echoed, a haunting melody that dripped with certainty.

As if on cue, figures emerged from the shadows—friends turned foes, people I had trusted now standing against us, their eyes hollow and set with purpose. My breath caught in my throat as I recognized faces from our community, their allegiance now a weapon aimed directly at us.

"You don't get to choose your allies or your enemies," our adversary declared, eyes gleaming with twisted delight. "Welcome to the new reality. It's all a game, and you two are the pawns."

"Why?" The question burst from my lips, raw and desperate. "Why would they side with you? We've fought for this town together! We've built something worth saving!"

"They're merely pawns as well, but they choose to believe in my vision." Their voice was like silk, wrapping around each word, spinning a web of deception that threatened to ensnare us. "And you? You're the lingering reminder of their failures, the embodiment of what they could never achieve. You're the perfect scapegoat."

Panic surged through me as I glanced at Nathan, his face a mask of determination mixed with disbelief. "This isn't just about us anymore. They've turned the entire town against us."

A heavy silence hung in the air as we faced our former allies, their expressions a mix of confusion and resolve. I could see the flickers of doubt in their eyes—some were reluctant, but many seemed resolute, convinced that betrayal was the only path forward.

"We need to regroup," Nathan said, his voice cutting through the chaos. "Find a way to break this hold over them."

As we backed away, the shadows shifted, the figures closing in on us. My heart raced, every instinct screaming that we were on the precipice of something dire. Just as we turned to flee, the lights flickered again, this time plunging us into darkness.

In that moment, time seemed to stretch, each second lingering as uncertainty wrapped around us like a heavy fog. And then, with a sudden crackle, the lights blazed back to life—illuminating not just the warehouse but a trap that had been laid with precision.

The familiar face stood at the center, flanked by our erstwhile allies, their expressions steely. "Welcome to the endgame," they declared, an unsettling smile curling their lips.

I felt the air thicken with dread as the realization settled over us. This was no longer a mere confrontation; it was a battle for our very souls, and the lines of loyalty had blurred into a chaotic dance of shadows.

With nowhere left to run, I glanced at Nathan, our determination mingling with fear as we braced ourselves for the impending storm. The warehouse echoed with the silent screams of what once was, and I steeled myself, knowing that the next move would change everything.

Before I could form another thought, the lights dimmed once more, plunging us into a sudden, suffocating darkness. A single voice echoed through the void, chilling and relentless, a whisper that pierced through the chaos, lingering in the air like a haunting refrain. "You'll regret this. You will all regret this."

The darkness pressed in around us, and I felt my heart drop as I realized we were no longer just fighting a battle—we were fighting for our very lives.

Chapter 20: The Breaking Point

The storm whipped through Windward Bay like a restless spirit, sending waves crashing against the jagged cliffs. I could taste the salt on my lips as I sprinted, each footfall a race against the heartbeat of the tempest that had turned our world upside down. Nathan was beside me, his presence a fierce anchor in the swirling chaos. I could feel the warmth of his arm brushing against mine, a fleeting comfort in the midst of uncertainty.

"Faster!" he shouted, his voice barely piercing the howl of the wind. His determination was infectious, igniting a spark of defiance within me. I pushed harder, my breath coming in sharp gasps, a rhythm set to the pounding rain that battered my skin like a thousand tiny fists.

The confrontation earlier had been a catalyst, tearing through the carefully constructed facade of our lives. Each word exchanged with our adversary had ignited the unspoken tension between Nathan and me. I had always thought of him as a rival, an obstacle in my quest for independence, but standing there, shoulder to shoulder, I saw something more—a partner forged in the fires of conflict. The fear in his eyes mirrored my own, and it was a strange comfort to know I wasn't alone in this.

"Turn left!" I yelled, pointing to the narrow alley that cut through the labyrinth of old buildings. It was a gamble, a desperate choice that could either lead us to safety or further into danger. Nathan nodded, trust evident in his gaze, and we veered off the main street, the noise of the storm swallowing us whole.

The alley was dark, the shadows creeping like whispering ghosts around us. I could barely make out the outlines of the buildings, their weathered bricks soaked in rain and sorrow. The air was thick with the smell of wet earth and something else—fear, perhaps? Or the remnants of our shattered hopes? I couldn't tell anymore. All I knew was that the adrenaline coursing through my veins screamed for action, and I wasn't about to let it fade into the backdrop of our tumultuous lives.

"Do you think they saw us?" Nathan asked, his voice low, almost swallowed by the storm. I could sense the tension radiating off him, a taut string ready to snap.

"I don't know," I admitted, slowing for a moment to catch my breath. "But we can't stop now. We have to keep moving."

As if on cue, a loud crash echoed from the street we had just left, and I could hear shouting—angry, desperate voices mingling with the storm. My heart raced, a drumbeat of panic pushing me forward. The chase had begun, and it felt like we were merely players in a game we didn't fully understand.

Nathan grabbed my hand, his grip firm and reassuring. "We can't let them catch us. Not now."

"Not ever," I whispered, trying to sound braver than I felt. The truth hung between us, an unspoken acknowledgment of everything we had risked to get here.

We pressed deeper into the alley, our footsteps echoing against the cobblestones. The rain poured relentlessly, drenching us to the bone, but it was the least of my concerns. My mind raced with thoughts of what would happen if we were caught, if the shadows finally enveloped us. I stole a glance at Nathan, his jaw clenched, eyes narrowed with focus.

I had always seen him as a challenge, a rival in a world that demanded perfection and control. But in this moment, I saw him as a fierce ally, a man who could stand beside me against the storms of our lives. My heart fluttered, a traitorous feeling that whispered of deeper connections.

"Where to next?" he asked, pulling me closer to a doorway that loomed in the shadows. It was an old shop, its sign barely hanging on, swaying gently in the wind.

"Let's see if we can find a way inside," I replied, my voice steady despite the chaos outside. We crept toward the door, the hinges creaking in protest as I pushed it open. A musty scent wafted out, the smell of old books and dust mingling with the freshness of rain.

Inside, the dim light revealed shelves lined with dusty tomes, their spines cracked and faded. It felt like a sanctuary, a brief respite from the storm outside. "We could hide here," I suggested, though uncertainty knotted in my stomach.

"No. We need to keep moving. They'll find us eventually," Nathan countered, his voice resolute. I admired his determination, but a flicker of doubt danced in my mind.

"Then what do we do?" I asked, scanning the room for an exit. The thought of being trapped in this tiny space sent a jolt of fear through me.

"Let's see if there's another way out," he said, moving deeper into the shadows, his instincts guiding him.

I followed closely, our footsteps muffled by the thick carpet. The shop felt alive, every creak of the floorboards echoing with secrets. I couldn't shake the feeling that we were being watched, the walls themselves holding their breath in anticipation.

As we reached the back of the shop, we discovered a narrow door, its wood splintered and worn. Nathan pushed it open, revealing a small alley that led to the rear of the building. The rain still poured, but at least the storm's fury was muted here.

"We can slip out this way," he urged, and I nodded, the tension between us thick enough to slice. I stepped out into the storm, the rain hitting my face like a thousand tiny needles. The world beyond was chaotic, but I felt alive, electric with possibility.

"I'm glad you're with me," I said, glancing over at Nathan. The honesty in my voice surprised even me, but the moment felt monumental. The stakes were high, the world outside spinning out of control, yet here we were, a team against the darkness.

"Me too," he replied, and there was a sincerity in his voice that sent warmth coursing through me.

As we prepared to run again, I knew that whatever lay ahead, we would face it together. The lines that had once divided us began to blur, and in the heart of the storm, I found something I hadn't expected—hope.

We dashed down the alley, the storm's fury swirling around us like an angry beast. My heart raced not just from the thrill of the chase but from the exhilaration of shared danger. Rain splashed against my face, each drop an urgent reminder of the chaos that surrounded us. The sharp sound of footsteps echoed in the distance, the unmistakable growl of our pursuers growing closer. I could feel Nathan's presence beside me, a solid force that both grounded and electrified me, and I leaned into it as we tore through the rain-soaked streets.

"Do you think they've figured out where we went?" I called out, my voice strained but determined, desperate to break through the tension that hung like fog between us. The alley opened up into a wider street, littered with debris from the storm—a chaotic scattering of old newspapers, leaves, and even a few overturned trash cans. The familiar buildings loomed like ancient sentinels, their windows darkened by the tempest.

"Only if they have a psychic," Nathan shot back, his grin flashing like lightning in the gloom. It was a fleeting moment of levity, and I appreciated the humor, even as dread gnawed at my insides.

We turned a corner, and I skidded to a halt, nearly colliding with Nathan. Before us stood the old library, its stone façade glistening with rain, a place I had always considered a refuge. The irony struck me then, that here we were, seeking shelter in the very heart of our memories, surrounded by countless tales of escape and adventure.

"We can hide in there," I suggested, nodding toward the heavy oak doors that looked as though they hadn't been opened in ages. A flicker of doubt crossed Nathan's face, but the sound of angry voices reached us, snapping him out of it.

"Fine, but only for a minute. We can't stay in one place too long," he said, and together we rushed toward the entrance. The door creaked ominously as we pushed it open, and the scent of old books and damp wood enveloped us, a stark contrast to the storm outside.

Inside, the library was dimly lit, the heavy curtains drawn against the tempest. Dust motes danced in the air, illuminated by the flickering light of a few flickering lamps. It felt like stepping into a different world, one where time stood still. I loved this place, had spent countless afternoons getting lost in stories that transported me far from the confines of Windward Bay.

"Did you ever think we'd be hiding out in a library?" Nathan quipped, glancing around as if he expected a ghostly librarian to appear and shush us.

"Only in my wildest dreams," I replied, unable to suppress a smile. It was moments like this—moments of levity amidst chaos—that made me feel alive, deeply alive. But reality quickly descended as the sound of footsteps echoed from outside, muffled yet insistent.

"Let's find somewhere to hide," I urged, my voice dropping to a whisper. We hurried through the labyrinth of bookshelves, ducking low and slipping between rows of dusty volumes. The air was thick with nostalgia, and I felt a pang of longing for the days when my biggest worry was whether to check out the latest fantasy novel or the new thriller.

Nathan and I found refuge behind a tall shelf, the titles a comforting barrier between us and whatever chaos awaited outside. I could hear the rain hammering against the roof, a relentless percussion that matched the thumping of my heart.

"Do you think they'll come in?" Nathan whispered, the tension in his voice palpable.

"They'll have to," I replied, trying to sound more confident than I felt. "We can't let them find us. Not here."

As we waited, I caught a glimpse of Nathan's profile, the way his brow furrowed in concentration, the slight twitch of his lips as he contemplated our fate. There was something profoundly captivating about him, the way he seemed to embody both strength and vulnerability. It struck me that our rivalry had morphed into something else entirely, a shared journey filled with complexities I hadn't anticipated.

"So, what's your plan?" he asked, a teasing edge creeping into his tone. "We could always start reading a book and hope the plot gets us out of here."

"Please," I laughed softly, "as if our luck is that good. No, we need a real plan. Something clever."

"Clever? That's my specialty," he replied, a mischievous glint in his eye. "How about we create a distraction?"

"Like throwing a book at them?" I raised an eyebrow, half-serious and half-amused.

"Not exactly what I had in mind, but it could work," he grinned, his enthusiasm contagious. "We just need to lure them away long enough for us to escape out the back."

Before I could voice my concerns, we heard the door creak open, a rush of wind followed by a sudden stillness. My breath caught in my throat. A moment later, voices drifted through the dimness, low and conspiratorial, cutting through the silence like a knife.

"They can't have gone far. Check the back," one voice commanded, the urgency unmistakable.

"Right," another replied, sounding reluctant. "I'd rather be outside in the storm than stuck in here. It's creepy."

"Creepy? This place is a treasure trove. Just imagine what we could find if we look hard enough," the first voice replied, a hint of excitement lacing his words.

With a glance at Nathan, we silently agreed on our next move. We had to act quickly. Nathan pulled out his phone, the glow illuminating his determined expression.

"Let's create that distraction," he whispered, a plan already forming in his mind. He typed furiously, and I could see the gears turning in his head.

"Just be careful. We can't risk getting caught," I reminded him, my voice barely above a whisper.

"Don't worry. I've got this," he replied, a glimmer of mischief in his eyes.

As he hit send, a loud crash erupted from the far side of the library, the sound of books tumbling to the floor, a symphony of chaos echoing through the stillness. The voices outside froze, uncertainty lacing their tones.

"What was that?" one of them exclaimed, and I could practically hear the gears turning as they processed the new threat.

"Let's check it out," the other replied, and the sound of footsteps retreated, a rustle of fabric and hesitant laughter echoing through the space.

Nathan and I exchanged quick glances, the momentary distraction igniting our instincts. "Now!" I urged, and together we slipped out from behind the shelf, the adrenaline spiking as we moved swiftly toward the back door.

The rain pounded outside, a relentless symphony as we stepped back into the storm, the chaos of Windward Bay welcoming us like an old friend.

The storm raged on as we fled into the night, the wind howling like a banshee, but somehow it only fueled my determination. The streets of Windward Bay had transformed into a surreal landscape, water pooling in the cobblestone cracks, glimmering under the intermittent flashes of lightning. It felt like we were racing against fate itself, and every gust of wind seemed to push us forward, propelling us into the unknown.

Nathan glanced back, his expression a mix of excitement and concern. "If they catch us, I'll let you talk your way out of it," he quipped, the corners of his mouth twitching into that infuriating smirk I had come to find charming.

"Funny. I'd prefer to avoid that altogether," I replied, matching his pace. It was absurdly comforting to banter with him, even in the face of danger. The chemistry between us had morphed from mere competition to an electric connection that thrummed in the air.

We ducked into another alley, where the rain seemed to collect in heavy puddles, reflecting the streetlights like a distorted painting. The world around us faded to a blur as we navigated the twisting passages, breathless and exhilarated. But just as the narrow space opened up into a small courtyard, a sudden flash illuminated the sky, casting stark shadows that danced along the walls.

"Wait," Nathan hissed, holding out a hand. We froze, the echoes of our footsteps swallowed by the relentless sound of rain. I peered around him, squinting into the darkness beyond the courtyard. The hairs on the back of my neck prickled, an instinctive warning that something was amiss.

"What is it?" I whispered, scanning the edges of the courtyard.

"I think I saw someone," he murmured, his voice tight. "Over by that dumpster."

I nodded, my heart thumping loudly in my chest. My mind raced with possibilities, each one more terrifying than the last. We needed to move, to get out of the open. "We should—"

Before I could finish, a figure emerged from the shadows, cloaked in darkness and rain, eyes glinting with an intensity that sent a chill down my spine. I instinctively took a step back, colliding with Nathan, who immediately stiffened beside me.

"Don't run," the figure called out, voice smooth as silk, yet edged with menace. It was a woman, her silhouette sharp against the backdrop of the storm. "You won't get far."

I felt Nathan tense beside me, the heat of his body radiating like a beacon of strength. "Who are you?" he demanded, his voice unwavering despite the obvious danger.

"Just a friend," she replied, her lips curling into a smile that didn't reach her eyes. "I've been waiting for you both."

"Waiting for us? Why?" I shot back, my courage faltering as the reality of the situation sank in.

"Because you're the key to everything," she said, stepping closer, the light catching her features. Rain slicked her hair back, and despite the circumstances, there was an eerie beauty to her. "And I'm here to make sure you realize it."

"Realize what?" Nathan asked, his brow furrowed with confusion and defiance.

"That you're on the brink of something monumental," she said, her voice almost hypnotic. "You think this is just about survival? It's about so much more."

The air thickened with tension, a palpable weight that pressed down on us. I felt a rush of anxiety, the kind that clouded judgment and left uncertainty in its wake. "We don't have time for games," I snapped, desperate to regain control. "We need to get away from here."

"Ah, but that's where you're wrong," she replied, tilting her head as if considering a puzzle. "You're already involved, and there's no escape from destiny."

Nathan exchanged a quick glance with me, a silent conversation passing between us. I could see the worry etched on his face, mirroring my own. "What do you know?" he pressed, his voice steady, as if willing to face this unknown head-on.

The woman took a step back, assessing us with a predatory gaze. "More than you can imagine. This town, its secrets, they're alive. And you two have stirred something—something powerful."

I was about to ask her what she meant when a loud crash resounded from the direction we had just come. The unmistakable sound of footsteps—heavy, purposeful—approaching fast.

"Time's up," the woman said, her expression shifting, something dark flickering in her eyes. "You can either come with me, or face them. Choose quickly."

The rain intensified, a deafening roar around us, drowning out my thoughts. My mind raced as I weighed our options, my heart pounding against my ribcage. I could feel the pull of danger from behind, the urgency of the moment tightening around us like a noose.

"Nathan," I whispered, desperation creeping into my voice. "What do we do?"

His eyes searched mine, a mix of fear and determination igniting a fire within me. "We don't have much time. If we go with her, we might uncover the truth. If we stay, we'll be caught."

The footsteps grew closer, the tension thickening the air. My instincts screamed at me to flee, to abandon this unknown woman who seemed to hold secrets far darker than the storm that raged around us. Yet another part of me—the part that had seen how far Nathan and I had come together—yearned to discover what lay ahead.

"Are you ready?" Nathan asked, his voice barely audible above the chaos.

I hesitated, the weight of the choice pressing heavily on my shoulders. But as the shadows lengthened, a final, thunderous crack of lightning illuminated the night, revealing the true nature of our pursuers—a dark figure emerging from the storm, cloaked in menace and intent.

In that split second, I realized we were standing at the edge of something irrevocable, a precipice that would determine our fate. Whatever happened next would change everything.

"Let's go!" I shouted, as the figure lunged forward, and together, we plunged into the unknown, racing toward destiny with our hearts in our throats and the storm at our backs.

Chapter 21: A Heart Unveiled

The lighthouse stood as a sentinel against the tempest, its beam slicing through the darkness like a sword of light. Rain pelted the rocky ground, each drop a reminder of the chaos swirling around us. I could feel the tension coiling within me, tightening like a spring ready to snap. The ocean roared below, waves crashing against the cliffside with the ferocity of our own unspoken fears. Nathan's presence beside me was a balm, anchoring me as the storm raged on both sides of the glass doors.

"Are you ready for this?" he asked, his voice low and steady, a soft rumble against the howling wind.

I glanced at him, his brow furrowed with concern. There was a wildness in his eyes that mirrored the storm outside—a flicker of uncertainty that only heightened my own. But as I took a deep breath, inhaling the scent of salt and rain, I felt my resolve hardening. I wasn't just standing against the tempest; I was standing for something bigger than myself, bigger than the both of us.

"Ready as I'll ever be," I replied, my tone betraying a confidence I didn't quite feel. The truth had been laid bare, like a wound exposed to the air, and now it was time to confront the festering darkness that had haunted us for so long.

We stepped inside the lighthouse, the warmth enveloping us like a hug. The air was heavy with history, whispers of those who had come before us—lovers, sailors, lost souls. I brushed my fingers along the cool, worn railings as we ascended the spiral staircase, the sound of our footsteps echoing against the stone walls. Each step felt monumental, a deliberate movement toward the confrontation that awaited us.

At the top, the lantern room awaited, a panoramic view of the tempestuous sea that stretched into the horizon. The glass was fogged with moisture, but I could see the storm swirling outside, lightning illuminating the sky in jagged flashes. There was a raw beauty to it, a reminder of nature's power—and our vulnerability in the face of it.

"Let's get this over with," Nathan said, his voice a mix of determination and dread. I nodded, my heart pounding like the waves below us. As we pushed open the heavy door, the wind howled through the space, a mournful cry that echoed our own fears.

Standing at the center of the room was our enemy, cloaked in shadows and cloaked in menace. His presence was palpable, a darkness that seemed to absorb the very light around him. "I've been expecting you," he said, his voice dripping with malice, as if he relished this moment.

"What a surprise," I replied, my tone sharper than I intended, fueled by adrenaline. "You've been expecting us, and yet here we are, ready to end this." The words hung in the air, heavy with the weight of our shared history.

"End this?" He chuckled, a sound devoid of warmth, reverberating against the walls. "You think you can end what you barely understand? The darkness is deeper than you can fathom."

I could feel Nathan's hand find mine, our fingers intertwining, a tether to sanity in the face of this chaos. "Maybe you're right," I said, trying to project more confidence than I felt. "But that doesn't mean we won't try."

With that, I stepped forward, fueled by a fire that burned brighter than the storm outside. "You've taken enough from us. You've twisted our truths and turned our fears into weapons. But we're done letting you control our narrative."

His eyes narrowed, the shadows shifting across his features. "You don't know what you're asking for."

"Actually, I do," I shot back, feeling a surge of strength flow through me. "I'm asking for our lives back. For the chance to reclaim the love and hope you tried to shatter."

In that moment, the air crackled with tension, a palpable energy that made the hair on my arms stand on end. Nathan stepped closer, his presence a fortress at my side. "We're not afraid of you," he added, his voice low and steady.

The enemy's laughter rang out, harsh and mocking, a sound that sent chills down my spine. "Fear? Oh, you should be afraid. You stand on the precipice of your own destruction."

A shiver danced along my spine, but I refused to let it consume me. "Maybe you're right," I said, my voice steady, "but I'd rather face destruction than remain a puppet in your game."

As the winds howled and the storm raged outside, I realized that our confrontation was more than just a battle of words. It was a reckoning, a reclaiming of our power, our narrative. The lighthouse, with its flickering light, symbolized our hope. In its glow, I saw the reflections of all that we had endured—the lies, the fears, the heartache—but I also saw the strength that had carried us through.

"Enough of this," he spat, and with a wave of his hand, darkness swirled around us, threatening to consume. But I felt a rush of defiance coursing through me, a surge of warmth that pushed back against the encroaching shadows.

"No!" I shouted, channeling every ounce of courage I possessed. "You will not win."

With that, I released the fears I had carried for too long, embracing the light that flickered within. As the darkness collided with my newfound strength, the storm outside roared louder, but I held my ground, my heart pounding in time with the crashing waves.

The confrontation spiraled into a dance of wills, the very essence of our souls clashing in a battle that was as much physical as it was emotional. And in that moment, amidst the chaos of wind and water, I discovered a strength I never knew existed—a fierce love that could weather any storm.

As the storm began to subside, I felt a clarity settle within me. We had chosen to confront the darkness together, and no matter what happened next, I knew our love would emerge unscathed. In that lighthouse, under the watchful eye of the heavens, I found the courage to unveil my heart, unearthing the power that comes from vulnerability, and the unwavering belief that love, even in its fiercest trials, could illuminate even the darkest of nights.

As the tempest howled outside, the darkness in the lighthouse seemed to thrum with energy, an unsettling heartbeat of the very shadows that sought to consume us. I stood at the epicenter of this swirling storm of emotions, the air thick with tension as our adversary glared back at us. The light from the lantern flickered, casting dancing shadows across the room, illuminating the determination etched on Nathan's face.

"What's the matter?" I shot back, my heart racing yet somehow steady. "Afraid of a little competition?" The audacity of my words surprised even me, but in that moment, I felt emboldened, as if the very essence of the lighthouse had seeped into my bones.

"Competition?" he sneered, his voice dripping with disdain. "You're nothing but a child playing dress-up, thinking you can wield powers you don't understand."

"Funny, I thought I was the one holding all the cards," I replied, crossing my arms defiantly. Nathan chuckled beside me, a soft sound that grounded me further.

The enemy's gaze flickered between us, uncertainty creeping into his facade. "You think your bond makes you strong? Love is a weakness, a liability in this game. Look around you."

I followed his gaze to the chaotic sea beyond the glass, waves crashing violently against the cliffs, as if the very world were torn between fury and despair. But in that moment, I recognized the truth; love wasn't a weakness. It was the flicker of hope that could light even the darkest of nights.

"Maybe you've never known what real love is," Nathan said, his voice a low growl, pushing forward. "We don't need to understand the depths of darkness to know that it can't extinguish the light we've built together."

I felt a surge of warmth at his words, a flame igniting within me that chased away the lingering shadows. "You don't get it, do you?" I said, locking my gaze on our adversary. "Love isn't about strength in the traditional sense. It's about the courage to be vulnerable, to face the unknown together."

His laughter echoed, a discordant sound that grated against my resolve. "Courage? Vulnerability? You're grasping at straws. When the chips are down, it's power that matters, not your sentimental notions."

"Then let's see how far your so-called power gets you," I challenged, feeling the rhythm of my heart in tune with the thunder outside. The storm outside was losing its ferocity, but within these walls, it felt as if a maelstrom was building.

With a swift movement, I reached for the lantern's lever, illuminating the room with a blinding light that flooded the darkness. "This isn't just our fight; it's a declaration. We choose to stand against you, no matter the odds."

The brightness pushed against the shadows, and I felt the shift in the air, a pulse of energy radiating from my words. Our adversary staggered, momentarily blinded by the brilliance we had summoned together. Nathan gripped my hand tighter, and I could feel the steadiness of his heartbeat syncing with mine.

"What have you done?" he spat, confusion momentarily cracking his bravado.

"Nothing you can't handle," I replied, my voice steady. "But I'll give you a tip: you should try embracing a little light in your life. It might do wonders for that sour disposition of yours."

He glared, his features twisting in a mixture of anger and surprise. "You think this is a game? You're playing with fire."

"Good thing we brought our marshmallows," Nathan quipped, his smirk a spark of levity in the tense atmosphere.

In that moment, as the tension hung in the air like an unbroken promise, I realized that our strength wasn't just in our love for each other but in our ability to confront the chaos head-on, to transform our fear into something tangible. The shadows quivered at the edges of the lantern's light, an acknowledgment of our defiance.

"Why do you think I'm here?" the enemy demanded, regaining his composure. "I thrive in chaos. It's where I find my power."

"Maybe that's your problem," I replied, stepping forward, emboldened. "You see power as dominance rather than collaboration. You'll never understand how to truly wield it."

He hesitated, and I sensed a flicker of doubt in his eyes. "You think you can defeat me with mere words?"

"No," Nathan interjected, his voice firm. "We're here to show you that words can be weapons too."

With a sudden rush of resolve, I found myself drawing upon the memories we had forged together—the laughter, the moments of tenderness, and the strength that had blossomed in the cracks of our vulnerabilities. "Your power can't hold a candle to the light of love. It's time you learned that."

The air shifted as if the very fabric of the room was responding to our unity. I took a step closer, feeling the warmth radiating from the lantern, its glow growing brighter, pushing back against the encroaching shadows. "You think darkness is your ally, but it only masks your own insecurities."

For the first time, a flicker of uncertainty crossed his face. "What do you know about me?"

"Enough," I said, my voice steady. "I see through the mask you wear. Beneath it, you're just as scared as the rest of us. You're clinging to power because you're terrified of being vulnerable."

The storm outside had calmed, the winds whispering softly against the walls of the lighthouse. In this moment, I felt the gravity of our words sinking in, binding us in a web of shared understanding.

"Vulnerability is strength," Nathan said, his voice unwavering. "You can choose to let go of the darkness. It's never too late."

He took a step back, the shadows recoiling at his words. "You're fools if you think I'll change."

"No," I countered, my resolve solidifying. "You're the fool if you think we'll let you dictate our fate. This is our story now, and we refuse to be mere footnotes in your twisted narrative."

And as those words hung in the air, an unexpected quiet enveloped the lighthouse. The world outside had shifted, the storm receding into a gentle hum, but the energy within the lantern room crackled with anticipation. In that silence, I felt a profound understanding settle over us—a shared acknowledgment that together, we could dismantle the darkness that had threatened to consume us.

In that moment, the lighthouse became more than just a structure; it morphed into a bastion of hope, a testament to our fight against despair. As the shadows danced at the edges of our light, I knew that whatever lay ahead, we would face it together, our hearts unveiled and our spirits unbroken.

The darkness in the lighthouse swirled around us, a palpable tension that crackled like electricity. The enemy's confidence had begun to falter, yet he still wore a mask of contempt that obscured the flicker of doubt in his eyes. "You truly believe you can defeat me with your sentimental nonsense?" he sneered, but his voice wavered, betraying a hint of uncertainty.

"Sentimental?" I echoed, incredulity lacing my tone. "What's sentimental about standing up for ourselves? What's weak about choosing love over fear?" I glanced at Nathan, who nodded slightly, the strength in his gaze reassuring. We were in this together, a tandem force against the encroaching darkness.

"Love is just a word," he countered, his bravado returning in waves. "It means nothing in the grand scheme of power."

"Maybe you should try it sometime," Nathan shot back, the corners of his mouth quirking upward in a playful smirk. "It might loosen that perpetual scowl of yours."

The enemy's glare intensified, the shadows around him pulsating in response. "You dare mock me?"

"Mocking you? No, I'm merely pointing out that your villainous act could use a little levity. You're making it hard for us to take you seriously."

I couldn't help but smile at Nathan's wit, the absurdity of our situation somehow lightening the atmosphere. It was almost as if we had stepped into a bizarre play where the villain had taken himself too seriously. The absurdity of it struck me—a storm outside, chaos at every turn, and here we were, exchanging quips as if we were at a coffee shop instead of a lighthouse standing on the edge of a stormy cliff.

"Enough of your games!" the enemy roared, advancing toward us, shadows swirling like dark tendrils. The air thickened with his wrath, and I felt Nathan's hand tighten around mine, grounding me in the moment. "You have no idea what you're up against."

"Then enlighten us," I challenged, taking a step forward. "Show us what you've got. But be warned, the more you unleash your darkness, the brighter our light will shine."

With that declaration, I summoned every ounce of strength within me, feeling the warmth radiate from the lantern as if it recognized our resolve. The glow enveloped us, a shield against the encroaching shadows, and I dared to push further, inviting the light to flow through me, illuminating the corners of my heart that had once been consumed by fear.

The enemy hesitated, momentarily caught off guard by our audacity. "You think this light can save you?" His voice dripped with disdain. "It's just a flicker in the grand scheme of chaos."

"Maybe," I conceded, my heart racing, "but it's a flicker that can ignite a fire." I stepped closer, feeling the energy shift, the shadows faltering under the weight of our courage. "And we will burn bright enough to blind you."

As I spoke, I envisioned the memories of our love—the laughter, the quiet moments, the fierce determination that had woven us together in this battle. I felt the surge of those memories coursing through me, intertwining with the light, pushing back against the darkness that threatened to consume us.

"Foolish girl," he spat, a snarl curling his lips. "You don't know the depth of my power."

"Maybe not," Nathan chimed in, his voice steady. "But we know the depth of our love. And that's a force you'll never understand."

In that moment, the shadows flickered, as if responding to Nathan's words. I seized the opportunity, launching a wave of light toward our adversary. The energy crackled through the air, illuminating the room in a blinding flash.

He recoiled, and I sensed the shift in power as the shadows began to retreat. "You think this is the end?" he barked, his bravado unraveling before our eyes.

"Not by a long shot," I replied, emboldened. "But it's certainly a start."

With the shadows retreating, the air lightened, and I could feel the lighthouse coming alive around us, an ancient entity pulsing with newfound energy. The beam of light intensified, illuminating the space in a warm embrace, wrapping around us like a protective cocoon.

But the enemy wasn't finished yet. "You may have won this round," he growled, his voice a low, dangerous whisper, "but this isn't over. The storm isn't just outside; it's within you. You can't escape it."

And with that, he lunged forward, a dark blur against the radiant light. In an instant, the space erupted in chaos. The lantern flickered violently, shadows clawing back, the air thickening with an ominous presence. My heart raced as I felt the weight of his power pressing against us, the shadows threatening to pull us back into their abyss.

"Stick together!" Nathan shouted, his voice slicing through the cacophony. We instinctively moved closer, our hands still linked, a lifeline in the tempest of darkness.

"Where's the light?" I yelled over the din, my voice strained. The brilliant glow of the lantern flickered, dimming as if it were struggling against an unseen force. "It can't end like this!"

But the shadows surged, hungry and relentless, wrapping around us like a living creature. I felt the pull, the pressure, an almost magnetic force drawing me into the depths. "Nathan!" I cried, desperation clawing at my throat.

"I've got you!" he roared, his grip tightening as we fought against the encroaching darkness. I could see the determination etched into his features, a fierce resolve that sparked a fire within me.

Yet, in the eye of the storm, the shadows twisted and writhed, drawing closer, whispering doubts that tangled in my mind. "This isn't your fight," they hissed, echoing my fears. "You'll never win against the darkness inside."

"No!" I shouted back, shaking off their influence. "I choose my own path!"

As I pushed against the shadows, I sensed a flicker of light within me, a pulse that throbbed in time with the heartbeat of the lighthouse. I drew upon that strength, willing it to expand, to push back against the shadows threatening to consume us.

But then, just as I felt the tide shifting, the lantern dimmed, its light flickering like a candle in the wind. I gasped, the realization crashing over me—something was siphoning its power, drawing it into the darkness.

"Nathan, we have to!" I began, but my words were cut off as a wave of shadows slammed into us, sending us sprawling. The world spun, darkness encroaching at the edges of my vision, and I could barely hear Nathan's frantic voice calling my name through the chaos.

"Stay with me!" he shouted, his voice growing fainter. I clawed my way through the haze, desperately reaching for him, but the shadows were relentless.

In a final, desperate bid, I grasped for the remnants of the light within me, pouring everything I had into it. The shadows recoiled for a moment, and I caught a glimpse of Nathan, his face determined yet shadowed by fear.

But before I could grasp his hand, the darkness surged again, pulling us apart with a force that felt as if the very earth were splitting beneath us.

"Don't let go!" Nathan cried, his voice a lifeline in the storm, but the shadows were closing in, wrapping around him, and I could feel myself slipping into the void.

And then, just as I thought I'd lost him to the darkness, a brilliant flash of light erupted from the lantern, illuminating the entire lighthouse in a blinding white. The force of it surged through me, pushing back against the shadows, but as the light engulfed the room, I realized I was no longer standing in the lighthouse.

I was suspended in darkness, my heart racing as I searched for Nathan, the blinding light fading as the shadows threatened to swallow me whole. Just before the darkness consumed me entirely, I heard Nathan's voice echoing through the void.

"Find me!"

And with that final plea, the world shattered into a million pieces, leaving me suspended in an abyss of uncertainty.

Chapter 22: A New Dawn

The morning sun broke over Windward Bay, casting a golden hue across the landscape as if the world had been dipped in honey. I squinted against the brightness, the warmth pressing against my skin, a stark contrast to the chilling memories of the night before. The air was thick with the smell of salt and damp earth, a reminder of the storm that had swept through our lives. Standing beside Nathan, I felt the ghost of fear linger, but it was overshadowed by something warmer—something like hope.

As we stepped onto the cobblestone path leading away from the lighthouse, the town buzzed with activity. People emerged from their homes, blinking like newborns in the harsh light of day. I could see the familiar faces of my neighbors: Mrs. Thompson, who always had a pie cooling on her window sill, and Mr. Jenkins, the gruff fisherman who never failed to share a tale taller than the last wave he caught. Today, their expressions were a mosaic of concern and cautious optimism, and I couldn't help but feel a swell of affection for this quirky little town that had wrapped me in its arms through the storms of life.

"Are you ready to face them?" Nathan asked, his voice low, almost a rumble beneath the brightness. His grip tightened on my hand, grounding me.

"Do we have a choice?" I replied, trying to infuse my words with a feigned bravado. I could hear the echoes of our shared struggles whispering between us, a melody woven from the threads of our past. It was incredible how quickly everything had changed—from adversaries in a petty rivalry to allies in a life-or-death battle against a common enemy. We had been pulled into a whirlwind, but we emerged not just intact but transformed.

The crowd began to gather, their murmurs like the rustle of leaves in a gentle breeze. It felt as though all of Windward Bay had come to witness our reckoning. I scanned the faces, looking for familiar comfort amid the uncertainty. A knot tightened in my stomach. How could I possibly explain everything—the revelations, the danger, and the unexpected bond forged in fire?

Before I could overthink it, I stepped forward, pulling Nathan with me. He mirrored my determination, his jaw set and eyes fierce. "We need to talk," I announced, raising my voice to carry over the crowd. The murmurs quieted, curiosity knitting brows and widening eyes.

"Last night, everything changed," I continued, my heart racing. "We uncovered a truth that threatened all of us. The darkness we faced wasn't just an isolated incident; it had roots right here in our beloved town." Gasps echoed in response, a ripple of shock coursing through the crowd.

"Are you saying it was the old lighthouse keeper?" someone called from the back, and I recognized Kelly's voice, always ready to dive into a story, even if the stakes were life or death. I smiled faintly at her, appreciating her eagerness.

I nodded, pressing on. "Yes. But it was more than just him. There were forces working against us, hidden agendas that sought to manipulate our town for their gain." I glanced at Nathan, whose presence anchored me. "But we fought back. Together."

A murmur of disbelief floated through the crowd. I could feel their skepticism like a cool breeze on a hot day, brushing against my resolve. I continued, laying bare the truth of our harrowing night. "Nathan and I...we didn't just survive; we learned. We discovered that we're stronger together than apart."

Nathan interjected, his voice cutting through the murmurs like a knife. "And it's not over. There's still work to be done to secure our safety, to heal the wounds this darkness has left behind." His intensity stirred something within the crowd. They shifted, the air thickening with a shared understanding that we had more than just our stories—we had a fight ahead.

An older gentleman stepped forward, his face creased like an ancient map. "What do you suggest we do?" he asked, his tone somber yet tinged with the flicker of determination. The question hung in the air, heavy with the promise of collective action.

"I say we reclaim our town," I replied, my heart pounding in my chest as the weight of my words settled over the gathering. "We need to unite, share our experiences, and make sure that what happened to us doesn't happen again. We'll form a community watch, open lines of communication. No more secrets."

The crowd's reaction was electric, a surge of energy coursing through the gathering as people nodded, murmuring in agreement. I could feel Nathan's eyes on me, a mix of admiration and surprise. It was a new dawn for Windward Bay, and I could sense the possibility of something extraordinary forming amidst the remnants of fear.

Just as I felt the tide of hope rising, a shout pierced the air. "What about the lighthouse?" It was Mr. Jenkins, his voice gruff yet tinged with genuine concern. "That place has been a beacon and a curse. Do we really want to keep it standing?"

The question hung like a storm cloud, casting a shadow over the newfound resolve. Nathan and I exchanged a glance, and I could see the wheels turning in his mind. It was a moment of vulnerability, one that felt oddly intimate in front of the crowd. "We need to decide together," he said, and his voice had that same rough edge I had come to admire. "But what if we can transform the lighthouse into a symbol of resilience instead of a reminder of what we lost?"

There was a palpable shift in the crowd, a collective reconsideration. "A community center?" someone suggested, the idea like a soft breeze igniting kindling. "We could turn it into a place for gatherings, a hub for our stories and our futures."

"Yes!" I exclaimed, the idea blooming in my mind like the first crocus of spring. "A place where we can share knowledge, hold events, and remember the past while building for the future." The energy was infectious, sparking hope and excitement as discussions erupted among the townsfolk.

With Nathan at my side, I felt invincible. The lighthouse—our lighthouse—would no longer be a symbol of fear but a beacon of unity, a testament to our strength in adversity. As I gazed out at the faces before me, I saw more than mere townsfolk; I saw friends, allies, and family, each heart beating in sync with the promise of new beginnings.

The energy of the crowd wrapped around me like a warm blanket, bolstering my courage as we began to plot the resurrection of our beloved lighthouse. Laughter mixed with earnest conversation, a symphony of voices rising and falling like the tide. It felt surreal, as if the storm that had ravaged our lives had finally swept away the clouds, revealing a sky full of possibilities. I caught Nathan's eye; his smile was a beacon amid the chatter, one that suggested he believed in me even more than I believed in myself.

"Who knew you were such a natural-born leader?" he teased, a playful glint lighting his expression.

"Don't get used to it," I shot back, unable to keep the grin off my face. "I'm only here for the cookies and community drama." A chuckle erupted from him, and the lightness of the moment washed away the remnants of our fears. It was refreshing to see humor flicker to life again in the aftermath of our ordeal.

As we brainstormed, a sudden thought struck me, like a bolt from the blue. "What if we host a town meeting this weekend?" I proposed, feeling a thrill of excitement bubbling in my chest. "A chance for everyone to share their ideas about the lighthouse and how we can strengthen our community."

The murmurs morphed into enthusiastic agreement. People nodded, voices overlapping as they voiced their support. It was thrilling to witness their engagement, the energy palpable as they bounced around suggestions. The fear that had gripped us all seemed to dissolve into something tangible—something we could mold together.

"I can bake," Mrs. Thompson offered, her voice a delightful blend of excitement and pride. "And I'll bring my famous apple pie. It'll draw everyone in."

"Just make sure to leave some for us this time!" Nathan quipped, grinning at her.

"Only if you promise to wash the dishes afterward," she shot back, her laughter infectious. It was moments like these that reminded me why I loved this town. In the midst of uncertainty, humor and camaraderie flourished like wildflowers breaking through asphalt.

As the meeting plans solidified, the group began to disperse, each person weaving their way back to their respective lives, emboldened by the prospect of change. Nathan and I lingered for a moment, watching the sun rise higher, its rays warming our skin, almost as if it were embracing us after the darkness we had endured.

"Do you think they'll really come?" I asked, my voice tinged with vulnerability. The prospect of facing my neighbors with the weight of our shared history felt daunting.

"They will," Nathan assured me, a quiet confidence in his tone. "You're giving them something to believe in, something they can be part of. People love to rally behind a cause, especially when it's one that strengthens their community."

His words resonated deeply, igniting a spark of determination within me. Together, we turned to walk back to town, the gentle sound of waves lapping against the shore echoing our thoughts. The day unfurled before us like a canvas waiting for vibrant strokes of color.

Later that evening, as I prepared for the meeting, I found myself lost in the rhythm of the kitchen, the comforting scent of cinnamon and sugar filling the air as I whipped up a batch of cookies. Each swirl of the wooden spoon felt therapeutic, a grounding ritual that calmed my racing heart. I could almost hear the laughter of the townsfolk as they reminisced about their lives in Windward Bay, shared over warm treats and camaraderie.

Just as I placed the cookies on a cooling rack, my phone buzzed, breaking the comforting silence. It was a text from Nathan, a simple message that made my heart race: Looking forward to our first town meeting. Maybe we can save some time to brainstorm a better name for the lighthouse.

I chuckled, imagining the possibilities. "Beacon of Hope" seemed a tad cliché, while "The Light House of Awkward Encounters" felt too personal. Before I could respond, another message popped up. Also, I'm bringing the coffee.

As the evening wore on, I found myself engulfed in a wave of anticipation. The town meeting was tomorrow, and with it, a chance to rewrite the narrative of our community. The more I thought about it, the more my nerves transformed into excitement, each thought sparkling like the stars beginning to dot the twilight sky.

The next day dawned bright and clear, the kind of day that made you feel like anything was possible. I slipped into my favorite sundress, its fabric soft against my skin, and set out for the community center, a lively energy thrumming beneath my feet. The building, usually quiet and unassuming, was transformed into a hive of activity. Tables were arranged in a welcoming circle, adorned with colorful banners and twinkling fairy lights strung around the ceiling, casting a warm glow over everything.

As I entered, the buzz of conversation swirled around me, laughter mixing with the clinking of cups and the rich aroma of freshly brewed coffee. It felt like stepping into a festival, a celebration of resilience and renewal. I spotted Nathan at the refreshment table, his sleeves rolled up, expertly pouring coffee into mugs while engaged in a friendly debate with Mr. Jenkins over the best fishing spots around the bay.

I couldn't help but smile. The sight of him so at ease with the townspeople brought warmth to my heart. I joined him, ready to dive into the conversations, to embrace the unpredictability of the evening.

"Looks like you've got it all under control," I teased, grabbing a mug and enjoying the rich scent of coffee as it enveloped me.

"Just trying to keep everyone caffeinated for the brainstorming session," Nathan replied, his eyes twinkling with mischief. "You know how much they love their coffee. It might as well be the fuel of democracy."

With laughter dancing in the air, we welcomed each person who entered, their faces lighting up with the promise of change. One by one, they shared their hopes and fears, pouring their hearts into the conversation, creating a tapestry of dreams and aspirations for Windward Bay.

But just as the energy reached a fever pitch, an unexpected guest arrived, a figure stepping into the doorway with an air of authority. The room fell silent, a wave of uncertainty rippling through the crowd as the newcomer surveyed the gathering. My heart raced, a pulse of apprehension thrumming beneath my skin.

It was Mayor Henderson, his reputation for pragmatism and sharp critiques known throughout the town. He cleared his throat, the room hanging on his every word. "I hear there's a plan to revitalize our beloved lighthouse," he began, a hint of skepticism lacing his tone. "And I'm here to discuss the potential hurdles we might face."

A heavy silence enveloped the room, tension coiling like a spring. Nathan and I exchanged glances, uncertainty flickering in the depths of our eyes. The meeting, which had begun with so much promise, was suddenly fraught with the weight of the mayor's scrutiny. As he launched into his concerns, I felt a sense of resolve hardening within me. We had come too far to let fear define our path now.

"Let's hear what you've got," I said, stepping forward, my voice steady. The room shifted, the warmth of camaraderie morphing into something more palpable, a shared courage that dared to challenge the shadows once more.

The room buzzed with an energy that felt almost electric as I stood before Mayor Henderson, the air thick with tension and anticipation. His gaze swept over the crowd, a mixture of skepticism and authority radiating from him. It was clear he was here to challenge us, to poke holes in our newfound optimism like a skilled fisherman looking for the tiniest crack in a net.

"I appreciate the enthusiasm," he began, his tone both measured and wary, "but revamping the lighthouse isn't as simple as a community meeting and some cookies. There are regulations, funding issues, and not to mention the restoration efforts needed to bring the old girl up to code."

A collective murmur rose among the townsfolk, and I could feel their hopeful energy wavering. Nathan stepped up beside me, his presence a solid reminder of the strength we had found in each other. "With respect, Mayor, we're not just asking for permission," he replied, his voice steady. "We're proposing a community initiative. With enough local support, we can tackle the hurdles together."

A slight smirk tugged at the corner of the mayor's mouth, his skepticism palpable. "And if the funding falls through? What then? Who will bear the costs?"

"Us," a voice from the back chimed in. It was Kelly, her hands raised as if to push the mayor's doubts aside. "We'll raise funds through community events, bake sales—whatever it takes. We're all invested in this town."

The murmurs transformed into a chorus of agreement, the initial fears ebbing away as a wave of solidarity surged forward. The energy in the room swelled, each voice becoming a thread woven into the fabric of our resolve. I felt a thrill race through me, my heart syncing with the rhythm of the townsfolk's determination. This wasn't just about the lighthouse; it was about reclaiming our spirit, our home.

Mayor Henderson regarded us, his brow furrowed. "And what if it all goes south? You're risking your own finances, not to mention the town's resources."

"Sometimes you have to take risks to see change," I shot back, surprising even myself with the fierceness of my response. "This town deserves to thrive, and we're willing to fight for it."

"Fight for it? Is that what you call this?" he retorted, crossing his arms, his expression inscrutable. "You think waving a few flags and having a bake sale will fix what's broken?"

A wave of uncertainty rippled through the crowd again, but before I could dwell on it, Nathan leaned closer to me. "You got this," he whispered, his confidence wrapping around me like a warm shawl. "Channel that fire."

I took a deep breath, feeling the heat of determination surge through me. "We've faced darker times," I said, addressing the crowd directly. "And if we've learned anything, it's that together we can rise from the ashes. If we commit to this, if we truly believe in our community, we will find a way. We always do."

The crowd erupted into applause, the sound echoing off the walls of the community center. Encouraged by their enthusiasm, I felt the mayor's resolve waver, his expression shifting slightly as he surveyed the crowd's reactions.

"I'll support a proposal," he finally said, the words begrudgingly escaping his lips. "But it needs to be a well-structured plan. I can't risk the town's reputation on a whim."

"Deal," Nathan and I said in unison, the agreement sparking a fresh wave of excitement. The mayor nodded, perhaps begrudgingly, and I could see the gears in his mind turning, weighing his next move.

As the meeting began to wind down, a tangible sense of accomplishment hung in the air, our determination thick enough to cut with a knife. We tossed around ideas for fundraising events—fishing tournaments, bake-offs, even a community garage sale—each suggestion building on the last, each name adding a flicker of life to our vision.

Later that evening, as the sunset painted the sky in hues of orange and pink, Nathan and I walked along the beach, the sand cool beneath our feet. The laughter of children echoed from the park nearby, the sound a soothing balm against the raw edges of our recent struggles.

"I can't believe we actually pulled that off," I said, glancing at Nathan, whose expression was a blend of pride and disbelief. "It felt almost too easy."

"Don't let that fool you," he replied, a playful glint in his eye. "It's just the calm before the storm. You know they'll come up with new challenges to keep us on our toes."

"Oh, please," I scoffed, though a shiver of apprehension tinged my words. "We've faced down crazed lighthouse keepers. What could possibly scare us now?"

He chuckled, a low rumble that vibrated through the evening air. "Famous last words, right? Besides, I think you underestimate the power of small-town politics. They're capable of turning even the simplest idea into a colossal mess."

"True," I admitted, glancing back at the horizon, where the last rays of sunlight dipped below the water. "But we have the support now. We've rallied the community. If we keep the momentum going, we can make this happen."

As if to punctuate my point, my phone buzzed in my pocket, interrupting the moment. I fished it out and glanced at the screen, my heart skipping a beat when I saw a message from Kelly. You won't believe what I just found out about the lighthouse... Meet me at the café ASAP.

A knot tightened in my stomach. "What's wrong?" Nathan asked, sensing the shift in my demeanor.

"Kelly wants to meet," I said, my voice barely above a whisper. "She says she found something about the lighthouse."

His brow furrowed in concern. "Do you think it's about the history, or—"

"Or something else," I finished, the weight of uncertainty pressing down on me. "What if there's more we didn't uncover? Something that could jeopardize everything we just started?"

"Let's not jump to conclusions," Nathan urged, his hand finding mine, a reassuring squeeze that steadied me. "We'll figure it out together. You're not alone in this."

We reached the café, the warm glow spilling out into the darkening street, and the feeling of dread settled in the pit of my stomach. The bustling interior felt strangely vibrant, alive with the chatter of patrons sipping their coffees. But amidst the lively atmosphere, my focus was solely on Kelly, seated at a table near the window, her expression tight with urgency.

"Hey, you made it!" she exclaimed as we approached, but there was an edge to her voice that sent a chill up my spine.

"What did you find?" I asked, my heart racing.

Kelly glanced around the café, her eyes scanning the room as if the walls held secrets. "It's about the lighthouse—something from its past. Something that could change everything."

My pulse quickened, and Nathan shifted closer, the intensity of the moment enveloping us. "What do you mean?" he pressed, the gravity of her words settling like a weight on our shoulders.

She leaned in, her voice barely above a whisper. "There's a reason it's been abandoned for so long, and it's not just about the structural damage."

I held my breath, the tension in the air thickening. "What are you saying?"

Kelly took a deep breath, her eyes locking onto mine with a seriousness that made my stomach churn. "There are rumors... legends about the lighthouse that involve more than just the light."

"What kind of legends?" Nathan asked, his voice low.

Before Kelly could respond, the café door swung open with a bang, a gust of cold air following. My heart dropped as I turned to see a familiar figure step inside, a shadow from our past that had somehow found its way back into our lives.

As our eyes met, the realization hit me like a punch to the gut. This wasn't just a conversation about the lighthouse anymore; it was a reckoning, and I wasn't sure if I was ready for what was about to unfold. The air crackled with tension, a prelude to chaos waiting to be unleashed.

Chapter 23: The Road Ahead

The ocean air wrapped around me like a comforting shawl, mingling with the warmth of Nathan's presence beside me. The waves rolled in with a soft whoosh, whispering secrets of the deep as they kissed the sandy shore. I squinted against the dying light, where oranges and pinks bled into the sky, their vibrant hues mirrored in the gentle ripples. Each breath I took felt like an inhale of new beginnings, though the past still clung to my heart like stubborn barnacles. Nathan was my anchor, yet he was also the storm that churned my insides.

"Do you remember that summer we snuck out to the lighthouse?" he asked, breaking the comfortable silence between us. His voice was a rich baritone, tinged with nostalgia that warmed my chest like a shot of whiskey.

"Which summer?" I shot back, a grin forming as I recalled the reckless abandon of our youth. "You'll have to narrow it down."

He laughed, the sound deep and infectious, and I felt the tension of the past few months ebb away just a little. "You know, the one where we nearly got caught by Mr. Patterson. You had that ridiculous flashlight—"

"Which was crucial for our operation!" I interjected, my smile widening as I leaned against him, my shoulder brushing his. "You were the one who insisted on exploring the creaky old staircase in the dark. If it wasn't for my trusty beam of light, we'd still be trapped in there!"

Nathan chuckled, his laughter echoing through the fading daylight. "Right. And if I recall, you didn't mind too much when we found that old journal hidden in the lighthouse. It was like we'd uncarthed treasure."

I turned to face him, the seriousness of the moment creeping back in. "It was a treasure, wasn't it? Just like you." There was a pause as we exchanged a look, his eyes darkening slightly. In that instant, I could see the flicker of something deeper—an awareness of the road we had ahead of us, the obstacles we still had to face.

"Sometimes, I think about that journal," he admitted, the lightheartedness of our earlier banter drifting away like the last rays of sun sinking into the horizon. "How much we thought we knew back then. But this? This is different. We've grown. We're not kids anymore."

The honesty in his tone made my heart ache with a mix of hope and fear. "No, we're not. But that doesn't mean we can't make our own story now." The salt of the sea hung heavy in the air, but it was the weight of our shared history that felt the heaviest.

As if on cue, a flock of gulls swooped overhead, their cries breaking the stillness. "We should probably head back soon," Nathan suggested, casting a glance toward the dimming sky. I could hear the reluctance in his voice, a yearning to stay, just a moment longer, wrapped in the intimacy of our own world.

"Just a few more minutes?" I pleaded, turning my gaze back to the waves, watching them crash against the rocks like the turbulent feelings we were navigating. "Let's let the ocean remind us how to let go of the past."

With a resigned sigh, he nodded, though I could see the way his muscles tightened. "Okay, a few more minutes. But I get to choose the next memory we relive."

"Deal." My heart fluttered with anticipation. There was something exhilarating about these little exchanges, the way our pasts intertwined, binding us together like a patchwork quilt, both warm and fraught with reminders of what we had lost.

The silence stretched, comfortable and filled with unspoken words. As I watched the sun sink lower, I felt a swell of determination. "Nathan, I know we have to face the town and everything that happened with… with Emily," I stammered, the name hanging between us like a ghost. "But we can't let her define our future."

He turned to me, his brow furrowing in concern. "I don't want her to define us, either. But the truth is, the town is still healing. People are still whispering, and we can't ignore that. Trust doesn't just rebuild overnight."

"I know." My heart raced at the thought of confronting those whispers, the judgment that hung thick in the air like a fog. "But we can show them that we've moved on. Together."

"Together." He repeated the word, his lips curling into a small smile that lit up his features. "I like the sound of that. But it won't be easy."

"Nothing worth having ever is." I stood a little taller, letting the courage I felt wash over me like the tide. "We'll show them we're stronger than they think, and we won't let our past mistakes dictate our future."

"Then let's start with the people we trust most," Nathan suggested, his tone shifting to something more resolute. "We need to gather our friends, the ones who believe in us. They're our foundation."

My heart swelled at his words. "Yes! We can host a gathering—some casual get-together. A barbecue, maybe? Something to remind everyone that we're still the same people they love, despite everything."

He raised an eyebrow, a smirk tugging at the corner of his mouth. "You just want an excuse to grill burgers."

"Maybe I do," I replied playfully, nudging him with my shoulder. "But it's also about connection. About rebuilding what we've lost."

Nathan's gaze softened, a mixture of admiration and something more profound swirling in his eyes. "Then let's do it. We'll create a space where we can be honest, where we can share the good, the bad, and everything in between. A place to remind ourselves and them that we're still us."

A sense of excitement coursed through me, lighting up my spirit like the stars that would soon emerge in the twilight. "Then it's settled. We'll host a barbecue, and we'll make it a night to remember."

As we turned to head back, I felt a new weight lift from my chest—a sense of purpose igniting the way ahead. Yes, it was going to be challenging, but as long as we faced it together, I believed we could build something beautiful from the ashes of our past. The horizon stretched before us, shimmering with endless possibilities, and in that moment, I knew we would rise together, stronger than before.

The next morning greeted us with a wash of golden sunlight, filtering through the sheer curtains of my bedroom and casting playful shadows on the wall. I blinked against the brightness, the warmth creeping into my bones, stirring me from a sleep that had been deeper than I'd anticipated. In the aftermath of our beachside conversation, I felt an unusual buoyancy, as if the world outside my window held secrets that promised adventure. I rolled out of bed, my heart still dancing to the rhythm of possibility, and padded to the kitchen, the cool tiles awakening my senses.

The smell of coffee greeted me like an old friend, and I was grateful for the small pleasures of life in Windward Bay. As I poured myself a steaming mug, I couldn't help but wonder what today would hold. The lingering tension of the town's whispers had yet to fully dissolve, but the idea of our barbecue felt like a beacon, lighting the way through the uncertainty. Nathan had been the catalyst for this newfound resolve, and I felt a spark of excitement at the thought of reaching out to our friends.

Just as I settled down at the kitchen table, my phone buzzed with a message. I glanced at the screen to find a text from Sarah, my best friend and partner-in-crime since childhood.

Can we talk? I have something to share!

I couldn't suppress a smile. Sarah always had a flair for the dramatic. Setting my coffee aside, I replied, Always. Coffee shop in 30?

Her response was instant, a flurry of enthusiasm. Perfect! Bring your best ideas!

Within the hour, I found myself nestled in our favorite corner of the café, the aroma of freshly baked pastries swirling around me. The walls were adorned with local art, each piece telling a story as vibrant as the people who inhabited this town. Sarah arrived, her dark curls bouncing as she waved, a lopsided grin spreading across her face.

"Coffee first, gossip later?" she suggested, plopping down across from me.

"Always," I agreed, my heart racing with curiosity. "So, what's the big news?"

With a dramatic flourish, Sarah lifted her cup to her lips, taking a slow sip before leaning in, eyes gleaming. "I think I might have a lead on a new job opportunity! The library is looking for someone to help with their community programs, and you know how I love organizing events."

"That's amazing!" I exclaimed, feeling a genuine thrill for her. "You'd be perfect for it. They'd be lucky to have you!"

"Right? But here's the twist—" she lowered her voice conspiratorially, "they want someone who can also help with their social media presence. I have zero experience in that department."

"Nothing a little research and a dash of your charm can't fix," I encouraged, my enthusiasm bubbling over. "Plus, you've always had a knack for connecting with people. You're practically a walking advertisement for Windward Bay."

Her laughter danced through the air, infectious and uplifting. "Okay, you're right. Maybe I'll just channel my inner influencer and hope for the best. But back to you! How are you feeling about this barbecue? I heard the grapevine has been buzzing, and I'm pretty sure they're still talking about you and Nathan."

The shift in conversation tugged at my heartstrings. "We're trying to build bridges. I just want our friends to remember who we are and what we stand for, not the mistakes we've made."

"Good luck with that." She rolled her eyes, the playful smirk returning. "But seriously, I think it's a great idea. Just remember, people can surprise you. Maybe you'll win them back one burger at a time."

We shared a laugh, the tension easing as we dove deeper into the plans for the barbecue. The more we brainstormed, the more excitement bubbled within me. We tossed around ideas for food, games, and even a bonfire, weaving a tapestry of camaraderie that felt invigorating.

"Okay, I'm officially excited," I declared, leaning back in my chair. "Let's make it a night to remember. If I can win back the town's trust, I'll do it over a plate of perfectly grilled burgers and a side of laughter."

"Just be prepared for the unexpected," Sarah cautioned, her eyes narrowing playfully. "Like when we had that summer cookout and the raccoons raided the food. I'm still not over that horror show."

"Never forget." I laughed, shaking my head at the memory. "I'll have my eye out for any sneaky raccoons this time."

We finished our coffees, the conversation shifting from whimsical to serious as we discussed our dreams and aspirations. For Sarah, it was about finding her footing in the community; for me, it was about healing. I wanted to take a step forward, not just with Nathan but with the town, embracing the collective heartache and turning it into something beautiful.

Once we left the café, Sarah and I wandered through the town square, admiring the autumn leaves painting the sidewalks in fiery reds and oranges. It felt like the perfect backdrop for our plans, a reminder that change is constant and beautiful. Just as we reached the park, I spotted Nathan chatting with a few friends near the playground.

"Look who it is," I said, nudging Sarah with my elbow. "Our fearless leader."

She grinned, her eyes dancing with mischief. "Should we crash the party?"

"Absolutely." I felt a surge of warmth, a sense of belonging that wrapped around me like a favorite sweater. As we approached, Nathan caught sight of us, his face lighting up as if the sun had just burst through the clouds.

"Hey, you two! Come join us!" he called, his voice carrying over the laughter of our friends.

As we settled in, I couldn't help but notice the way Nathan's hand instinctively found mine, our fingers interlocking seamlessly. The laughter, the chatter, the occasional bursts of chaos from the children playing nearby—it all felt so right, a piece of the puzzle I had almost given up searching for.

The conversation flowed easily, each laugh peeling back layers of doubt, reminding me of why we were doing this. In that moment, surrounded by friends, I understood that the road ahead wouldn't be without its bumps, but together, we could navigate any storm.

As the sun dipped lower, casting a golden glow that bathed the park in warmth, the laughter of our friends became a comforting backdrop to the swirling thoughts in my mind. Nathan leaned closer, his presence grounding me as we settled into our small circle. The familiar faces of our friends surrounded us, and for a fleeting moment, I felt a sense of normalcy return. It was a fragile peace, one that could easily shatter under the weight of our past, yet it felt like a new beginning.

"Okay, everyone!" Nathan clapped his hands, drawing our attention. "We've got a barbecue to plan, but I think we should start with an icebreaker. Let's share our most embarrassing moments."

A collective groan echoed, but a smile crept onto my face. This was classic Nathan—always eager to lighten the mood.

"Fine," Sarah said, crossing her arms dramatically. "But if I end up reliving the great raccoon debacle, I'm holding you personally responsible."

"Raccoon debacle?" one of our friends, Mark, raised an eyebrow, intrigued. "Now I have to hear this."

"Let's just say, it involved an uninvited dinner guest, a very surprised group of teenagers, and a whole lot of chaos," I explained, my laughter mingling with the others.

With each story shared, the atmosphere shifted, laughter washing over us like a refreshing tide. Nathan shared an anecdote from his high school days when he accidentally set off the fire alarm during a chemistry experiment gone wrong. "I thought I was going to be the next Einstein," he chuckled, shaking his head. "Turns out, I just became the school's 'Fire Starter.'"

The camaraderie felt invigorating, stitching the wounds of the past with threads of laughter and shared history. Yet beneath the surface, I sensed the whispers still lurking, like shadows waiting for their moment to leap out.

As we turned to food preparations, Nathan and I worked side by side, grilling burgers while trying to keep the flames from licking too high. "You know, I'm really glad we're doing this," he said, glancing at me, the warmth of the grill casting a flickering light on his face. "It feels...normal."

"Normal is good," I replied, my heart racing at the idea of what we were building together. "But we have to remember, it's not just about the food or the laughter. We need to be honest with everyone, especially if we want to rebuild trust."

"Agreed." He nodded, his expression turning serious. "But I think honesty can be a gradual process. Let's not throw everything out there at once."

"Right," I said, catching his gaze. "We ease them into it, like the perfect marinade. Give them time to absorb what we're trying to do."

As the aroma of sizzling burgers filled the air, a few friends gathered nearby, playful banter erupting around us. I couldn't help but admire how easy it felt to slip back into the rhythm of friendship. It was a world I desperately wanted to protect, even as the specter of our past loomed over us.

"Hey! Grab the buns!" Sarah called out, nudging my arm as she darted toward the table. "And make sure to check for raccoons first!"

The playful jest sparked laughter, but it also reminded me of how quickly things could turn. Just as I turned to grab the basket, the sky darkened abruptly, the sun retreating behind a wall of ominous clouds. A chill raced through the air, shifting the mood as the laughter dimmed.

"Did anyone check the weather?" Nathan asked, his brow furrowing as he glanced up.

"Nope! It's Windward Bay; what's the worst that could happen?" I replied, trying to keep the mood light, even as my stomach twisted with unease.

As if in response, the wind picked up, sending a gust that scattered napkins and toppled drinks. My heart thudded in my chest as I grabbed a nearby table to steady myself. "Alright, everyone, maybe we should pull things together just in case."

But before we could regroup, a distant rumble echoed, sounding less like thunder and more like a heavy engine. The ground vibrated slightly beneath my feet. "What is that?" I asked, my voice rising in uncertainty.

Nathan narrowed his eyes, focusing on the horizon where the clouds swirled ominously. "I think it's coming from the harbor."

A knot formed in my stomach as I recalled the rumors about the old shipyard—a once-thriving port now lying dormant, shrouded in mystery and whispers of strange happenings. "What do you think it is?"

Before he could answer, the ground shook again, this time with more intensity, causing the trees to sway and a few people to stumble. The laughter faded as everyone turned their attention to the harbor, the laughter replaced by a growing sense of dread.

"Everyone, stay calm!" Nathan shouted, his authoritative tone cutting through the panic that threatened to rise. "Let's move away from the tables. It's probably just a heavy truck or something."

But just as he finished speaking, a brilliant flash of light erupted from the direction of the harbor, momentarily blinding us all. The air hummed with electricity, and a collective gasp echoed among our friends. When the light faded, it left a trail of confusion in its wake, shadows dancing like wraiths.

"What the hell was that?" Mark exclaimed, his eyes wide.

I felt my heart race, a mixture of fear and anticipation coiling tightly within me. "I don't know, but it can't be good."

Suddenly, a distant shout pierced through the air, rising above the murmur of confusion. "Help! Someone's in trouble!"

Without thinking, I grabbed Nathan's hand, our instincts kicking in as we dashed toward the commotion, hearts pounding with adrenaline. The crowd began to disperse, a wave of panic washing over them as we sprinted toward the shoreline.

"Stay close!" Nathan urged, his grip firm around my wrist.

We reached the edge of the harbor, and my breath caught in my throat as I took in the scene. A small fishing boat was adrift, smoke curling from its engine, while a figure flailed desperately in the water nearby, thrashing against the churning waves.

"Is that...?" I whispered, the dread pooling in my stomach as I strained to see.

Before Nathan could respond, a surge of water crashed against the dock, and I stumbled back, heart racing as the world spun around me. I felt the tension tighten around us like a noose, uncertainty filling the air with a palpable weight. Whatever had emerged from the harbor, it was far from ordinary.

"Someone has to help!" I shouted, adrenaline surging through me.

But before we could make a move, the figure in the water let out a piercing scream, and then everything shifted. The ground trembled again, and I could feel the chaos unraveling around us like a thread pulled too tight.

I turned to Nathan, but his expression had shifted from determination to sheer terror. "What is happening?" he shouted, his voice barely rising above the tumult.

Just then, a shadow loomed over us, massive and dark, cutting off the fading light. My pulse quickened, and I felt my breath hitch as I realized that this was just the beginning. Whatever storm was brewing was not just in the sky; it was here, and it was about to change everything we thought we knew about Windward Bay.

Chapter 24: Embracing the Future

The salty tang of the ocean air wrapped around me like a long-lost embrace as I stood at the edge of the pier. Each wave kissed the weathered planks beneath my feet, a rhythmic reminder that the world continued its dance, even as I wrestled with the torrent of emotions swirling within me. I turned to Nathan, the sunlight catching the angles of his jaw and the depths of his warm, hazel eyes. In that moment, the chaos of the past faded like the receding tide, and I felt a surge of hope that resonated deep within my bones.

"Isn't it beautiful?" I asked, nodding towards the horizon where the sky melted into shades of gold and coral, a watercolor masterpiece splashed across the canvas of evening.

He smiled, a playful quirk of his lips that made my heart flutter. "You mean the sunset, or my breathtakingly handsome face?"

I rolled my eyes, though the laughter bubbled up from my chest, pushing aside the shadows of doubt that had lingered too long. "Oh, it's definitely the sunset. Yours is a close second, though."

Nathan chuckled, his laughter harmonizing with the soft roar of the waves. "Well, if I can only be second to a sunset, I suppose I can live with that."

The warmth of his hand wrapped around mine felt like an anchor in the unpredictable sea of life. I was reminded of the countless moments we had shared—battles fought in boardrooms, arguments over logistics that had turned into debates about our dreams and futures. Each quarrel had stripped away the barriers we had constructed, revealing layers of vulnerability beneath. We were no longer just adversaries in a relentless competition; we had become partners, willing to navigate the uncharted waters of our emotions together.

As the sun dipped lower, a flicker of apprehension danced in my stomach. The future loomed ahead, cloaked in uncertainty, but with

Nathan by my side, it didn't seem as daunting. I took a deep breath, inhaling the heady mix of salt and adventure. "What do you think it will be like?"

He shrugged, his eyes fixed on the horizon as if it held the answers to the universe. "I think it will be like this moment—uncertain, yet beautiful. We'll have to navigate it together, make our own rules as we go."

I squeezed his hand tighter, letting his words settle in my mind. The thought of forging our path excited me, but there was also a gnawing fear that our past might resurface, like a phantom haunting our new beginning. Would we be strong enough to withstand the storms that could arise?

Just then, the sound of footsteps interrupted my thoughts. A familiar voice called out, slicing through the evening calm like a knife. "Well, if it isn't the star-crossed lovers at the edge of the world!"

I turned to see Grace, her bright smile illuminating the dusky pier. She approached, her hair a wild halo in the gentle breeze, embodying the vibrant spirit that had always been a beacon of light in our lives.

"Shouldn't you be celebrating your new position at the firm instead of playing lovebirds?" she teased, hands on her hips, but her eyes sparkled with genuine affection.

Nathan released my hand, stepping forward to embrace her. "Just enjoying a moment before plunging into the chaos of office life."

"Chaos? I thought you thrived in it!" Grace shot back, winking at me.

I laughed, the tension of the evening ebbing away. "You know, I think we both do. But there's something to be said for taking a moment to breathe before diving headfirst into the deep end."

Nathan nodded in agreement. "Exactly. Besides, with all the plans we have, we'll need a break before the madness begins."

Grace tilted her head, curiosity dancing in her eyes. "Plans? What plans?"

I exchanged a glance with Nathan, our unspoken agreement swirling in the air. We had dreamed of starting our own business—a bold venture where we could merge our skills, tackle challenges together, and create something truly ours.

"Nathan and I were just talking about launching a consultancy," I said, unable to suppress my excitement. "Combining our expertise could bring a fresh perspective to the industry."

Grace clapped her hands together, her enthusiasm infectious. "That's brilliant! You two together could take on the world. Just make sure you don't kill each other in the process."

Her teasing sent a warm rush through me, the kind that wrapped around my heart like a cozy blanket. "Oh, I'm sure we'll find ways to keep things interesting. Like deciding whether to file taxes in the morning or the evening," I replied, my voice laced with sarcasm.

Nathan laughed, the sound deep and comforting. "And figuring out who's actually the boss."

"Good luck with that," Grace replied, chuckling. "I've seen you two argue over a single decision before."

I feigned a pout. "Those were just passionate discussions!"

"More like epic battles," Nathan added, his expression turning mock-serious. "But they only brought us closer, right?"

"Right," I said, smiling back at him, the weight of the world shifting ever so slightly. The fears and doubts that had once loomed large began to shrink under the light of possibility.

The sun sank beneath the horizon, and the sky transformed into a canvas of deep blues and purples. The stars began to twinkle, shy at first but gradually finding their confidence, much like the newfound strength blooming within me. With every moment shared and every laugh exchanged, I felt the future opening up before us, a vast expanse of opportunities waiting to be seized.

We stood together at the edge of what could be, ready to plunge into the depths of our shared dreams. The past, once a weight upon our shoulders, became a foundation for what lay ahead. Embracing the future felt less like a leap into the unknown and more like a dance into the familiar rhythm of hope and love, hand in hand, as we stepped forward into the night.

The cool evening air wrapped around us, laced with the scent of salt and adventure. As the stars blinked into existence overhead, I felt the weight of possibility pressing against my chest, both exhilarating and terrifying. Nathan and I turned away from the pier, letting the distant sound of waves recede into the background. The laughter of Grace faded too, a soft echo of friendship that hung in the air like the final notes of a symphony. With a shared look that spoke volumes, we headed towards the nearby café, a charming little place with fairy lights strung above, casting a warm glow over the outdoor seating.

The clatter of dishes and the murmur of patrons filled the air, creating a lively ambiance that contrasted the stillness of the night. I settled into a chair, and Nathan pulled one closer, leaning in as if to share a secret. "You know, I've been thinking..." His voice dropped conspiratorially, an edge of mischief dancing in his eyes.

"Oh, now I'm scared," I teased, raising an eyebrow. "What is it this time? Are you planning to reinvent the coffee wheel or something equally as ludicrous?"

He laughed, shaking his head. "Not quite. But how about we spice up our consultancy name a bit? 'Consultancy A' sounds about as exciting as watching paint dry."

I rolled my eyes dramatically. "Fine, give me your best shot. But it better be good, or I'm sticking with the boring option."

"Okay, how about 'Dynamic Solutions Duo'? Has a nice ring to it, don't you think?"

I pretended to ponder this, tapping my chin. "It does sound like we'd be solving crimes in our spare time. Next, you'll suggest we wear capes and save the world."

"Capes are so last season. We need matching outfits, something that says 'professional but also here to party.'"

Before I could respond, our waitress arrived, a bright smile and a notepad at the ready. "What can I get for you two lovebirds?"

I shot Nathan a warning glance, my lips curling into a grin. "Let's stick with coffee for now before he starts planning a themed outfit for our meetings."

"Oh, but I can make it sound so much more enticing!" Nathan interjected, adopting a mock-serious tone. "How about 'espresso-based invigorators' to fuel our brilliance?"

The waitress laughed, and I shook my head, smothering my giggles. "Just two coffees, please. Strong enough to keep us awake through our brilliant brainstorming session."

As she walked away, Nathan leaned back in his chair, a satisfied smirk on his face. "You know, I could get used to this. We might actually turn out to be the next big thing in consulting."

I tilted my head, a playful smile teasing my lips. "You mean, aside from being the next big thing in fashion?"

"I don't want to be known for my fashion sense," he said, feigning a serious demeanor. "That would be too much pressure. I'm more of a 'let's hope my shirt matches my pants' kind of guy."

"True, but you've mastered the 'I just rolled out of bed' look remarkably well."

"Why, thank you! I aim to impress."

Just then, the waitress returned, two steaming mugs in hand, the aroma enveloping us like a warm hug. She placed them on the table, and I wrapped my fingers around the warm ceramic, savoring the moment.

As I took a sip, I felt a twinge of nervousness knot in my stomach again. The idea of launching our consultancy was thrilling but also fraught with the weight of expectation. What if it all fell apart? What if we failed? I glanced at Nathan, his brow furrowed in thought, as if he was picking up on my unspoken fears.

"Hey," he said softly, pulling me from my spiral. "Are you still with me?"

"Yeah, sorry. Just... thinking."

"About the business?"

I nodded, tracing the rim of my cup with my fingertip. "What if we're not ready for this? What if we mess it all up?"

Nathan leaned forward, his expression earnest. "We won't. We've faced tougher challenges. This is just a new adventure. Plus, we'll have each other. That makes a world of difference."

I met his gaze, finding solace in his conviction. "I guess you're right. Together, we're a force to be reckoned with."

"And if it doesn't work out, we'll just move to a tropical island and open a smoothie shack."

The image made me laugh, and for a moment, I could almost picture it—the two of us, sun-kissed and carefree, surrounded by palm trees and turquoise waters. "Okay, but only if we can call it 'Sippin' Sunshine.'"

"Deal!" He raised his mug in a mock toast, and I followed suit, the laughter filling the space between us, banishing my lingering doubts.

As we settled into our coffees, our conversation flowed effortlessly. We brainstormed names, tossing around ideas like confetti, each one more outrageous than the last. The world around us began to fade into a backdrop, a kaleidoscope of laughter and chatter that underscored our growing excitement.

Amid our laughter, the café door swung open, a gust of wind carrying a chill that sent a shiver down my spine. I turned, caught off guard by a familiar figure stepping inside—a tall man with an unmistakable presence. My heart sank as recognition washed over me like cold water. It was Ben, the very embodiment of the rival I had left behind, the one whose shadow had haunted my every decision during those tumultuous early days of my career.

I felt a rush of panic surge through me, my mind racing as I considered the implications of his sudden appearance. He spotted us almost immediately, a surprised expression flashing across his face. I could see the wheels turning in his head, calculating the best way to approach us.

Nathan must have sensed the shift in my demeanor. "Hey, what's wrong?"

I struggled to find the words, the fear of facing my past settling like a heavy fog. "It's… it's Ben."

His eyes flicked towards the entrance, and I held my breath as our former adversary made his way to our table, a mixture of determination and unease etched across his features. "Fancy running into you both here," Ben said, his tone casual, but the underlying tension crackled like static electricity.

"Ben," I managed, forcing a smile that felt more like a grimace.

"Glad to see you're both doing well," he replied, his gaze lingering on Nathan, a hint of challenge in his expression.

"We're busy, actually," Nathan interjected, his protective instinct flaring.

"I can see that," Ben replied, a wry smile creeping onto his lips. "But I'd love to chat for a moment, if you don't mind."

I glanced at Nathan, uncertainty coursing through me. Would this be a confrontation or a reconciliation? The air was thick with unspoken history, the remnants of rivalry clawing at the edges of my confidence. I felt Nathan's hand on mine, grounding me in the chaos, and I took a deep breath, steeling myself for whatever lay ahead.

As Ben settled into the chair across from us, the atmosphere shifted palpably. The cheerful clatter of the café faded into a distant murmur, and all that remained was the tightrope of tension strung between the three of us. I could feel Nathan's grip tighten around my hand, a silent reassurance that we were a team, ready to face whatever fallout came our way.

"Ben," I said, striving for casual indifference, "what brings you here?"

He leaned back, his expression an unsettling mix of charm and challenge. "Oh, you know, just enjoying the ambiance. The coffee here is fantastic. But I must admit, running into you two is the highlight of my evening."

"Lucky us," Nathan muttered under his breath, but I caught the hint of sarcasm in his tone, and it made me smirk despite the situation.

"I actually wanted to discuss something important," Ben continued, his gaze fixed on me, an intensity flickering in his eyes. "I hear you're starting a consultancy. Impressive move. Bold."

"Thanks, I guess," I replied, cautiously measuring my words. "But I'm not sure what you want from us."

He waved a dismissive hand. "Oh, I'm not here to sabotage or anything. I just think it would be wise for us to... collaborate."

I blinked, genuinely surprised. "Collaborate? With you?" The words came out sharper than I intended, but I didn't care to hide my disbelief.

"Why not? You and Nathan have proven you can take on the world together. I have resources and contacts that could benefit all of us." His smile was smooth, but there was a glint in his eye that made my skin crawl.

"Resources?" Nathan's tone turned icy. "The last time we collaborated, it didn't end well for either of us."

"Ah, but we've all grown since then, haven't we?" Ben's expression shifted slightly, revealing a flicker of something unspoken. "Life has a funny way of changing perspectives. We could be a powerhouse—just think of the potential."

I felt a rush of anger and confusion surge within me. "You mean you want to join forces after everything? After all those cutthroat games? How can I trust you?"

"Trust is overrated," he shot back, his voice almost flippant. "What matters is results. We could make quite the impact if we combined our strengths."

A flicker of doubt settled into my mind. Had he really changed, or was this merely another ploy? I glanced at Nathan, whose jaw was clenched tight, the tension radiating off him in waves.

"You're not the same person I knew," Nathan said slowly, his voice steady but laced with warning. "What's really in it for you, Ben? You don't strike me as the benevolent type."

"Touché," Ben conceded, his smile faltering just a fraction. "I suppose I'm still the opportunist you remember. But think about it. This could be mutually beneficial. You want to make a mark in the industry, and I can help you do that."

I leaned forward, my heart racing. "And what's your angle? What are you not telling us?"

He held my gaze, the flicker of mischief in his eyes morphing into something more serious. "I'm trying to change, okay? I know I haven't been the best influence in the past, but maybe I'm not that person anymore. We all have to evolve, right?"

"Change is great, but I'm not sure we can take that risk," I countered, a knot tightening in my stomach.

"Fine," he snapped, his expression shifting to one of frustration. "Then what's your plan? Going up against the industry giants alone? You think you can take them on without some backup? You're walking into a minefield."

Nathan bristled at the insinuation, and I felt the weight of his protective instincts bear down on me. "We've fought our battles, Ben. We're not looking for your approval or your help."

The air crackled with tension, and for a moment, I felt caught between the past and the promise of a new beginning. Ben leaned closer, his voice dropping to a conspiratorial whisper. "What if I told you that there's a bigger player in the game, someone who's been eyeing both of you? Someone who wants to sabotage your plans before you even get started?"

My heart raced as the implications of his words sank in. "What do you mean?"

"There's a chance you'll be facing more than just competition. I've heard rumors—heavy hitters are watching you, waiting for a misstep."

"Why would you tell us this?" I shot back, skepticism tightening my voice.

"Because," he replied, his demeanor shifting again, the bravado fading, "it could be mutually beneficial. You help me regain some respect, and I help you navigate the treacherous waters ahead. It's a simple business proposition."

I glanced at Nathan, who was now observing Ben with a mix of wariness and intrigue. "And what's in it for you?" Nathan asked, the challenge lingering in the air.

Ben straightened, his confidence returning. "Like I said, respect. I'm tired of being the villain. It's time to change the narrative. Help me help you, and we could all come out on top."

The table grew silent, and I could feel the weight of the decision pressing down on me. On one hand, the idea of teaming up with Ben felt like inviting a storm into our lives, but on the other, could he actually provide insights that would help us secure our footing?

"Let's say we consider it," I said cautiously, "what's your plan?"

His eyes sparkled with a dangerous gleam. "Let me set up a meeting with a few key players. You'll see I'm not the enemy here. Trust me."

A chill ran down my spine, and I felt Nathan tense beside me. "Trust seems to be your favorite word," I said, my voice laced with uncertainty. "How do we know you won't turn on us the moment it suits you?"

"Ah, trust is earned, not given," he said, his tone smooth, yet I sensed a shift in his demeanor. "You'll have to take a leap of faith if you want to play in the big leagues."

A deep breath filled my lungs as I weighed my options. Just then, the café door swung open again, this time accompanied by a gust of wind that sent a shiver down my spine. A figure stood silhouetted against the fading light, and my breath caught in my throat as recognition surged through me—Leah, my former mentor, her expression unreadable.

"Looks like the plot thickens," Nathan murmured, eyeing Leah's determined stride as she made her way toward our table.

"Mind if I join?" she asked, a hint of curiosity sparking in her eyes.

I felt my heart race. What was she doing here? Had she come to warn me, or did she already know about Ben's proposition? The energy shifted again, the weight of decisions suddenly overwhelming.

"Um, we were just..." I stammered, my mind racing.

Before I could finish, Leah leaned in, her voice low and urgent. "I need to talk to you—both of you—about what's really going on."

The air thickened with tension, and I exchanged a glance with Nathan, who looked just as unsettled as I felt. The night was growing darker, but the stakes were suddenly illuminated in stark relief.

"Right now?" I asked, my voice barely above a whisper.

"Yes, right now," she replied, the urgency in her tone undeniable. "We don't have much time."

And just like that, the future I had been so eager to embrace began to unravel, a delicate thread pulled tight, threatening to snap at any moment.

Milton Keynes UK
Ingram Content Group UK Ltd.
UKHW031347011224
451755UK00001B/58